QUIET ECHOES AT NIGHT

L. G. JENKINS

BOOK THREE OF THE MERIT-HUNTERS SERIES

Grace & Down
PUBLISHING

First published 2024 by Grace & Down Publishing
an imprint of Malcolm Down Publishing Ltd
www.malcolmdown.co.uk

28 27 26 25 24   7 6 5 4 3 2 1

British Library Cataloguing in Publication Data
A catalogue record for this book is available from the British Library.

ISBN 978-1-917455-03-9

Cover design by Liz Carter
Map illustrations by Sarah Jenkins
Art direction by Sarah Grace

Printed in the UK

Dedication

For Mum, and for anyone who
feels chained down by the past.

PART ONE
THE CITY

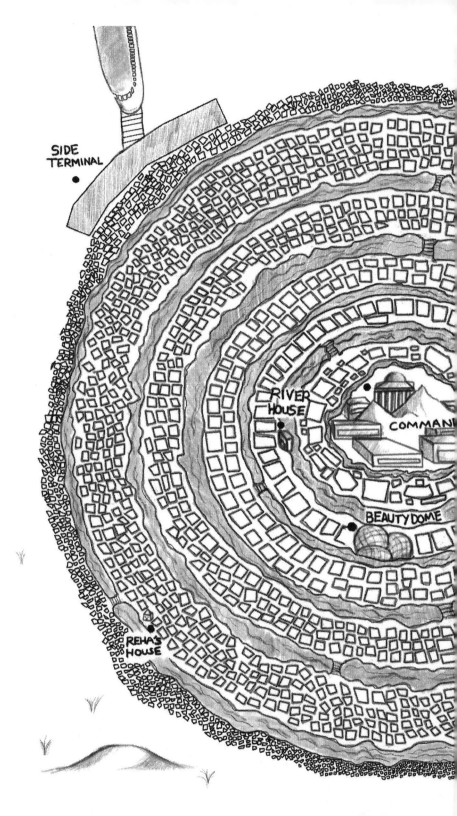

Tulo City

PROSPER

PROLOGUE

You're listening to 'All That Motivation' with Colli Bloom.

'I think all of us can admit we're not our best selves every day.'

'Yeah.'

'I think it takes courage to say I didn't meet my merit target today. Or I feel unproductive or inefficient. That's not to say we shouldn't address the problem, but there are ways we can try to help each other.'

'Absolutely. For those just joining us, welcome back to 'All That Motivation', I'm Colli Bloom and I'm here with the lovely Georgie Ghatty, Tulo's favourite and *award-winning* motivational speaker and author. We're chatting about those times when you don't feel your most effective self. Where should someone turn when they can't hit a merit target? What helps you, Georgie?'

'Well, different methods work for different people. For me, it's always going back to basics. That's the way I've been brought up. It might feel frustrating at times, but Progress is Strength and we all have a part to play to build a greater Tulo. The more of us who strive to meet that M-500 mark, the more is fed back so we can all live better lives. So that's it for me, just taking a quick second and grounding myself back to those foundations.'

'Right, that's so key, isn't it? I remember when I was M-499. It must have been ten, eleven years ago. That's making me feel old, but I—'

'Ha, don't, that means I should be in the Village.'

'Not at all, Georgie, I can't see even a silver hair.'

'It's all natural.'

'I don't doubt it. But I remember being that close to Glorified, and man, that last merit point just seemed to take forever.'

'Yep.'

'And it obviously took the same amount of time to earn a point – well, it could have even been quicker, but it felt like it was trickling up and I remember thinking, *I'm never gonna make it.*'

'But you did. You got there, and everyone can; it just takes a bit of extra grind, motivation and passion, you know?'

'Definitely, and there's something in getting there and still having that drive to go even further. That's mega-rewarding.'

'Of course. We still need to aim for the next thing. Whatever that might be for each of us – probably going for M-600. But it makes us the strong community we are.'

'On that, then, before we go for some thoughts from our listeners, I did just want to talk about the current unrest, Georgie.'

'Isn't it awful?'

'Terrible, terrible. We're all *still* trying to navigate our new City after the Liberation Day Attack, and it's very raw for a lot of people.'

'Sure.'

'So I just wanted to touch base with you on how to stop it distracting us from our goals. How can people ignore all that and merit-make efficiently? Because I'm hearing a lot about it setting people back, this uncertainty and fear, and they're failing to meet their yearly score targets. What's your take on it?'

'Pfffft, well it's so tough because in reality, we can't ignore what's happening around us right now.'

'No. OK.'

'The restrictions on our freedoms make it hard to ignore; having our Watches constantly checked and monitored for whatever we do, even just buying a coffee now, you know, it seems crazy, doesn't it?'

'It happened to me the other day while leaving my own apartment.'

'I've not had that yet, but it's developing all the time. So we can't ignore it. And we can't ignore the noise around it all and how our City just feels different.'

'We're living somewhere we don't recognise.'

'Exactly. All of this is unprecedented, especially the growing distrust of Command.'

'Right, what—'

'But I would say we've got to remember that all these changes are for our security, and it's only happening because a group of Unworthies, The Rogue, if you want to give them a name – personally I don't think they even deserve that recognition – but *they* decided to trespass into *our* lives to tear down what we've all worked hard for and frankly, that should spur us on even more.'

'And resting on that will motivate us to protect what our ancestors did during the Revolution.'

'Precisely. It's just about turning it all on its head. Negative into positives.'

'That's so valuable to hear. Ah, man, I could just sit and talk to you all day but time is pressing on and I wanted to open this conversation around perseverance to our listeners. And we've got Timm from the Outer-Inner-Ring on the line. Thanks for tuning in, Timm. What tips have you got for us?'

'A tip? Yeah, I've got a tip. Everyone, including you two should be asking themselves the question: what have Command been doing? They've been fu—'

'Timm, Timm, I'd like to remind you we have a family audience, please lower your tone.'

'It's disgraceful, though. All these cases of Command officers turning out to be part of The Rogue. And that lad Ambers who worked at Prosper and killed his colleague before making a run for it. These are working professionals, living among us and I want to know *why* Command hasn't done more—'

'OK, Timm, can you just—'

'No, Colli, don't. The constitution is a beautiful thing, but The Rogue are still out there despite this new Watch model – where is that, by the way? They've been promising it for months – it might be alright for you Glorified folk, but what about the rest of us? We don't have any walls or mountains around our houses.'

'You will once you're Glorified, to be fair.'

'Excuse me, Georgie? You're saying just because I don't carry that M-500 badge of honour, my kids don't deserve to be protected too, you lit—'

'We do apologise to our listeners, especially if you had any children listening. We'll ensure merit deductions for that listener take place for his negativity.'

'Can I just say something, Colli?'

'Of course, Georgie, go ahead.'

'I want to reassure people that Command *is* looking to protect us. I don't mean to offend anyone, but the latest update from Arneld Hevas is very comprehensive and accessible through your Watches, so please make sure you listen to that and not misguided individuals.'

'Thank you, Georgie. Well, that's all we have time for; it's been fabulous to have you in today. I think you'll have inspired people. Have a happy merit-making day, and no doubt we'll have you back soon. Would you like to introduce our next song?'

'I'd love to. It's been a pleasure, as always.'

'The pleasure is mine.'

'Inspiring us to keep pounding the treadmill, this is The Tulip Twins, coming in hot with a tune boasting a massive 95 per cent promoter score. This is "Back on Track".'

CHAPTER
ONE

She felt uneasy as she saw him checking his Watch. She was sad, disappointed.

The feelings grew stronger, like a dark fog moving in, peppered with the temptation to check her own wrist. Even then, in a moment where nothing else should matter, they still couldn't pull themselves away from the constant desire for merit.

Genni Mansald could feel a tight web of guilt spinning in her thoughts as she sat on the soft-backed chair. *Progress is Strength. Missing merit opportunities is weakness.* She could see the irritation move across the room in hot ripples as every funeral guest started to fidget. Disgruntled faces turned towards the back of the large open space, all of them expecting the funeral coordinator to appear. She could see it clearer than ever before; when it came down to it, life was about selfish productivity and there was no space for anything else, no empathy or sacrifice or decency or respect.

Despite it all, Genni managed to fabricate a smile for Blake as he looked up from his wrist, addressing her with alert eyes and a subtle wave across the rows of funeral attendants. Pearl, Jaxson and Mila were beside him. They now saw her too. It was only for a moment, before they were all pulled back in, working from their devices or posting something on *Personi*, or both.

Is Ace, your friend who hasn't even been dead a week, not worth your full attention?

And don't I deserve more than a wave? I haven't seen you since Ajay, the love of my life, murdered Ace because he found out Ajay was a fraud and had been lying to us as long as we've known him, and my life has fallen apart and you can't even stop working for a second to come and give me a hug? Some friends.

What she hated more than anything, though, was how much she wanted to join them. The woman's words on yesterday's 'All That Motivation' broadcast echoed in her head: 'Progress is Strength and we all have a part to play in building a greater Tulo.'

That's what I should be doing, but it all feels so dirty.

She wanted to shake off the desire to gain points, but the culture had its ropes wrapped so tightly around her neck, she could only choke rather than breathe. What she'd seen in the Side over the last few days with Ajay's family had helped her see things more clearly. The people in the Side, Unworthies, weren't everything Command claimed they were. They weren't lazy or selfish or worthless. Memories of Ajay's mother running around after her own mother and ladling endless scoops of soup into boxes for others confirmed the contrary. A shiver tingled down Genni's back as she wondered whether her thoughts were a crime. She hated that now she was back, breathing in the toxic City air, the clarity she felt in the Side was lost in a fresh cloud of merit lust.

I don't need merit. Of course I do. It's everything I know. Stop thinking. These ten minutes are about Ace. Does he not deserve my time and attention to say goodbye?

She glanced down at her legs, wiping the trousers of her silver pantsuit, as if to wipe away her accessory of persistent sadness. So much about the City felt twisted. Even the tradition of wearing silver to the funeral of someone with a M-400 plus score and only donning gold for the Glorified was perverted. *Is their memory not worth as much?* They weren't worth as much as they'd achieved less. That's what Genni had always known, but she couldn't forget what she'd seen.

She could still hear her brother's voice, coarse and evil as he toyed with the Blythefens, as if they were nothing. It was hard to believe he was an undercover Command detective, not an events executive. But he was disgusting; he, Rod, just casually told that family he arrested Tara, Ajay's sister, years ago.

And then Command *dealt* with her. He treated her execution, or whatever it was, as simply as a pass in a football match.

She had tried to imagine Ajay's parents' faces but she couldn't. It was funny how she didn't really know them, but she still cared deeply, which also made her feel unhinged.

This is Ajay's family. Ajay, the narcissistic liar who destroyed your life, broke your heart and ran away from it. Not to mention the fact that he killed, killed, the friend you're supposed to be honouring right now.

Genni could feel her arm hairs standing on end as she held back the tears.

Is this why Command is taking so long to find Ajay or The Rogue? Because they're too busy with corrupt vendettas against the Side? How can I stop it? I can't. I'm just a woman, with no power, trapped in a system.

She picked at her nail cuticles and swallowed the lump in her throat as she looked considerately at the head of Ace's mother a few rows in front. Her dyed brown hair shone under the tasteful, fluorescent lights, curling under at the back with the smooth curvature of a bowl. Genni wondered whether her eyes were welling with tears or just held their usual sharp and intimidating glare. It was hard for Genni to believe Ace came from such a ruthless woman, though she could see some of her stubbornness and vanity in him. She knew from her own mother, whose mouth wouldn't ever stay shut, about the drama when Ace was a baby. His father cheating and leaving, the merit deduction for his bad behaviour not enough to warrant any real punishment. Perhaps all that resentment had formed a solid mass within his mother and so she carried it around like a heavy burden, forcing her to treat Ace as a project rather than a son.

All parents seem to carry that burden.

At that moment, Genni's eyes gravitated towards the second row to meet her own mother's persistent stare, two large pearl earrings sitting gracefully either side of her plump face. Instantly and predictably, her mother fussed and tapped the broad shoulder of Genni's father beside her. He twitched his head in her direction, his silver hair combed back. He stared at Genni, irritated, with a disciplinary look. Genni watched his lips mouth over the rows of heads: 'Where have you been?'

She wasn't going to respond, merely moving her gaze to the front of the conference room where the Prosper logo spun on a hovering screen. Turning her thoughts to the room, she admired the quality of the painting on the cool, eye-catching feature wall; the three shades of the Prosper purple complemented each other in an asymmetric pattern. The ceiling was high and the room airy and bright with a view of the City through the windows on her left.

If she died, she wasn't sure if the room in the Beauty Dome would have a view, having heard that they used the basement rooms for funerals. Though she'd never thought much about it, she wouldn't have imagined anyone she knew would die young enough for their funerals to be at their workplace rather than in the Glorified Quarters. Suppose it was only right, though; if there was any building worthy enough outside the Quarters, Prosper was it. Genni had never been in before, despite always asking for a tour. Ajay, who worked there for half of their three-year relationship, had promised her one once. Genni breathed through the circle of her mouth, feeling the anger brewing with the recognition of another way he'd let her down. Her suspicions were correct about the building; it was just as impressive inside as out.

Genni didn't even hear the swooshing of the double doors as the funeral coordinator bounded into the room, filling it with a silent relief. As he stood before his agitated audience between two hovering drones, he adjusted his silver tie knot, his voice coming out dry through the drones' microphones. Genni watched him, the sweat visible in his black locks and his blotching skin.

Genni reckoned he was mid-forties, and no higher than M-300 with his worn-out suit and general tardiness. She was surprised; she assumed helping citizens move on from grief would be a Worthy contribution. Perhaps he was well-merited and was just having a bad day. Genni closed her eyes, damning herself for the jerk reaction of merit judgement.

None of this even matters. Ace matters. Use this time for him. Don't think about anything else. Not Ajay, his family, Rod, Command or my questions. And not about the coordinator's merit score. It doesn't matter. But it has to. Doesn't it? Somehow.

'To begin the celebration of Ace's contribution, here is a short reel of his highest merit achievements.' The coordinator shuffled away as the drones swirled around to project the film.

The video flickered through Ace's jobs, his community efforts and overall statistics, but it still failed to change Genni's thought pattern. Her trip to the Side and everything after it was absorbing her; in the four days since her return, everything took her back there. She felt guilt press into her like a relentless boss; Ace deserved her full attention and she couldn't give it to him. Even as a picture of him volunteering with kids at an Education Centre stole the room, Genni saw the playground in the Side; a young girl celebrating with her father as he lifted her body across the climbing frame. *Are the Blythefens still alive? Would they have killed them already?*

She could still hear the struggle of Ajay's mother as they pulled them from their own home.

Genni tried to clear her mind, not letting the images of Rod, the drones, the arrest and their destroyed garden steal her focus. She looked back to the screen where Ace's work statistics were appearing and they managed to distract her, finally. *He was a power station.* Genni had never noticed but his work-hour tally was monumental, making her feel inadequate. *Is this why Command promoted funerals?* The service wasn't about Ace at all, but about throwing someone else's achievements around to make others compare, and work harder as a result. It felt like a Command thing to do. The Command she now knew.

She closed her eyes again, trying to erase the memories, and fill them with ones of Ace. She couldn't. As more images of Ace appeared, she was reminded of what she did when she returned from the Side and what it could mean for her future.

CHAPTER
TWO

She had been breathless, having run from the Side terminal back into the Outer-Rings of the City. Genni had leaned against a wall, allowing people and drones to flock past her. Trying to steady her arm, she swiped at her Watch to find the newest contact in her files.

'She'll help you,' Kelli, Ajay's kind-hearted mother had said, as she transferred the details for 'Reha' between their Watches and pushed Genni out of the back door before Rod and Command smashed through the front one.

When Genni had rung, she held her breath as the woman's face came into view.

At first, Genni thought it was a dodgy Watch camera or an error in the pixelation, but as the woman peered in closer, she understood that the dishevelled-looking woman had a dark-red mark that ran down her right cheek and over her chin. She'd never seen a skin defect like it, and she was curious as to why the woman wouldn't have opted for surgery to remove such an imperfection.

'Hello? Who are you?' Reha's voice was brusque and dry over the noise of a fox yapping. 'Alpha, stop that.'

Genni hadn't been able to speak, still fixated on the woman's appearance; her head of ungroomed greying hair filling most of the screen. It made her feel more nervous, but she had nothing else. No one else.

'I . . . yes, I'm . . .' Genni fought through her dry throat. 'Genni. My name's Genni.'

'Are you from the Centre?' Reha asked, eyes persistent.

'No, no.' Genni blinked. 'I'm a . . .' she paused, '. . . acquaintance of the Blythefens.'

'Ah.' Reha squinted at Genni through the camera. 'You're the boy's girlfriend.'

Genni's legs turned weak beneath her.

'Don't look so frightened, girl.' Reha's eyes seemed to soften momentarily. 'Where are you?'

'By the Side terminal. Something's happened to them and I don't know what to do.' She wobbled, bidding tears back.

'They took them?' Reha's eyes turned urgent.

'Yes, and they—'

'Did anyone see you?' Reha said after shushing her.

'I . . .' Genni could feel her heart crashing against her chest. 'I don't think so.'

'OK.' Reha relaxed her shoulders but maintained her tone. 'Come here, I'll send you my location. We need to get you off the streets, in case.'

Genni only subtly nodded before Reha ended the call and a location pin appeared spinning above Genni's Watch. Not too far from Downtown, over the bridge. She questioned herself; how could she go to a stranger's home in the Outer-Ring? It was reckless. Stupid. But she was too freaked out to think logically, so she wound up shakily knocking on the door to a house by the river.

She was pulled through it and stumbled into a messy living space; sofas were draped in clothes, with a strawberry-red fox settled on top of them. Reha had stood expectantly, sadness in her sharp, wrinkled eyes.

'They took them . . . and Tara . . . they . . .' Genni frantically wiped her tears away as she tried to steady her breath.

'You know about Tara?' Reha blinked rapidly.

'Do you?' Genni struggled to process everything, including the sore, red splash across Reha's face, brighter than on camera.

'She was here a lot, before.'

'But the others, Kelli, Karlane, didn't seem to know?' Genni had managed to slow down. Despite feeling vulnerable and panicked, she managed to say Ajay's mother and grandmother's names without breaking down.

'Confirmation of your worst fear is a painful thing.' Reha had shown Genni a seat on the sofa. *Why isn't she more upset?* 'Most of the City turn a blind eye to the Side, girl.' She pulled a mug from the kitchen cupboard. 'Even when people just disappear.'

'But that's been happening for years. Wait . . .' Genni had shivered. *All of those vanishing Side citizens Command claimed moved to the City were killed?*

'Here, you need this.' Reha had offered Genni the steaming mug too casually. She didn't drink from it.

For a while they spoke amicably about the disappearances, the Side and The Guiding Light, the holographic device with an ideology that stifled progress. With an arm smoothly draped over the armchair she sat in, Reha sipped calmly from her own mug, not offering any solutions or action. She continued waffling on about how not everyone in the Side even followed The Guiding Light, which Genni could see was contrary to everything she'd known, but it didn't help the Blythefens. Reha then played with the fox while cooing and saying that Tara had been part of a group spreading the devices across the City, but Genni didn't care; she eventually boiled over with Reha's seeming indifference.

'Do you not care about them, or Tara?' she'd said, bolting up from the sofa. 'It's not like she was part of The Rogue or killed anyone. She didn't deserve to die.'

'Of course she didn't.' Reha placed her own mug on the coffee table, tension in her eyes. 'But Command have tabs on anyone distributing Guiding Lights, and it's a risk Tara took.'

'And what about the others? The ones in the Side? Surely they weren't all breaking the law?'

'No.' Reha gazed at the crumb-ridden floor.

'And the Blythefens?' Genni hadn't struggled to say their last name, but its difference to Ajay's surname continually reminded her of his betrayal.

'Pawns in Command's game.'

'So, what are you doing about it?' Genni hadn't been able to control herself, the revelations and anger going so deep.

'What I can.'

'It doesn't seem like it.'

'We can't stop what Command is doing.' Reha's voice turned sharp. 'But we can make a difference slowly through small things.'

That can't be enough.

'I think it's time for me to leave,' Genni said, standing and stepping over an old pizza box.

'Why don't you come with me and I'll show you?' Reha had followed her to the door, speaking softly.

'I'm not going anywhere with you. I don't know you.' Genni's hand hovered over the door release. 'I never should have come here.' She slapped her palm against the controls, the door slid open and she stormed back into the Outer-Ring crowds without looking back.

As the funeral ended, her every muscle was tense as she remembered Reha's refusal to help the Blythefens. It was exasperating. Genni knew it would be dangerous, but Reha wouldn't even toy with the idea. They were her friends, weren't they? Why wouldn't she try?

She felt the tears tickling her cheeks, and it was only as the funeral coordinator bumbled off the stage and left a picture of Ace in his place that she noticed the glancing eyes. Her gasping sobs filled the room; all that raw emotion and frustration merging to become only the loss of Ace. It was almost a relief as she stared into the eyes on her friend's photo, Ace's charming smile overtaking her. She knew some of the tears were for him. Despite all the other 'stuff', she finally reflected on his absence without distraction. Yet it was only for a moment, because as she started to control her tears, the rest of it was back again. Genni was grieving more than his death; it was the death of a life she once lived, where Command was a righteous power, and Ajay was *her* Ajay, not Karle Blythefen from the Side. Where was he? Was he even alive? Did he care? He had to; it must have been an accident. The Ajay she knew wasn't a murderer, and whether any of what she knew was the truth, the friendship he had with Ace was undeniably real.

She would never see Reha again. Her stomach twisted then, because she realised that the woman was self-assured and knew things. *And so, I could find a way to help the Blythefens through her, without her help. They're people who don't deserve how they're being treated. I know how that feels.*

As she pulled tissues from her trouser pocket and people started to rise from their seats and instrumental music faded through the drone speakers, Genni saw Blake and the others coming towards her, everything still battering through her brain.

'We're going for a quick drink, want to come?' Glancing up at Blake, Genni smiled slightly at his orange-speckled tie and followed his tailored silver suit down over his prosthetic legs.

A quick drink? How can they ask for a quick drink?

Blake, no legs, the attack. The Rogue, hidden. Public, unhappy. Security, everywhere. Ace, gone. Ajay, gone. Command, lies.

The broadcast was back again, Georgie's voice fluttering into Genni's headspace.

'Watches are constantly being checked and monitored for whatever we do.'

'The Rogue decided to trespass into *our* lives.'

'We have to fight for what our ancestors gave us during the Revolution, and not let those who didn't work hard enough bring us down.'

Genni felt like it was all empty words. Their history meant little to her, not when Command had been killing Side citizens for years. And even despite the fact many would agree with Command's 'culling of the dead weight', she could also see how much the system pulled people apart. When she overdosed on electrically enhanced *SkipSleep* last year, she could have ended up Unworthy like them – *would some people believe that's what I deserved?* Or Blake, standing there now, on legs he wasn't born with, who had given up his love of dancing because it wasn't Worthy enough and whose merit compensation was so inadequate that he was made to feel Unworthy . . . *It isn't right. And it isn't good.*

A drink? I can't slip back into a life where I do something as ordinary as a quick drink.

'Not today,' she stuttered before collecting herself and making her exit.

CHAPTER
THREE

The twinkle of the billboard shone into her bedroom. Genni lay on her back, blinking at the ceiling, watching the purple and black shapes spin over each other. She couldn't sleep. The noise of the City was usually a calming presence, but tonight, it was a storm. Everything was. After the funeral, she'd gone to the office and stared at her three screens as if they weren't even there. She'd come home, hoping to focus. Instead, she painted a City street with the tones of how she felt; black, grey with a dash of red for her anger. Then she decided sleep would do her good. It always had in the past. But nothing. As she lay there, all stewed up, she considered how she didn't even need *SkipSleep* to stay awake. That's what people were missing. They didn't need drugs to continue merit-making, they merely needed frustration, angst and a complete distrust of everyone and everything. She shook herself and slid from the bed, the hems of her thin shorts rising up her legs.

Dragging herself through the kitchen into the living room, she peered over the shopping centre outside, watching small people filter in and out in the night light. *All of us just living in the darkness.* Again, she tried to shake it off and find something positive in life. Her eyes scanned over a billboard as an advertisement for Rogue reports faded into a teaser for pomegranate salad. Food. She liked food. Plonking herself on the sofa, she tapped at her wrist, trying to focus on the menu and not on Reha or the Blythefens or Ajay or Ace. *Kale or spinach? Why wouldn't Reha help them? What did she mean about showing me how to make a difference? If it's not to do with Joon and Kelli, or exposing Command, I'm not interested. It's dangerous, anyway. She said it herself. Tara got killed. Kale. Do I really want a salad? No. Pasta. More comforting.* She watched as the Watch validation sequence ticked over, bored with its new additional steps. *I'm hungry. This was a good decision.*

It was only five minutes later that the drone arrived at her window and she had to slide out from her irritated comatose state. She took the box from its metal arms and breathed in the fresh, tomato steam. It made her feel sick. Sighing, she dropped the box onto the kitchen counter, trying to remember the last time she ate a proper meal. She squeezed her waist, feeling the bone beneath. Things were getting unhealthy, she knew that, but she had nowhere to go. She couldn't move to the Side; that would be sacrificing everything she'd worked for, and if the system did have moral principles, which she believed, overall, it did, then she shouldn't neglect that. Although it would be more of a statement. Not that anyone would know. She was a nobody. She certainly couldn't try to break the Blythefens out alone, that would be a death sentence. The only person she knew who *could* help was Reha, and she was uncooperative. Though, she hadn't completely rejected Genni; she had reached out once after they met, offering her support. But she couldn't collaborate with her, whatever it was she did, because after all, Genni knew it wasn't safe. None of the options were safe. She swore loudly at the ceiling, the purple and black from the billboards filling the apartment again.

A work email about lab reports on the new skincare range came in on her wrist. The latest tests showed the new recipes didn't help improve scar concealment. *Do I even care?* She sat on a breakfast stool, staring at the blinker on her screen, wondering whether to go over to her desk and log in. She glanced past it to look at her painting, dark and gloomy figures walking between dark and gloomy buildings. No. She couldn't stay here. *I'll try the office again. It'll be less busy at this time.*

It had taken her two minutes to get ready as she threw her hair up, lobbed some trousers on, marched past her untouched meal and bumbled into the street. As she merged into the City's current of people, something felt off as she boarded the sky train. It was much busier than she expected for this time of night. People looked at one another suspiciously down the carriage and it only took her a few seconds to notice the man in the blue hoodie to the right of her. He was sat on the disabled seat with a cardboard sign between his legs. She then noticed there were more like him. She instantly felt something like a rock drop in her chest. The train continued to slide with its simplicity past the glinting diamond windows of skyscrapers, but the inside felt anything but sparkling. There was a tension. Hot and fierce.

Genni stood her ground, clutching the purple pole by the door, ready to depart when her stop came. When it did, she skipped quickly off onto the platform, but many people followed her and she was caught in the rush. She went with them towards the Retail District and the Beauty Dome; as the crowd split, there were more of them, people in indistinctive hoodies carrying foghorns and more cardboard posters. Some boarded the train, headed for the Financial District, the Social Sphere and the Glorified Quarters. They arrived at the plaza outside her office, and some of them joined others by the fountain. Many stood on its walls, shouting and chanting over the night. It was only then that Genni saw the posters.

It was Ace's face.

She felt a hollowness as she nervously licked her dry lips.

She slowly moved past them, shaking right down to her feet. Managing to stop a gasp, she grew teary as she saw a young girl in a black dress, waving around cardboard boasting the words:

WITHOUT AMBERS IN A CELL,
WE'RE NOT SAFE AND WELL.

Genni quickly scanned into the office, the subtle pink walls of the Beauty Dome feeling as black as the girl's dress. She stood there as the bustle of the office continued around her. *Well, at least people are unhappy with Command. Maybe then we can see change, but they're using Ace's face to symbolise their shortcomings. And Ajay. He was never part of The Rogue. He can't have been. I still don't believe that – Command are lying there too.*

She became alert to her colleague's questioning eyes as she made her way to her desk. Before she'd even sat down, a news alert vibrated on her wrist and was projected above the staff board. Pictures of Joon, Kelli and Karlane shone over the rows of desks. *What?* They all looked pale and broken. The kindness in Karlane's eyes that Ajay had always said about his grandma had faded into nothing. Just a lifeless stare. Genni tried to stomach the squirmy voice of Arneld Hevas as he explained their 'progress with the Ambers case'. It seemed they'd be conducting thorough interviews with his family and they were in custody. Genni wanted to scream as their faces disappeared. *They'll kill them. They're from the Side and they'll find a way to kill them with the public's approval. They'll probably brand them part of The Rogue.* She was quickly corrected when Arneld announced there was no reason to believe they were members of The Rogue like their son, but his next words stole her breath.

'We will stop at nothing to locate Ajay Ambers and The Rogue in order to make Tulo safe again.'

What does 'stop at nothing' mean? Torture? Genni sensed the vomit rising in her stomach and her jaw turned stiff. She ran to the toilet and let it out. As she wiped her mouth with a tissue, still holding her head over the basin, she watched her tears fall onto the white porcelain. *I can't escape from this. I can't go back. Somewhere I've got to take a risk. I'll start with Reha. If she won't help me, maybe she can introduce me to someone who will.*

CHAPTER
FOUR

A week later, Genni held on tightly to the plastic box; the smell of warm bread was wafting from it, but it arrived to her as nothing. Walking slowly across the Outer-Outer-Ring bridge, she hoped the brim of her sunhat was low enough to cover her face. *I shouldn't be doing this. This isn't going to end well.*

'So Reha said you work in the Retail District?' His voice made her twitch.

She had barely noticed him shuffling along beside her, so deep was her trepidation of being seen.

'Huh?' Genni finally looked at him, one of Reha's friends who happened to be heading the same way she was. She noticed a sweet mole on his neck.

'Your job.' He laughed as they walked over the bridge towards Downtown, the river flowing beneath their feet.

'Sorry.' She grew distracted by the hard thumping of her heart as she scanned the neighbourhood through her sunglasses. 'I'm at the Beauty Dome.'

'My brother works at the fashion one.'

She concentrated only on sliding through the increasing crowd of Unworthies; their smell brushing on her as their shoulders clapped. *I should never have agreed to this. When Reha said to provide aid to Unworthies, I didn't consider how exposing it would be. I might not even meet anyone who could help me help the Blythefens, no matter how connected she is.*

'My name's Lorcan, by the way.' He smiled with his slightly crooked teeth.

She nodded subtly as they passed a cordoned-off house with blown-out windows. It hit Genni straight on; these streets were people's homes and Command left the houses of Rogue suspects derelict and destroyed. Across the door was Ace's face with Ajay's name plastered next to it:

WITHOUT AMBERS IN A CELL,
WE'RE NOT SAFE AND WELL.

How long is it going to be like this?

'It's great what you're doing, ya know. With the food and everything. We needed more help.' Lorcan's voice floated past her. 'Genni?'

Genni snapped back as they walked, with one eye still on the blown-out house.

'I just said it's great what you're doing.' He spoke lightly.

'Oh,' Genni breathed through her anxiety. 'Thanks.'

'Not many people like you bother with people like us.'

'Like you?' Genni jostled the box in her arms, keeping her head low.

'M-250 and falling.' Lorcan shook his wrist, his Watch screen lighting up with the movement. Genni felt instantly stupid – why ask such an obvious question that exposed him like that?

'But that's the least interesting thing about me,' he said, seeming not to care.

'What's the most interesting?' Genni managed, despite another thing making her flinch. She thought a drone was circling towards them before it simply flew in the opposite direction. They crossed a road not far from the old Downtown market stalls.

'Well, I *love* hot dogs, probably have two a week—'

'Two a week?' Genni said, trying to figure out the merit deduction that much cholesterol would demand.

'Yeah, you can probably tell.' Lorcan sighed jovially, and patted his moderately protruding belly. Most men in their mid-twenties were hard as a brick in that area; six-packs, eight-packs, ten-packs. Genni didn't respond, glancing behind her.

'What about you?' Lorcan hoisted up his rucksack. 'What do you like to do?'

'Work, I suppose.' Genni held his blue eyes as she spoke; they reflected the way the white sun shone on the river in speckled, moving light.

'Oh, come on.' He stretched out his words. 'You're obviously different from the rest of them. That can't be all you like to do.'

Genni went quiet; no one had ever asked her that question so openly before.

'You can tell me.' He nudged her softly on the shoulder of her green, floral dress. 'What is it? Do you sleep all day, every day?'

'Not all day,' she mumbled before smiling. 'I paint.'

'Paint?' He raised his eyebrows.

'Yeah, landscapes; sometimes people.'

'You'll have to show me.'

Genni hesitated. *His interest is unnatural. Be careful.*

'I don't know you.'

'Oh, so you want more?' He nodded. 'OK, well, I fix cars and am sometimes drafted in for sky train maintenance, like my dad. I'm one of five kids and was born round the corner.' He pointed down the side of the alley they were emerging from.

Genni tried to stop him. She wasn't asking for his life story.

'I'm a strong swimmer too,' he said, showing no signs of slowing down. 'Though I don't get to the pool as much as I would like. It's not well-maintained.' He plunged his hands into the pockets of his baggy jeans. 'It was better when we were kids, when we could get into The Tower with my mum.'

What? Genni's sudden confusion must have shown in her face.

'She works at Prosper,' Lorcan explained with a laugh.

'Are your parents still together?' Genni had never met anyone whose partner was even fifty points below them. Those relationships didn't work . . . But clearly that wasn't true, either.

'Twenty-five years strong.'

Genni looked down at the dirty ground beyond the box in her hands.

'What else can I tell you about me? I like hanging out with my best people, I take these to people who need them.' He jostled his backpack, the metal of The Guiding Light devices clinking together as he spoke. It instantly pulled Genni back to the reality of her vulnerability. She took two steps away from him as they walked.

'Oh, and I have to scan the pad on my front door three times every time I leave, just to make sure it's still working.'

Genni only gave him a questioning look.

'I know. It's obsessive, but what if I get home late and find it's not working and then I'm locked out?'

She said nothing as her mind turned back to the bread, not sure who it was really for. *I only did it because of the peer pressure. I never should have gone back to Reha's house, but how was I supposed to know there were groups heading out and Reha would immediately pull me in? She's manipulative.*

'There, now you know everything, can I see your paintings?'

'Maybe.' Genni anxiously counted the bags of bread in the box for the third time. *Sixteen.*

'Are you alright?'

Genni nodded and a nervous, awkward tension fell between them, the sun suddenly streaming down. She longed to wipe some sweat from her brow. They walked further down the river, edging closer to the Side terminal.

'You don't recognise me, do you?' Lorcan's voice was quieter, more tentative.

'What?' Genni glanced up at him before avoiding some broken glass on the ground. She couldn't place him.

'A few months back, I found you Downtown. In the markets; you were upset.'

Genni stopped still, recalling the incident instantly. She didn't want to think about it, but he had seen her at her worst; he'd had an instant image of her as a broken woman, crying and desperate for knock-off *SkipSleep*. It wasn't far from here, a few street rings across, in the room behind the old Downtown markets. When her addiction to enhanced *SkipSleep* had been at its peak, it was like her second home, other than the office. She couldn't go a day without a fix, and even after months of being clean, finding out about Ajay's lies had driven her back to where Lorcan had found her. She remembered feeling ashamed but he was kind, almost easing the pain of Ajay's betrayal – fresh, new and all-absorbing.

'That was you?' Her mouth went dry.

He nodded as a woman in a nearby house twitched her curtains. There was a new silence, one even more awkward than the last.

'You look better now.' A compassionate look grew on his face. Genni wondered what he'd gone through to be so kind, or whether it was all a front.

'I'm getting there.' She smiled, hoping that was enough to end the conversation.

He got the message and graciously moved on. 'So that lady looks like she could need some help.' His lighter tone was back as they reached the top curve of the river and he pointed at an older woman with a thin, stretched face who was hanging her legs over the water. She looked dirty, uncivilised and Unworthy.

Genni instinctively took a step back, placed the box on the ground and tipped her hat down. *Breathe. She's just a person.*

'Do you want me to come with you?' Lorcan tightened the tatty straps on his backpack.

She shook her head beneath the rim of her hat. *I don't want to be with him and those illegal devices any longer than I need to be.*

Before she knew it, he'd gone and she was tip-toeing her way across the riverside. She barely looked up but shakily held onto a small bag of bread rolls she'd recovered from the box. Arriving by the woman, she was hit with the smell. Months of dry body odour.

Genni took a quick look around, seeing the crowds pass by uninterested.

'Can I help you?' the woman croaked.

Genni almost jumped. Only after seeing the length of the woman's scrawny body and a fabric trolley beside her did Genni realise how close she was. She scurried away, dropping the bread bag by the woman's side. She said nothing. Turning on her feet, she wasn't even embarrassed by her impoliteness; it was a defensive instinct. The woman shouted after her but Genni merely kept walking, stroking her arms before retrieving the big box of bread and dashing down an alley, cursing herself for ever agreeing to the task. There was no way she could deliver the remaining fifteen. It didn't feel worth the risk. It wasn't helping Unworthies that was the problem, it was the association with the people she was helping them with. People like Tara. People whom Command killed. Of course, she wanted to save the Blythefens, but throwing bread at a helpless woman wasn't going to make a difference. It wasn't worth her time. Nor was it worth her life. It truly was meritless.

CHAPTER
FIVE

Joon Blythefen didn't know his name, the Command man with serpent-like eyes.

As he felt the heat of his breath on the plastic over his mouth, he couldn't stop seeing his face; he saw him every time he thought of Tara, his sweet girl. He'd always held a small hope that one day, she might swing back into his arms. Every time he closed his eyes, he was back in their cosy kitchen, where he would sit her on his lap and tie her pigtails. But that's not what he saw. Instead that kitchen was where he listened to that man's harrowing laugh and it penetrated every part of him with the pain that his daughter was gone. It was all so fresh, as if it had happened seconds ago, not hours. In the drive across the desert, it all played over in Joon's head like a constant, tortuous song. And it hadn't stopped. He'd once vowed to protect his children, but they were both lost in different ways. Karle, or Ajay, pulled by the lure of the City and now, where? Tara, gone. A sense of inexplicable failure fell over his shoulders along with the tight rubbing of the cuffs around his wrists. *I'm sorry.*

He lifted his welling eyes to watch the grey walls pass, trying to breathe and console his unsteady heart. *She's up there. We'll be OK.* He closed his eyes again, struggling to wipe from his mind the trepidation of their situation and *her*. A woman he hadn't seen for twenty years. He could hear the groans of his mother-in-law behind him and the frantic breathing of Kelli, his wife, on his right. All he wanted was to hold her hand. It was as if time caught up with itself as they abruptly swooped to a seamless stop and he jerked open his eyes.

The sudden invasion of light was alarming, exposing the impressive room around them. It had floor-to-ceiling windows, with a view of the Glorified Quarters, the mid-morning sun rising high above the mountain peaks. He followed the large, oval space, big enough to fit several of their kitchens inside. Along its walls were posters decorated with bold, calligraphic letters. Their words were fuzzy at first, before Joon adjusted to the harsh light – 'To get there, be effective', 'Progress is Strength' and 'Never stop striving'. Then came the muffled sound of *her* voice. He saw a scrawny body drowning in a black suit, standing in front of a blue-lit tank – a growing baby bobbed in it.

She turned to face him. A breath caught in his throat. She looked like a twisted version of her former self.

'Hello, Joon,' she said softly, calmly, with an unnerving smile on her ageing face. Walking towards them, her heels clipped across the white, mosaic tiles. Joon hadn't expected her to look so different. So old, skinny, unhealthy.

'We've got a lot of catching up to do,' she sighed, clasping her twig-like hands together before stopping still and waiting for one of the guards to pull over a red sofa. She fell into it as the other guard pushed Joon, sending him stumbling forward.

He stared into the artificial blue of Esabel Hevas' eyes, trying to ignore the sound of the guard harshly moving his wife and mother-in-law before the elevator disappeared behind them. Esabel commanded the other man to rip the plastic from his mouth. Joon hissed from the pain.

He said nothing as she threw her spindly legs over the armrest of the sofa, darting her fake eyes between him, Kelli and Karlane. The guards shoved him and the other two into hard seats, and all of them fell into a toxic silence.

'Oh, I can't take it.' Esabel eventually flung her legs down. 'You're so rude. Why don't you introduce me to your wife?'

Joon had told Kelli about Esabel, the one he once knew, but the memories felt irrelevant.

'And this must be Karlane.' Esabel leaned forward to get a better look at Karlane behind him. 'She's had better days.'

He winced as he heard Karlane's struggle as the guard manhandled her to sit up.

'Don't fuss.' Esabel flapped her hand. 'You'll get your hands dirty.'

Joon closed his eyes to settle his anger before managing to ask her what she wanted. Esabel stood and tilted her head inquisitively at him. 'You used to be much chattier.'

Joon stared at the scuffed fabric of his brown shoes, marred by desert dirt.

'I shouldn't have had such high expectations, I suppose.' She wandered over to a fridge on the near wall, pulling out a bottle of water. 'You never did like being coerced into anything.' She twisted the cap from the bottle and lifted it to her lips, staring at Joon as she sipped. *She knows how thirsty we are.* Joon tried to compose himself and looked back out through the window over the Quarters.

'Beautiful, isn't it? You must regret giving it all up.' She walked beside him, staring out at the view.

Joon turned to his wife. Her eyes were focused on only one thing – the tank in the corner of the room. *Stop it, Kelli. Don't.* It had been a while since he'd seen a tank baby and he bet Kelli never had; women in the Side weren't Worthy enough for that privilege.

'We've got a problem here, Joon, haven't we?' Esabel came closer, bending down to him as if he were a small child.

He stayed silent, smelling the coffee on her breath.

'Answer my question.' She slapped the armrests, rattling his chair. Her erratic nature triggered memories; the way she scrambled through work at the Centre; the time she accidentally ordered 100 meals by drone instead of ten. Merit rushed her, maddened her somehow.

'Do you agree that your son has caused me a problem?' Her face quickly turned sour as she finally caught Kelli in her gaze. 'What do you think you're doing?' She struck Kelli's cheek with the back of her hand all too quickly. Joon winced, unable to do anything as Esabel roared into his wife's face. 'Did I give you permission to look at my daughter?'

CHAPTER
SIX

Only Joon Blythefen would marry someone who could be so obnoxiously entitled to believe they could stare at another's developing flesh and blood. *She's not a proper mother. There is no way she knew what it meant to see a child grow from a single-celled organism into an able-bodied being. She'll have missed out on all that glorious development by having them grow inside her, all the while draining her body of its resources and ending up with nine months of unproductivity and illness.* Plus, *she* didn't even give her children the chance to be spared of their flaws. At least Esabel had tried.

Arneld's genetic manipulation wasn't as effective as she'd hoped. She had missed the characteristics of stubbornness and rebellion, but still, they'd managed to get through to him in the end. By rebuilding his contribution, and by it, his reputation, they'd kept the family name healthy in the public eye. It was one of her husband's better ideas, but her son still existed as a sour taste in her mouth. She didn't trust him. That's why she needed to try again so the future of Command wasn't left to that waster, should he choose to accept the constitution mandate that the Hevas bloodline had rights to control. So, this time, she would make sure with the geneticist that her daughter wouldn't be so boisterous.

And yet, Joon Blythefen's wife had the audacity to look at her growing child with a stare of judgement. She would never understand. She was deluded. They all were. Kelli had her wicked ways with Joon when she picked him up in his Unworthy state, and brainwashed him into the life of The Guiding Light.

It's a shame, really. Joon had potential. She shook out her hand after knocking the freckles off his wife's face.

'I'm sorry,' Kelli stuttered. 'I've just never seen one.'

Esabel watched her swallow and enjoyed the developing red marks on her cheek. She leaned down and stroked her swelling skin, adopting a playful tone.

'That looks sore. Let's get you some ice.' She eyed the fatter of the two guards, who marched across the room towards the freezer, returning quickly to dab ice over Kelli's bland features.

Esabel returned to the sofa and on collapsing into it, felt the familiar ache of her back and a flurry of fatigue. She glanced over at the *SkipSleep* port on her desk. *Not now. Deal with them first.*

She played with the plastic wrap she'd pulled from Kelli's face between her fingers. 'You know, if you were open-minded and had frozen your eggs, like most women,' she paused, wanting the next line to hit them hard, 'you could replace the daughter you lost.'

'Don't talk about her.' Joon's eyes turned to fire, his entire body twitching.

'There he is.' Esabel pointed, ecstatic. 'I've been waiting for you. I was worried you'd lost that nasty temper.'

'Just stop it.' He stared at the ground. 'OK, just stop it.'

Esabel sat up straight, laughing under her breath. 'Yes, sir.' Her eyes suddenly darted to her wrist.

Wrap this up. Other things to do.

'Like I said, Joon, we have a problem.' She stood, waving her hand at the fat guard and gesturing towards the foul old woman, who had been slumping in her chair. He proceeded to shift her up again.

Joon squirmed and insisted they didn't know where Ajay was, as pitiful tears crawled down his wife's insolent cheeks. *This woman is unmanageable.*

'The problem isn't Ajay, or where he is.' Esabel watched a line of drones swoop past the window. 'But more what he's left behind.' She almost impressed herself with the grittiness in her voice. 'I've got unrest on every street corner.' She shook her head, walking back to her seat. 'So, what does a woman do when her capability is being questioned?' She leaned on the sofa's arm and pulled down the cuffs of her suit jacket.

They didn't respond. *Good, it's time for your kind to listen and bow. You deserve nothing more.*

'In order to settle people's doubts about our control over The Rogue and Ajay—'

'He was never with them, that's a lie,' Joon said, his lips trembling.

'Is it?' Esabel smiled. 'Truth doesn't have to be objective. We can make up any truth we like.' She broadened her smile, her tongue between her lips, catching his emotional brown eyes behind those stupid, slanted glasses. A sudden warmth of his familiarity unnerved her but she ignored it.

'I have to show the City we're not messing around—'

'By killing us.'

'Joon, I just wanted to say hello after so many years,' she said, placing a hand on her chest. 'And frankly, I feel rather hurt that you would think that this is anything but hospitality.' Esabel let the silence fester for a moment. 'With your daughter, it was different, you understand?' Her hand remained on her chest as she shook her head. 'She was doing something quite illegal.'

Esabel didn't want to go into the daughter and her distribution of those devices across her City. Because the Side Eradication Project would continue, as strong as before, after all the nonsense with The Rogue was over. She also didn't want to think about Rod Mansald and his disobedience; he should have arrested them *quietly*. They weren't ready for any public scrutiny; now they would have to find a way to use them quickly. All this thinking was a time soak. She lifted her wrist, flicked out her Watch, and swallowed hard when a merit reminder appeared. *Thirty minutes with no merit.*

'But if you want to be so straightforward and avoid any catching up or small talk, I suppose we'll cut straight to it.' She took a sharp intake of breath. 'Your son has killed a civilian. The public wants to bring Ajay and The Rogue to justice. But Ajay's little disappearing act is working fear into my people's hearts, and fear can drive people to do crazy things. That worries me. I haven't found your son yet, but what I do have is *you*, and you might just calm their nerves.'

QUIET ECHOES AT NIGHT

TWO MONTHS LATER

Personi Social Post

Nefi Mallie – Personi – M-299 – W-35/Y2462 – 12:33

How can we be sure we're safe if so many of *them* are in our apartment buildings, in our offices, around our children? Command needs to do more. They need to show us what they're doing to #FindAmbers.

30,569 loves

Reply from Melia Jacks – Personi – M-429 – W-35/ Y2462 – 12:37

It's astounding how much time people like you are dedicating to this. Suppose your score speaks for itself.

Reply from Nefi Mallie – Personi – M-299 – W-35/ Y2462 – 12:39

A high merit score won't stop The Rogue from killing you.

Reply from Melia Jacks – Personi – M-429 – W-35/ Y2462 – 12:39

Command is doing what they can. You'd know that if you had the brains to stay awake.

Reply from Tex Smath – Personi – M-311 – W-35/ Y2462 – 12:42

Sorry, @Melia Jacks but you obviously aren't concerned about the precious merit time you're losing by engaging in this conversation. Nefi is right when she says that Command isn't doing enough. It surely shouldn't be this hard for them to find a guy who literally killed someone in his own apartment. And what about the interrogations within Command? They've gone silent on that too. They're not interviewing the family anymore. It's unnerving and feels like they are out of their depth and that leaves us all vulnerable. #FindAmbers

Reply from Tex Smath – Personi – M-311 – W-35/ Y2462 – 14:42

@Nefi Mallie, with his silence, looks like we won this one.

Reply from Nefi Mallie – Personi – M-299 – W-35/ Y2462 – 14:56

Progress is Strength, eh, @Tex Smath?

CHAPTER
SEVEN

He'd experienced pain before. When he'd come second in his Quals or when his mother lectured him for being unmotivated. He knew pain, and this wasn't it. *This* was like a parasite eating him up from the inside and every breath, day, place, person and thought only fed its survival.

Rod Mansald stared depressingly at his merit count after two hours on the rower. He ran his hand over his sweaty forehead, scared by how exhausted he felt. Gathering his towel, he forced his way decisively from the gym and grazed past the playing courts. He arrived at the boost room, slamming open the door, not registering the startled people already plugged in. He slumped down in a seat and ordered the *SkipSleep* machine to rise from the table beside him. The needle was there, poised and ready for his arm. He whacked it down, tying the belts over it, and scanned his Watch over the panel. Drumming his fingers, he watched the loading circle whirl as it authenticated his Watch with the new security measures.

He stared at the ceiling, his anger barely controlled as he waited for the relief of the boost. It took him a minute to realise the needle was still, refusing to inject him with the drugs that would provide him with the energy he desperately needed. He prodded the screen, irritated by the voice of technology.

Daily boost limit reached. Try again in 5.25 hours.

He swore loudly, yanking the belts off his arm and wobbling the glass table.

His hands tight in fists, Rod slammed through the door, back into the Sports Tower's main thoroughfare. *I'm wrecked. What about my score? Dad will notice a drop. Will Genni become his more successful child?* The painful parasite bit harder.

One day Esabel Hevas would pay for this. They all would. Her, and her husband, and his incompetent colleague, Jona.

Rod did his job and he did it well. The Blythefens were in custody. So what if he made a scene by blowing up their poor little garden? He smiled at the memory. It was one of the best arrests he'd made. Tied up nicely with the fact that he'd already caught one of the family – that Tara girl. It was all perfect. Until Jona called him into his office, with his unfounded, self-entitled authority, and told him they were demoting him to a Watch administrator. So the parasite had its first breath.

Rod had read over the years, in inside reports and data, about Worthies losing it and slowly becoming pathetic, low-scoring Unworthies. People had said that time made the pain less stark. It had been a month and nothing had changed. And he didn't work all his life to be demoted from a Command compliance detective to a Watch administrator. Esabel had refused to see him, he was constantly angry and every time he saw the Blythefens on the news, with their tragic interviews, he seethed. The temper was sometimes so intense that saliva festered, frothing between his teeth. They still hadn't finished the job because there was still breath in that family's lungs. And it made his demotion even more unjustified. *So, they wanted a quiet arrest to hide the truth – that Ambers, a seventeen-year-old boy, outwitted them with an old computer in a dusty Side bedroom?* Using them in interviews hardly gave the illusion Command were close to finding Ambers and satisfying public demand. *No, this feels personal.*

Now in the shower room, Rod smacked the wall and water fired onto his head like rounds from a laser gun. They'd taken everything from him. One way or another, someone had to pay.

CHAPTER
EIGHT

Sometimes Esabel wondered if men were necessary; they annoyed her so much, it could only be natural they were some grave mistake. Her husband didn't function properly. She appreciated his quiet nature, always discreet in the background and imparting wisdom when she needed it, but of late, he'd turned into some overloaded announcement drone. Every time they'd been together over recent months, it had hung in the air: his disapproval. It was ridiculous and childish. What she'd decided to do with their daughter's life was her decision. Obviously, she could see he had some stakes in the matter, but he'd said at the four-week mark he was happy for changes to be made, starting with her immune system. So why all the sudden hostility? Esabel quickly returned to work as she watched him disappear into the office elevator.

It *was* the right thing. Her daughter wouldn't inherit her father's lack of organisation or her brother's unfiltered tongue, and not to mention her father's nose. She had spared her child from all of that. Plus, she'd have Esabel's determination and small appetite for anything sweet.

Stronger muscles, better stamina, greater confidence. It was all a gift.

'You're welcome, child,' she whispered towards the tank, her daughter's five-month-old foetus curled up tightly. 'Daddy's just being silly. He says I'm going too far, that you'll no longer be anything like us. But he's missing it; you'll get the best of us.'

She sat and reviewed several execution reports on suspected internal Rogue members from the previous day. It was time to speed things up, so she sent a note to increase the passable reliability score to 85 per cent – anyone who scored lower should be shot dead. As she nibbled through a fruit salad, she tried to read how many 'Ace's faces' had been cleared from her City's walls, but her mind was fluttering to her husband again. *Oh, no, no.* She should put her foot down: stop the thoughts before they got too distracting. *Esabel Hevas doesn't doubt herself.* She did not need to justify anything. It was preposterous that the new level of genetic engineering hadn't been pitched to the mass market, but it was only right she was setting the best example. There was a duty to procreate, to keep Tulo society flourishing, and those at the very top deserved to craft their children exactly as they chose. Her daughter would thank her for it. It was love. It was what a proper mother would do. Her father, on the other hand, didn't seem to understand and was probably too attached to his own overinflated ego. *That's right. Esabel Hevas does not doubt herself.*

With that, she returned to the video clips and details of that boy's face being lasered from Outer-Ring stalls, walls and pavements. They were all acting as if this Ace was some sort of martyr, a symbol for Command's lack of control, and the City couldn't rest easy until Ambers was found. It was rude, frankly, that anyone would question her leadership. She flicked at a screen and let the call ring out, pulling a grape off the end of her small fork.

'Yes, Ms Hevas?' Salli's squirmy little voice vibrated around the office.

'What are we doing about the graffiti?' She went in for another grape.

'We've made several arrests and are getting the paintings removed. Shall we broadcast the videos?'

Esabel dismissed her question, straightening her back. She took a moment to breathe, remembering why she made this woman vice-chair to the Board; she was efficient, but sometimes she asked the most stupid questions.

'We need to take stronger disciplinary action on the vandals.' Esabel chewed. 'Kill any of them under M-250.'

'Are you sure?' Salli seemed to stutter.

Another stupid question. Esabel poked her fork at the fruit salad, avoiding the brown pieces of pineapple. 'Just get it done. Discreetly, of course.'

'Right, OK, I'll send the update to the team.'

Esabel didn't hesitate and shut the call down as she tightened her jaw, squishing her face with the tartness of the last grape. *Who prepared this food? Get them fired.* Dropping the fork and pushing the bowl away, she reminded herself she wasn't losing control.

No one would miss anyone of such low merit scores and their contributory value was nothing for the City anyway. Once all the unrest was gone, they could get back to normal in ensuring the City was safe from The Rogue, and not waste too many of their admittedly stretched resources on them. The outcasts wouldn't last much longer. *We've stopped planes, we've taken their main camp, and we're finding their people, so I need to stop distracting myself.*

She needed to lift the City from the stagnant heap they'd been in for the last few months. Nothing made her more anxious. *We've been too weak. Progress is Strength. We can't exist without it.* There must be more they could do. Her eyes glanced at the date. It was almost a year since the Liberation Day attack. *Maybe we should give the victim's families an additional merit bonus? That would show sympathy, solidarity and all that compassionate stuff people seem to want.* It wasn't a bad idea. Esabel clicked her tongue as she thought more deeply. *Why have I only just thought of that? I've been too distracted. No, this isn't like me. Esabel Hevas doesn't get distracted.*

'Focus, focus,' she repeated while pressing her fingertips to her forehead.

Joon. Joon. Joon Blythefen. Exploding back into my life.

From her desk, she glanced over the view of the Quarters, thinking of him. The interviews had worked to a point. She was done with them, really; there wasn't much more she could get out of a sad man, his wife and a shrivelled old woman taking up a bed in a hospital. There was an obvious answer of what to do with them. The Side Eradication Project even had it down in writing: *The project aims to spare Tulo society from influencers of ideologies which teach against progress and who do not accept the generous offer of Purification.* Unfortunately, though, due to an inexcusable case of miscommunication between some lesser workers in publicity and admin, her plan to craft the Blythefens as part of The Rogue had fallen flat. The blockheads had even managed to publish that the family had no understanding of Ambers' allegiance to the terrorists. *No surprise, as Ajay was never part of The Rogue anyway. Lies get you nowhere,* she thought sarcastically, as a smile crept across her defined face, knowing how many lies had elevated her further. Here, though, a lie was stolen from her; they couldn't backtrack about the Blythefens' status with The Rogue, and unfortunately, the majority of the public wouldn't agree with blowing their heads off because as it stood, they appeared innocent. The very reason why only select teams in Command knew about the Side Eradication Project. *Pitiful, pitiful, pitiful. This is exactly why genetic modification needs to go up another level. Tulo shouldn't be home to people who make such mistakes. Better genes, better brains.*

However, as she began writing instructions for the anniversary merit bonus, an unwelcome feeling settled on her chest. It felt like . . . relief? As if the Blythefens' lives being temporarily spared was a good thing. Almost like she didn't want to kill them after all? *Especially not Joon.* She shook herself and buried the feeling. Deep. *Esabel Hevas does not doubt herself.* They'd have to find another way to kill them, but later, when the public had forgotten them and no one would notice their absence.

All this thinking is dangerous. She breathed, standing up at her desk and scanning her merit count. She was getting nowhere fast. *Not acceptable.* Getting some oxygen pumping round her veins would correct her demotivation, or lack of concentration, or overthinking, or whatever it was.

Soon, she'd donned her leggings and let the high-pitched voice of technology fall over her as her mirror noted the reduction in her pores since yesterday. She swiped it off. *Let's go.*

She stepped furiously into the open space at the side of her office and rattled on the control panel, syncing it with her Watch. She grew impatient as it validated her identity. *Surely I don't need these measures every time I scan. Esabel Hevas is no fraud.* After setting a target of 0.2 merit points for the session, the space digitised into a boxing ring with a virtual opponent ready for her onslaught. She shoved the gloves onto her hands, bashed them together and jumped straight in.

CHAPTER
NINE

'What did you do to your leg?' Caril's croak interrupted Genni's thoughts and forced her to glance at the scab on her left knee.

'I fell over.' Genni tottered down the steps towards the river's edge and popped the box of bread next to Caril.

'You rush too much. That's your problem.' Caril peered longingly into the box at the bread, but hesitated.

Genni tutted. 'Stop it, just help yourself.'

Caril, delighted, handled one of the rolls, split it open and sucked up its smell into her dried, cracked nose.

'Thank you,' she beamed, revealing her missing teeth and swollen gums.

'You're welcome. What happened to your trolley?' Genni peered at Caril's pull-along trolley behind her; it was worn, dirty and now had crosses of tape over a hole in its pink fabric.

'It was some shard of glass from a broken door or somethin'.' She chewed. 'Just lying there.'

Genni expressed her sympathetic distaste before taking a bite of bread and checking her wrist, groaning slightly at the amount of work emails. She used to feel motivated, even excited, at the sight of them, each one amounting to some sort of merit instead of the draining necessity they had become.

Flicking back, she glanced over the news to see more of the same spiel about unprecedented protests and arrests, but nothing else about Ajay's family, not since Joon's last interview.

'What's that sour face for?' Caril said, bits of bread falling down her chin.

'Nothing.' Genni smiled.

'Look, kid, I may be "Unworthy",' she gestured with her fingers, 'and terrified of folk from places like you come from, but I ain't daft.' Caril raised her eyebrows, so untamed they met in the middle. 'You're sad. It's all over ya face.'

'I just want to know if they're OK.' Genni remembered how Caril listened the week before. 'I just can't stop seeing that picture of Kelli, after they published her interview. She looked so jaded and pale. And it's just been silence for three weeks. I don't even think I believe that Karlane is in the hospital. She could be dead.' Genni stared into the river, feeling the weight of her own words. 'They could all be dead.'

'I wish I could tell ya, kid.'

'Do you think they'll interview them again?'

Caril shrugged her tiny shoulders and returned to the box for more bread.

'What about in the past? Did they tend to publish more than one interview for people on trial?'

'I don't remember,' Caril muttered. 'Never paid much attention. But the City never had so much trouble.'

'They've surely made an example of them already?'

'Kid, you're talkin' to the wrong lady,' Caril said bluntly.

'But they don't deserve to die for merely giving Ajay that computer. My mother bought me the shoes I often wore to go and get an illegal *SkipSleep* fix. Does that make her responsible for my mistakes?' Genni unloaded, her breath quickening with her words.

Caril blinked at her blankly as a quick breeze picked up off the river and passed them by.

Genni flicked off her wrist, closed her eyes, and sat in the acceptable silence, trying to tame her feelings. *This isn't enough.* For the last three weeks, Genni had lived in a merry-go-round state. After that first day when she'd been too scared to talk to Caril, she realised she was overly judgemental, and meeting some Unworthies would do her good. And it had. But then, like always, it never totally satisfied her because at the end of the day, the family who were kind to her at her lowest moment were suffering for Ajay's selfish betrayal.

Bread wasn't enough.

'You still mad with the birthmark lady?' Caril asked, circling her head on her neck.

'I was never mad at her,' Genni declared, thinking of Reha before noticing Caril's wide, condescending eyes. 'I wasn't.' She tried to lie better.

'Ya definitely had your Watch strap in a twist last time ya were 'ere.' Caril bent down and picked up a couple more pieces of bread before pulling out some old paper from her broken trolley to wrap them up in.

Before she could outrightly dismiss the comment and ask Caril whether she wanted a new trolley, her wrist pinged.

You haven't added to your merit score for sixty-two minutes. Is it time to do something of worth?

'I'm trying,' Genni said beneath her breath before she said goodbye to Caril and made her way back to the Inner-Ring.

'I don't want to keep fighting about the same thing, girl,' Reha said as they walked down the sloped steps to the River House. 'I know you're frustrated. I am too.'

Genni stayed silent and only focused on the end of the corridor, tightening her grip around the bag she was holding. She didn't want to say anything because she could feel the emotion in her chest. The truth was she didn't want to fight about it, either. She wanted Reha to be more courageous or passionate or even open to the idea of helping the Blythefens. That's all she was asking for, but it always fell flat.

Genni wanted to get them out; Reha would argue she could get killed. A fair point, though a coward's one. Genni said she would quit her job; Reha convinced her to keep it. *Use the system to your advantage.* She could see that, yet it felt hypocritical.

Genni argued that Command should be held accountable; Reha said she agreed, but they could never do that alone nor rally an army without again getting killed. It made sense, yet still felt unjust and uncomfortable.

She was tired of it so the two of them slipped into the River House without exchanging any more words. The first time she'd stepped into the River House, a nagging vulnerability told Genni she was going to die. It was the way the water rushed above her head; only a few panels of glass stopping it from crashing down on her like a collapsing building. Yet after a few visits, the water had become as intended: a tasteful and impressive feature of a large, welcoming room full of seating in the form of comfy sofas and secluded booths with round windows looking out into the water.

They were never taught about the Underwater Bar Disasters of Y-2357 at the Education Centre. The only reason she knew about it was because she read it once at the library. All those people injured or killed because they built the bars with cheaper materials. But the first time she'd come, she didn't think much about the fact they were never talked about.

As she dropped a bag of multipack vegetable crisps on the old bar, she smiled at Lorcan who waved while he was talking to another man at the far end of the room. Genni glanced at her Watch for today's merit count and the familiar dark weight came, clouding her mind as she saw her score slowly turning stagnant. Work and exercise had been enough to maintain it, but never enough to increase it.

She scanned the room and observed the moment: a couple of women were chatting on the sofas, probably with their Watches recording; a man was having a *SkipSleep* boost on the large, green armchair opposite, and another was bending over a table, rifling through papers and inspecting a large map of the City, drawing circles on it intently.

'Still here, then?' Trixy's voice broke through her thoughts, as she began stacking boxes on the counter.

'Looks like it.' Genni turned her head from the man with the map and gazed at Trixy's bushy eyebrows behind her square glasses. She didn't know Trixy well, but she knew enough to feel comfortable around her, especially with the way she was peculiarly open with Genni the first time they'd met. She'd told her how she lost her only child after he swallowed a loose drone part Trixy had left accessible on the kitchen table after working late one night. She didn't seem ashamed to let the tears fall in front of a stranger, one very much embroiled in the life of the City. It immediately convinced Genni to have immense respect for the woman. *How in Tulo did she manage to keep her Robotics job after all that trauma?*

'Reha has a way of keeping people around.' Trixy nodded as she examined the food with the thoughtful look of a hostess. 'We need a salad.' She peered back into the box and pulled out a crisp, green lettuce. 'Do you mind?'

Genni hesitated. It was like there was some unspoken agreement between these people that mucking in was part of life and there was no merit-worthy excuse to avoid it.

As the lettuce was forced upon her, her instinct was to lie and say something like 'I can't do that now, work is manic' or 'I'll be back in ten minutes'. That behaviour was normal, almost expected, to the point that, Genni considered, people rarely asked anything of others at all. Listening to the satisfying tear of the green leaves between her fingers, she still couldn't decide if she liked it. The change was unnatural, but not unwelcome. Disagreeable at times, but weirdly, warming.

'I am so ready for this.' A skinny man bounced over from the other side of the room and scooped up one of the empty plates from the table. Reha followed just behind him, nodding at Genni with some sort of approval at her lettuce tearing. It was hardly worth praising; she was pulling parts of a plant apart.

'Help yourself.' Trixy was making herself busy by moving the food boxes to make room for more. 'Nelly not joining us?'

'Probably not.' He battled through his stutter, spooning curry onto his plate. 'She got kept behind . . . with work. Something about one of her . . . colleagues' . . . Watches not passing the check getting in the . . . building. Held everyone else up.'

Trixy slid a bowl of steaming potatoes next to the curry as Reha tutted at the man for letting the spoon fall into the food as he moved on to the vegetables.

Genni smiled at the man as she placed the salad bowl down, watching him plunge his large hands into its leaves.

'Use a spoon.' Reha smacked his hand out from the bowl.

Genni suddenly felt helpless without a task, like a floating spare part, so she joined the back of the small queue next to Lorcan who was engaged in conversation with the same man as when she'd walked in. She watched Reha pile potatoes onto her plate, making her feel uneasy. *That's a lot of carbohydrates.*

Genni hadn't grown used to how relaxed these people were with food. It wasn't as if they were distastefully unhealthy, far from it, but they didn't seem obsessed with how sugars, carbohydrates and highly saturated fats could play havoc with your energy levels and squander your productivity.

Their conversation moved on and Genni zoned out, thinking about the Blythefens again. Did any of these people seem like someone who would help her, despite the risks? The skinny man appeared too clumsy but Trixy was an option.

'Hey, Genni, you work in this stuff.' Lorcan's voice brought her back to the moment as he handed her an empty plate. 'Tell him you can't share lipstick.'

Random. Slightly taken aback, Genni squinted at the man next to Lorcan, smaller than him and skinnier, with a head of untamed jet-black hair. Not unlike Ajay.

'No . . .' She hesitated before recalling the awful images of cold sores she'd seen in risk-assessment sessions after people had shared products. 'It's definitely not recommended.'

'Thank you.' Lorcan playfully smacked his friend's arm.

The man jerked away from Lorcan, turning to Genni while stroking his sore skin. 'My wife stayed over at someone's in the Side and forgot her lipstick. I thought it was reasonable to suggest she borrowed hers.'

'Did she listen to you?' Genni asked, starting to dish food onto her own plate.

'Of course not.' He licked the tip of his forefinger after splashing some sauce on it. 'But it's become another one for the list that proves I'm stupid, apparently.' He shook his head.

'That must be a long list.' Lorcan followed his friend around the table before shooting an amused look at Genni.

'I'm Yarin, by the way.' The man set down his plate and offered her a thin hand. 'Lorcan's never been good at introducing people.'

Lorcan let out a soft expletive and apologised as Genni felt the grip of Yarin's firm handshake. For the next ten minutes as they sat and ate, she learned that he helped Lorcan with distributing Guiding Lights; he had many questions about her life, as if he took a genuine interest, and there was no merit earned for the interaction. The way they all seemed to operate was unfamiliar, living without a focus on scores. Genni liked it in a lot of ways, but she couldn't lose her concentration. If Yarin and Lorcan risked their lives for The Guiding Light, wouldn't they risk it for the Blythefens?

CHAPTER
TEN

The first time he saw her, his first instinct was to push her into the river. With no regret, consequences or remorse. He wanted to feel like he was in control of something, *anything*. He hated happy people. They made his blood boil so hot he'd wonder if his cells might fry and turn to ash. He often wished they would, but somehow the empty vessel carrying him around persevered. And so did Kelli.

Joon Blythefen didn't push his future wife into the Outer-Outer-Ring river that day. It was a good job he didn't. *I would have had no life without her.*

He remembered exactly what she was wearing; a bland grey dress, not improved by the plain belt sucking in her waist, but her socks mirrored the bright blue of her eyes, which sat softly under a load of knotty brown hair. She would always wear bright socks back then, before the kids came along and her mother got ill. Time would run away and there wouldn't be enough of it for their once lengthy considerations over her footwear.

'Is today an orange or a yellow day?'

He smiled, feeling a chill, as he remembered the way she would hold up the socks by her ears, willing him to be the one to choose. Every pair had holes in them, but it didn't matter.

She got on with the life she'd been given. Mostly.

Joon stared at the door they'd taken her through, not even giving him a chance to say goodbye, if that's what it was. He'd watched her as she mouthed the words, 'It's OK.' That was a lie, he knew, because nothing would ever be OK without her. Even though the four walls around him hadn't changed since they'd taken her, they'd immediately felt darker and more enclosed. Staring at the blank ceiling, Joon had given up on crying. A month of hysterical sorrow proved it did nothing to ease the pain. It was messing with him and he had to hold onto the light.

As he lay, breathing in the musty air of the cell, he knew *it* meant he still had something to hold onto, but he felt as if he barely had grip. He peered down again at the score on his Watch.

M-0.

For years since he'd been in the Side, it had been capped at M-200, but frustratingly, it pained him to see it dwindle to a prisoner's score. *Merit always leaves you wanting.*

A sharp alarm startled him, the blinking red light by his hard bench filling the void. Next came the expected brown bag sliding across the dusty floor, hitting his bare feet after being launched through the opening in the wall. Joon didn't know if he could eat today. He'd managed a full meal only once in the last three weeks. Not because the food was bad, but because everything else was. The dinners were what he was used to, not too far away from the vacuum-packed meals they rationed in the Side.

Bending forwards, he hissed as he grabbed his swollen ribs. He'd almost forgotten about them. How long had it been?

Thinking about it, they'd given him at least three days. Three whole days without them bruising or breaking a part of his body. They'd stopped the interviews too.

'When did you last see Ajay?'

'You knew he hacked into his Watch?'

'You knew he was part of The Rogue?' They asked him that several times and unsurprisingly hit him harder every time he insisted it wasn't the truth.

Lies fell out of Command like merit; endless and destructive. They were arresting and killing his friends and family, and playing it as if they'd chosen Purification; that was a fact. He'd been losing people for years. So many times he'd longed to fight back, but realistically, what could he do? Who would believe people from the Side, anyway? Maybe now Tulo was changing, that would change too. He didn't know, like he didn't know where his wife was.

Stretching again and supporting his side with one hand, Joon scuttled his fingers across the floor of his cell and grabbed hold of the meal bag. He felt the weight of it on his lap, pressing into his sweat-ridden, Command-purple jail suit. He glanced up at the turning and twitching of the cell's camera. He felt a bad energy emanating from it, telling him that whoever was watching was someone who wanted him to suffer.

How is this ever going to get better? The Light always said it would, but was he a liar? Was it all a lie? Everything?

He felt too exhausted to face his doubt. Sliding the box out from the bag, he felt ready to eat. He lethargically pulled off the foil lid, letting it shriek across the box's plastic rim.

Joon took a struggling breath and swore.

It contained only a piece of rock with a note on top.

'Be careful not to break your teeth. Esabel x.'

Scrunching his eyes and feeling his body shiver, he screamed for everything he'd lost and for *them* as he launched the rock at the eye of the camera. The hard clunk of it contacting the lens echoed around his cell, and it dropped to the floor in pieces, the camera remaining unscathed.

'Why don't you just kill me?' Joon cried at the lens, saliva foaming down his chin. He marched towards it, his hands shaking into fists. 'Esabel, I want to talk.'

CHAPTER
ELEVEN

Trying to block out the noise of the table tennis behind her, Genni sat tensely in the armchair, enjoying being alone. She had no interest in games, when people were suffering outside.

The low, oval coffee table in front of her was housing countless books and mug stains; somebody's blue hoodie sat next to a biscuit tin on the far side, one of its arms draping down to the floor. Sitting up, Genni glanced at a book on top of the pile and scanned the title: *Being Productive in a Post-attack World*.

Disinterested, she turned her eyes to The Guiding Light beside it. For years, she'd never seen one; only heard of the devices that taught forbidden ideologies about rest and laziness. But she'd seen a lot of them since she'd first encountered its holographic glow in the office of Ajay's father. Shame still sat tightly around her stomach whenever she thought of that moment, the light of the hologram jumping up so quickly and her startled scream vibrating around their house in the Side. She never should have been snooping around in the first place, and so when Joon Blythefen caught her, the disgruntled look on his face was completely justified.

Moving past the memory and trying to ignore her rigid irritation over the situation with the Blythefens' captivity, she dropped one stack of books to the floor and looked back to ensure everyone was still engrossed in the game. She wasn't sure why she cared if anyone saw her. It wasn't like she was trespassing this time, but she wanted to explore it in her own way, on her own terms. Command had always warned against its influence. *Our constitution allows everyone to be fairly rewarded, according to the time they dedicate to moving society forward through technological reform, personal development and community spirit. Merit has become a statement of status. Earned, not simply given.*

Why did The Guiding Light hinder that?

Without hesitation, she pulled the black, oval device towards her and stroked her fingers over the engraved, swirled pattern on its top. *It's a tree.* Genni jumped slightly when the hologram flew up from the device, its light catching her eyes.

Before having the chance to debate about putting it back, Genni grew distracted by its beauty. The hologram was a figure, like a person, but its body was distorted by the way small sparkles danced in, through and around it. Staring at it silently, she didn't know what to do next.

'Hello,' she whispered, feeling stupid.

To her surprise, the device started to talk. A soft, non-mechanical voice flowed gently towards her, capturing her attention totally.

'Welcome. I am glad you are here.'

'You can hear me?' Genni's Watch buzzed at the thumping of her heart. She breathed with relief when the hologram failed to respond but merely continued.

'I have stories to tell.'

So, the material is just stories? That's all it is?

'In time and with the right heart, you will experience more of what these stories represent and my voice can carry them into your life. To get started, tap in the code number for your chosen story or hit play to start from the beginning.'

Genni sat in her initial confusion before noticing a small digital display had appeared near the figure's blurry, sparkly feet. There was a number sandwiched between two arrows, allowing her to go back and forth, and next to it sat a number pad to input a code. *There's no list. How do you know which code corresponds to which story?* Not caring too much over the answer, Genni typed a random three-numbered digit on the pad.

'The Story of the Waterkeeper,' the voice announced as a roar erupted from the far-end of the room.

Genni turned to see people's jovial condolences for Lorcan on another loss and their eyes made contact.

'Hey, Genni . . .' He shouted over, raising his bat in the air. 'Wanna play?'

'No, thanks, I'm good,' she called confidently, smiling. She watched as he nodded and passed the bat to Reha, mumbling something into her ear. *Are they talking about me?*

He then started to walk towards her. Quickly turning back to the glowing device, she frantically slapped at its controls, trying to silence it. She didn't want to invite any questions from Lorcan, and especially not from Reha, but the device continued to talk about some guy who looked after a water tower.

'Stop, stop.' Genni tried with no success, before remembering she'd swiped over the tree to turn it on. She slapped at the engraved image and the hologram sucked itself back into the case and suddenly everything felt dark and quiet.

Relieved, Genni pushed it back to the centre of the table and remained upright in her chair, flicking her eyes to the photos hanging along the wall.

'Well, that was embarrassing,' Lorcan sighed as he lowered himself into one of the empty armchairs.

'Only if you're already meant to be good at it,' Genni commented as she slowly drew her eyes towards him, her heart rate coming down after the adrenaline.

'How'd ya mean?' Lorcan leaned forward, retrieving a biscuit from the silver tin and munching his way through it.

'I don't get why we're embarrassed by failing at things we've never tried or practised.' Genni shrugged off the feeling she knew too well.

'Well, I've tried table tennis a lot. I've never got any better.'

'So you're not suited for it. Why should you care?'

'Alright.' Lorcan held his arms up in defence, his half-eaten biscuit crumbling between his fingers before he then threw it all into his mouth.

'Sorry.' Genni picked up and shuffled a deck of cards from the coffee table. 'I'm a bit irritable.' She sat back in her seat, wanting the sofa to swallow her.

Lorcan nibbled at another biscuit, like he wanted to eat through the tension.

'You know, everything you've been through sucks,' he said sincerely.

'Yeah, it does.' Genni couldn't place whether the comfort she felt with him was welcome or unnerving. She sat up and took a biscuit herself, snapping it between her teeth and staring back up at the photos on the wall.

'You knew her?' She'd spotted a photo of him and Ajay's sister; Lorcan's face was spottier but slimmer. 'Tara?'

'Yeah.' Lorcan swallowed.

'What was she like?'

'Fierce.' Lorcan nodded slowly. 'Loyal. She just had this thing about her, like you knew whatever trouble you got into, she'd be there for you, no matter what it cost her.'

Genni said nothing, sadness invading the moment.

'She was so hilarious, as well.' Lorcan laughed, putting the lid back on the biscuit tin. 'I remember she always had some story, things that wouldn't happen to anyone else. Like getting her foot stuck in a garden grate wearing only her underwear.'

'What?' Genni said. 'Why did she go out in just her underwear?'

'She was a risk-taker.'

'What did she do?'

'Called on her neighbour to help – a kind, elderly man. He must have got a shock.' Lorcan smirked. 'She then proceeded to tell everyone she knew, of course.'

Genni gave him a small smile.

'When did you meet her?'

'About, three, four years ago,' Lorcan considered as the tennis continued behind them. 'She had just finished her training, I think.'

'As what?'

'A teacher.'

'Right,' Genni closed her eyes for a moment. 'I knew that. What else did she like?'

'Er, I think, like just hanging out with people. You know, game cards and stuff.' Lorcan spoke hesitantly, before stroking his wide neck.

'And delivering those,' Genni nodded at the rucksack full of devices by his armchair, 'like you do.'

'Yeah.' Lorcan continued to nod, his voice fading. 'I wish I knew her better than I did. There wasn't enough time in the end.'

Lorcan looked away, staring at the water above them. Genni felt a strange excitement, like it was an opportunity.

'Doesn't it make you mad? What happened to her?' she said erratically, keeping her voice low.

'Course it does,' Lorcan whispered. 'I still think about her and the others . . .' He glanced at the photos, then at the entrance, '. . . and how one day they might walk back through those doors. And all those in the Side too.'

'Why don't you do anything about it? Like trying to save the Blythefens or exposing what Command is really doing?' Genni felt her teeth pressing together, all the anger of the last month building.

'I could try, but nothing would work.' Lorcan looked at her with pitiful eyes, as if she could never understand.

'How do you know if you've never tried?' Genni felt her hands clamming.

'We've never had a good enough plan.'

He was too casual about it and Genni felt irritability tingling up her legs. It wasn't only about the Side; it was becoming so much bigger than that. It was the broken nature of the system itself. She could feel the resentment and the need for change bolstering her confidence every day; it was about people's worth not being tied to a number on their wrist or what neighbourhood they lived in or who they were dating; it was about how she almost killed herself trying to meet a standard she never wanted to reach; about Blake giving up his dancing for something he had no desire or drive for; about Ajay feeling so outcast that he lost pieces of himself striving for opportunities the system was never going to offer him. And for what? *For this?* For Ace's death? For the death of hundreds in the Side?

'Well, why don't you make another plan?' She almost swore and raised her voice, stopping herself wisely.

Just then a point was won and Yarin cried out, 'Please have mercy.'

'No, come on, boy. Match point.' Reha's dry voice grated on Genni, like it had before. She respected her kindness, and leadership, and every other admirable quality she had, but her reluctance to do anything for the Blythefens left a stain on Genni's overall perception of her as a person.

She turned back to Lorcan. 'Well, why don't you?' Not thinking, she grabbed hold of his knee before immediately retracting her hand. But it didn't faze him, he was only calm.

'Because he said to wait.'

'He?'

Genni followed Lorcan's eyes as he referred them to The Guiding Light device sitting silently on the coffee table. She agreed that the voice sounded more male than female, but it was a mechanical device and it hardly felt appropriate to give it such a pronoun.

Lorcan nodded. 'He's been faithful before.'

'He's . . .' Genni paused. '*It's* a machine.' She fell backwards, hands on her head.

'Do you even know anything about it?' Lorcan squinted at her and then at yet another biscuit.

'No.' Genni wiped dust from her lap, her frustration preventing her from revealing her earlier interest. 'I don't want to.'

'OK.' He sat back easily, like she had merely refused a piece of cake.

'Look, I think there could be a way to get them out.' Genni sat up, leaning closer to him and not letting it go.

'How?' he breathed, the mole on his neck pulsing as he swallowed.

'I don't know yet,' Genni mumbled and he raised his eyebrows. 'But there has to be something.'

'It's not possible, Gen.'

She turned uneasy. *Gen? When did we ever get to the point of 'Gen'?*

'You'll get yourself killed. I'm asking you not to do that.'

'You don't even know me.' Genni sat back, tempted to flick up her Watch so she didn't have to look at him anymore.

'OK. But I'd like to get to know you.' He sounded so genuine. Genni both enjoyed and despised it. He didn't like her like *that*, did he? Because she was not in the place for that, so he was wasting his emotions. 'And I know that Reha cares about you, she's dealt with enough.' He stared into her. 'Karlane is one of her best friends.'

Are you kidding me? Genni couldn't cope with it. None of it made sense. There had to be a way.

'So let's freaking do something.' She bit her tongue, grimacing at the sharp pain.

It was at that moment she knew she was fighting a losing battle. Lorcan wore the same look as Reha, one that said, 'I'm sorry, but I can't help you.' They were all the same, these Guiding Light junkies. Completely irrational. They were willing to die to deliver those devices and yet, they wouldn't take a risk for their friends in a Detention Centre. But then, yes, she realised it was unreasonable to try to convince them to take that on with no plan or resources. She wanted to cry. She didn't, and opted to fall back into the sofa and consider if it was time to go back to work. Or maybe she should return Pearl's messages. Or Mila's. Or she could move back into her parents' house, merely exist in the Quarters and achieve nothing. She didn't know what would be worse: her current state of being so powerless it stung, or helping her mother choose what colour to paint the dining room for the rest of her life.

'I know it's horrific,' Lorcan said, making Genni want to scream. How could he possibly understand? Until she realised, he probably did. He'd had friends taken from him. He might not have been through what Genni had, but he'd faced hardship. Living where he had, knowing what he knew and yet he survived, and still managed to be one of the most cheerful people she'd ever met.

'How do you live with it?' she asked, concentrating on her breathing to stop the tears.

'Together.' Lorcan glanced over at the small group and let the moment hang between them like some sort of bond had been formed.

Genni met his gaze. *But the Blythefens aren't getting the enjoyment of 'together'.* She then felt her wrist vibrate as Lorcan looked down at his own. The table tennis immediately stopped and the tone of the room shifted.

'I'll get it up.' Reha threw her bat down before tapping and flicking her screen onto the back wall.

Arneld Hevas appeared on a large projection. Genni was so sick of seeing his face. Too many people considered the Hevas family as the exemplars, the end goal; attractive, healthy, accomplished, with merit rippling through their family tree like water. With their ancestors as the leaders of the Revolution, they were bound to be where all decisions ended up, the top of Command. Genni had never thought much about them, but recently, they inspired a nasty taste in her mouth.

She glanced at Arneld's blond-tipped, puffed hair for a moment before looking away, feeling his brittle voice was enough.

'At Tulo Command, we want to thank you for your patience and loyalty during these testing months.' Genni heard Lorcan sigh. 'As always, we are working tirelessly to prioritise your safety with Rogue searches continuing and more convictions happening daily. We are also pleased to announce we can now begin the Watch-3 roll-out.'

'Watch-3?' Lorcan grimaced. 'When was Watch-2?'

Reha shushed him and everyone continued to listen. Genni knew the answer as Ajay used to bore her with the intricacies of each model's interface. The current model was Watch-2.9, if she remembered correctly, and Watch-3 would be the first time in decades the actual hardware would change. Only now did she know the real reason why Ajay knew so much; to keep hacking into his Watch and hide Side-born Karle Blythefen from the City and from her. *Little naïve me just thought he was passionate.*

'Beginning tomorrow, Glorified citizens will be invited to Command for the initiation process. We ask for your utmost patience and cooperation so the roll-out can be executed as efficiently as possible. You are all helping us build a greater Tulo and as always, remember that Progress is Strength.'

Arneld disappeared as quickly as he'd arrived. Genni let the resulting conversations muffle around her, engrossed still in remembering Ajay and then the Blythefens. They've had their interviews – why was Command holding onto them? There was only one possible reason; something she couldn't save them from. Why did she ever go to the Side in the first place? If she'd only been strong enough to not let the pull of Ajay's past drag her there, she never would have met them, and would never have become so, inappropriately, attached. And yet, there was some joy there too. She was being shown a different kind of life and she knew her obsession with them was dangerous, but she wouldn't let it go. She would keep her eyes and ears open for something she might be missing.

CHAPTER
TWELVE

Four weeks later, Genni felt strange. She realised she hadn't been this deep into the Quarters since the attack. It all seemed the same: the streets were still lined with floral baskets, the people continued to flutter in and out of cafés and homes, hover cars roamed seamlessly, their blacked-out windows reflecting the harsh rays of the sun. Yet a haze of uneasiness sat beneath the surface. Genni glanced at the cruxes of the mountains and the winding driveway that meandered down to her childhood home; her parents had moved since then, deeper into the mountain side, a house she'd never been to nor did she plan to visit. Despite still knowing the comfort it was to live there, it all seemed smaller to her; the mountain peaks appeared lower, the pavements felt dirtier and the paintwork on the buildings looked faded and chipped. It all seemed the same, but it wasn't. Genni pulled her eyes away from her old driveway and closed them momentarily, breathing deeply and feeling the heat of the sun on her forehead. As she headed to Command, she barely saw the short woman with golden highlights straightening petals in a hanging basket, making sure even the flowers put their best selves forward. Her Watch vibrated and the voice of technology drifted upwards from her wrist.

You're expected at the Command Waiting Bay in ten minutes.

'Mansald.' The voice was crisp through the speakers, bidding Genni to move quickly towards the long white table, unchanged from her initiation when she was eighteen.

She spotted the voice's owner – an administrator at the far left of the room, with thin greying hair.

It was only when she got closer that she spotted someone she never expected to see; she stopped in front of him and the two of them were caught suspended in the moment with mutual surprise and discomfort; his serpent eyes pierced into her, the cheeks beneath them turning red, until Rod quickly flicked his face away.

He appeared ashamed, like he would run if he could, but he hurriedly continued administering a Watch to a blond man. *What is he doing here? Working in admin?*

She wanted to laugh. Not merely a small grunt, but a deep, hysterical laugh. *Serves you right. He must be dying inside.* If someone had told him to work in admin, he would have barked back some offensive remarks. He was never one to look vulnerable or spend time on anything 'beneath him'; he was always proud, cocky, entitled. *How hilarious.* A top Command detective serving the public, just one of the administrators, unspecial and sat doing the same mundane thing, again and again. *I wonder what Mummy and Daddy think.*

'Please have a seat.'

Part of her suddenly felt for him; she instantly rebuked herself. *He'd enjoyed it, destroying the Blythefens and their home and Tara and, I guess, many other Side citizens. I remember.*

'Have a seat.'

It was easier to focus on hating him, rather than letting some softer feeling confuse her into sympathising with the downtrodden look on his face.

'Mansald.'

His voice ricocheted through the moment, sharp and loud. Genni flicked her focus away from Rod to her own administrator, his eyes drilling into her with irritation.

'Sorry.' She quickly sat, one eye still on Rod, who was acting busy.

'OK.' The administrator sighed and spoke robotically. 'My name's Quain. As usual, any questions, just let me know.' He tapped at the desk. 'Usual procedure.'

'Sure,' Genni managed, watching Rod, who typed on the desk and welcomed another citizen at the end of the long table. *How could you be my brother? Someone like you. Related to me.*

With the snap of Quain's fingers in her face, Genni stared back at him, shocked at his rudeness.

'There are a lot of people waiting.' Quain spoke in a tired voice, peering down at the desk in front of Genni. She now realised two hand outlines had appeared. How long had they been there? She didn't speak, but placed her hands down, embracing the tickle of the fingerprint scan.

'Thank you.' Quain smiled hesitantly. 'Now, as was explained in the presentation, the new model works by recognising the skin on your arm, so we need to scan your wrist too.' Quain gestured towards a small, tubed machine on his right. Genni leaned forward, eyes focusing on it, and giving it her arm while her mind was still fixated on Rod. A crazy thought came, but it was too reckless to entertain.

'Just a reminder, this now means that only *you* can use the device, even after fingerprint validation. Unlike before. It might take some getting used to.'

Genni nodded at this, briefly thinking how she never let anyone use her Watch anyway.

'I need to make the data transfer.' Quain held out his palm without explanation. Genni's mind went blank, still thinking about Rod and wanting to make sure he didn't leave, even though she knew talking to him would be dangerous. She needed to focus. Quain was getting frustrated, made obvious by his groan and hard stare at the Watch on her wrist.

She clicked it off, smiling at him subtly and placing it in his hand. Glancing at Rod again, she barely noticed the drone hovering by Quain's shoulder. She only just registered the calibrating noises as he made the data transfer from the old device to the new.

'OK, we're ready.' He held up the new device, which finally took Genni's full attention. It was a lot nicer; thinner than before, almost like a sheet of glass, and as he lowered it onto her wrist, its mechanics tickling around her skin, it felt as light as a piece of cloth. She admired it on her wrist, noting how the fit was just right.

'A list of the new features can be found in the manual, but if you do have any questions, now is the time to ask.' Quain had stopped looking at her, just dismissing files on the desk and presumably getting ready for the next person.

As she still beheld it, she wondered if it would do what the last one failed to do: keep everyone safe. She supposed Command never expected such a threat as The Rogue to exist. Or that there were any Ajays out there, clever and motivated enough to manipulate the model's weaknesses. Command appeared vulnerable, not in control, and the thing sitting on her wrist was supposed to save them? Save their worsening reputation? It might work on most, but it wouldn't work on her. No fancy development or technological advancement would convince her that their motive was only to protect and preserve society.

'So you're absolutely sure it's safe.' A whiny voice cut into her thoughts. She turned to see a short woman in a yellow dress next to her, cradling her wrist and staring at her administrator.

'Yes, ma'am,' her administrator nodded.

'They fixed the issue that let them do it?' she persisted.

'Of course. Before, people's fingerprints were only registered to their devices and not to their identification on the server. Plus there's now the validation of your skin.'

'And so if they tried it again, it would be clear and obvious? No way they could get through?'

'No, ma'am. I assure you. We have covered all possible avenues of fraud detection.' The administrator smiled as the woman sighed with relief, spluttering her thanks. Genni couldn't help but feel sorry for the woman; she was like her once, bumbling through life oblivious to the atrocities going on at the top.

'Any more questions?' Quain said, anger now palpable in his voice.

'No,' Genni spluttered, not really thinking.

'Very good.' Quain sighed. 'As ever, you can always contact Watch support or visit the stores.'

'Right. Cool. That's fine, thank you.' Genni stood, noting that Rod's chair was now empty.

Her eyes darted to the back of the room, where she saw him disappear through the door. Without hesitation, she gave a rushed thanks to Quain again and broke from the room, almost barging someone out of the way. She didn't know what she'd achieve by finding him, or talking to him, or following him. But, maybe, just maybe, the scum who arrested the Blythefens might be the key to helping them.

She found herself in the wide foyer of the second floor, ignoring the glares of people waiting on large, set-back sofas. She found him at the balcony, straight-backed over the bright view of the Quarters. He was staring at the mountains, puffing his *SkipSleep Pro* with one hand and clutching the railing with the other. Nervously, Genni edged closer towards him, her desire to attack him rising with each step. As she saw his profile more clearly, all she could hear was his voice in that kitchen.

'*Take them.*'

What was she doing? She shouldn't go anywhere near him. He was detestable. How could she hold a conversation with him without giving away her disgust? A new strength seemed to somehow will her forward. Part of her knew there was nothing she could get from him, other than more frustration and angst, but it still felt like a chance for *something*. Even if only to prove she was bigger than he was.

She walked into the vapour of his last puff and opened her mouth to speak, but he beat her to it.

'Shouldn't you be getting back to your mascaras?' He didn't give her the courtesy of looking at her.

You allowed him to speak first, he has no right. He always did win their games. His voice sounded strained, almost emotional. Genni gripped the silver railing and stood beside him, seeing a couple walking away from Command below with their arms interlinked.

'So you're not on Ajay's case anymore?' She strained her neck, letting the sun baste her skin.

'I suppose I don't need to teach you about incompetent bosses.' Rod swore.

Silence between them was never tense or awkward, merely something of nature. Genni was confident he would have no suspicion of what she knew. He saw her as he always had: his pathetic little sister. An airhead who floated in her own dreamland and never took decisive action. *Well, he's wrong.*

'Saw they got his family.' Genni spoke softly, trying to appear sad, not angry or resentful. She saw Rod's eyebrows twitch above his villainous eyes. She imagined being inside his head. A dark place where his response lay but would never be spoken aloud: *I got his family.*

'No surprise, is it?' He shrugged and exhaled, the mist from his *Pro* disappearing. 'What with your mate's face layered on every brick wall.' He spoke nonchalantly and his reference to Ace cut deep. *How can he be so cruel?* Standing so close to him was starting to make her stomach twist.

'What will they do with them now?' she pressed as a drone with a small box swooped past them.

'Let them rot in their own waste downstairs.' Rod casually put his *Pro* back in his jacket pocket as Genni tried not to react. *Downstairs?*

'You really don't know where your Unworthy boyfriend is?' He gave her a deep, cold stare.

'He's not my boyfriend.' Genni flinched. 'And of course not.' She shook her head as she told the truth, trying not to think about Ajay. *Downstairs. The Blythefens are only downstairs? Somewhere in this building? Underneath my feet?*

Another silence dropped. Genni felt her heart pound harder and decided it would raise no suspicion if she just slipped away. Without saying another word to the man she no longer called her brother, she spun on her feet.

'Hey.' Rod grabbed her arm, hands around her new Watch, making her insides lurch. 'Don't tell them, alright?'

'I don't tend to tell them anything,' she said plainly. As she pulled her arm from his grasp, she thought about how great it would feel to inform their parents of his obvious demotion. But she was beyond those games. She smiled to assure him, making herself feel physically sick. He'd touched her. She would wash thrice over; get soap in between all the creases of her fingers and into the very pores of her skin. Genni walked away, knowing he was watching her, and she held her breath until she escaped into the clammy, desert air, armed with at least *some* new information.

CHAPTER
THIRTEEN

He popped another pill in his mouth. *Come on, act faster.*

Staring into the mirror, his red puffy eyes, encircled by deep purple rings and blotchy skin, became the subject of the red-lettered statistics on the screen. The hope of the Mood Enhancers was the only thing stopping him from throwing his fist through the reflective glass.

'Your skin oil production has increased by—'

Rod punched the mirror, silencing its voice and smashing its face. Breathless and seething, he bent over the sink, grunting as blood dripped from his knuckles over the white porcelain.

Pull it together. She won't tell them.

Seeing Genni had unnerved him in a way he didn't like. He'd never once felt intimidated by her or as if she had something to hold over him. What did he expect? People were always going to notice his demotion, even though most still believed he was an events executive, but Genni knew how far down they'd pushed him. From detective to nobody. From calling the shots to following a process with M-350 airheads. *It doesn't matter what she thinks. It doesn't matter what anyone thinks. You can do this. You're the best in your business, no one can match up to you. They'll allow you back in, this is a season. They'll change their minds, just remind them of what you can do.*

He puffed out air, knowing the mood drugs were doing their work. Wiping his face to gather himself and swirling water around the sink, he watched his diluted blood spiral down the drain.

They'll kill them soon too and everything will be as it should. Don't give up, Rod. Don't you give up.

CHAPTER
FOURTEEN

Downstairs. He said they were holding them downstairs.

Once she was out in the Quarters, away from Command, Genni stopped in between a café and a decadent gold gate enclosing someone's driveway. She flicked at her wrist, panting with nervous energy. Many times she had searched for where they were keeping The Rogue or prisoners like them, and she'd only ever been given the result that they'd likely be in one of six Detention Centres across the City and its borders. *He said downstairs, so they're in the one under Command.* Genni could feel the sweat gathering under her arms. Perhaps now she had their location, Reha would agree it was worth the risk. That with some planning, getting them out could be possible, as fantastical as that concept sounded.

Genni scrambled her fingers at her Watch, tutting at the incessant pop-ups on the screen. She couldn't give two drones about the newest features.

Have a tour around your new interface.

She pressed 'skip'.

Remember to select one of the newest themes.

She tapped 'remind me later'.

Don't forget you can now operate with multiple screens to improve your efficiency. Try it now.

Genni followed the finger motion of the animated demonstration and a second pop-out screen appeared to the left of the first. *That's helpful.* She left the next pop-ups there, telling her about the new metabolism tracker and the greater synchronisation options with her wardrobes, dressing tables and beauty tools.

She swiped her fingers over the first screen, ready to input a search for the blueprint of the Command building. But she hesitated, her newfound caution holding back any flippant behaviour. *Searching for that will appear incredibly suspicious. But maybe Reha or the others have some information.*

Genni flapped her hand to close the screen but it refused, showing her an ad for a Command-branded energy drink because it had 'detected low mood and falling energy levels'. *Seriously?* She rejected the offer and pulled herself together; surely now she could convince *someone, anyone* to help her to get them out.

Genni approached Lorcan in an empty River House after returning from Command. 'I know you said it wasn't possible, but—'

'Oh, you're still on that.' Lorcan trailed his finger down a list of names, copying them onto circled locations on an Inner-Ring map lying on their usual booth table.

Genni felt stung, offended at the dismissal, feeling her teeth grate against each other. 'It's not exactly easy to let go.'

Lorcan looked up at her softly. 'Sorry.' He put his pencil down. 'I was distracted.'

'I know they're in the Detention Centre under Command.' Genni shuffled along the cushioned seat opposite him.

'How?' Lorcan flicked his growing hair away from his eyes. 'They could be in any of the centres.'

'No, I know. Rod told me,' Genni remarked, cupping her hands around a fresh cup of tea Lorcan had prepared when he knew she was coming.

'Your brother? The one who arrested them?'

'Yes.' Genni leaned across the booth's metal table, as if that would help her argument. 'He said they were downstairs.'

'What are you doing speaking to him about this, Gen?' Lorcan looked worried for her. 'It's dangerous.'

'He can't hurt me.' Genni took offence again. *I never gave him permission to protect me.*

'You can't show any interest in them. No one knows you were there. It must stay that way.'

'It's fine. He wouldn't ever expect me to have anything to do with them.' Genni almost told him that Rod had been demoted, but the detail was irrelevant. 'If we can find out exactly where they are,' she persisted, 'how to get in—'

'You can't get in.' Lorcan raised his voice slightly.

Genni didn't feel offended this time, she felt wounded. In the few months she'd known him, he'd never spoken to her like that.

'Everything alright?' Reha had arrived at the opening to their booth, neither of them hearing her arrive through the main door. *Brilliant.*

'What's going on?' she asked, munching through a biscuit, the crunching adding to the tension.

'Nothing.' Genni looked away, finding comfort in the view of the river water through the booth.

'Genni wants to get into Command.' Lorcan sighed and sat back. Genni glared at him, not believing his betrayal. 'To get Karlane and the others. She spoke to her brother, they have them in the lock-up there.'

'He told you that?' Reha almost choked on her biscuit, placing its remains on the table.

'He didn't realise what he was telling me,' Genni confirmed, deliberately avoiding eye contact with Lorcan.

'What else did he say?'

'Not a lot.' Genni slurped her tea too quickly. 'Just implied they were leaving them there to rot. He was detestable, as always.'

'OK.' Reha flapped at Lorcan, who moved up to make space for her on the opposite side of the table. 'So he said they were downstairs in Command, yes? Those were his exact words?'

'Correct.' Genni sat up, surprised by Reha's interest.

'Hmm.' Reha retrieved her biscuit and crunched through it pensively.

'Reha, you can't be thinking we could do anything about this?' Lorcan shuffled uncomfortably in his seat. 'We don't have the resources, or the manpower—'

'Shush.' Reha held a hand to his face. 'You're right in my ear, boy.'

Lorcan retreated into his seat, looking like a young child sent to his room by his mother. Genni refused to feel as if she'd won some sort of battle between them, because she knew it was so much bigger than that, but she couldn't help herself from growing impatient. Watching Reha defeat another biscuit wasn't an ample use of her time, nor did it get the Blythefens out any quicker.

'What are you thinking?' Genni hurried Reha, whose eyes returned to her, soft and sympathetic.

'Genni, I'm afraid Lorcan's right.' Reha leaned forward and placed a hand over hers. 'I was trying to think about my contacts and who might be able to help us, but with the state of things, I can't see how this information gets us any closer to what we want.'

Genni pulled her hands out of Reha's and looked down to them, picking at her cuticles, in a bid to distract herself from the emotion rising inside.

Reha sat back and a silence hung above the table like a cloud of smoke none of them could dismiss.

'I'm going home,' Genni finally said, sliding out from the booth as the tears began to fall.

'Gen,' Lorcan pleaded softly.

'Stay, Genni.' Reha followed her and slowed her down by putting a hand to her shoulder.

'Please leave me alone.' She swiped her comfort away. 'Neither of you really know me.' Genni glanced at the names and maps on the table and thought of Lorcan, hiking across the City, those devices on his back. 'I shouldn't be here. If there's nothing I can do to help them ... ' Words failed her as gasping sobs took over.

Reha stepped forward, her arms out. 'We need to be smart. There might be a way; we just haven't found it yet.'

Genni nodded, barely able to hear her own thoughts through the struggle of her tears; if they could, they would. The way they did things for others; all the food, shelter, help for Unworthies. Why wouldn't they save them if there was a way? Maybe they'd even tried before? Maybe there was more to this that she didn't yet understand. Why wouldn't they tell her? She didn't think she could take any more. The questioning and the frustration. Genni couldn't help it. It was like a tidal wave of emotion plummeting through her as she fell to the floor, grabbing on to Reha.

'I hate him.' That was all she could muster. 'I hate him.'

'Who?' Reha clung on tighter, pulling Genni's hair away from her face.

'Ajay,' Genni breathed, seeing Lorcan's dirty trainers, not moving, standing firm.

It was all because of Ajay.

Drawing her in, breaking her apart, exposing her to a family who were paying for what he'd done. If it wasn't for him, everything would be easier. She'd still be living the merit-hunting life, albeit ignorantly, but at least it wouldn't hurt like this. The only way she could think to numb the pain was to take matters into her own hands.

She'd get the Blythefens out herself.

CHAPTER

FIFTEEN

He watched the fruit turn. Over and over. Only lifting one finger to press the button. The three neon wheels swizzled and stopped. He lost. He won. He smacked the button. They swizzled in the dark night. He lost. He won.

Whatever the result, Rod's reaction was the same. Nothing. Lifeless. Anger. Pain. His job didn't seem to be coming back, no matter how many times he'd tried to persuade Jona and the Hevases to see the grave error they'd made. Because of them, he was reduced to spending his nights Downtown, wasting away on the streets, playing games created by his high-merited acquaintances. It was another way to make credit. Corrupt. Clever. Manipulate those who were dumb and desperate enough to fritter away their time and credit on something that would, more often than not, take not give.

Whacking the button again, and watching the fruit roll, Rod tipped up the near-empty bottle in his hand. The ethanol hit his tongue and he hissed. It felt good to take the edge off, and even better, to avoid the 0.2 merit deduction for its purchase. The reinstated life of trades

Downtown was a welcome thing for him, where he could give in that 'M-500 and above' coffee machine in exchange for the strong stuff. He lost again and hadn't even noticed the fat, dirty man who had scuttled in front of the machine next to him.

'I'm not having a good night, either,' he croaked, his bucked teeth distinguishable under the flickering neon light on the street wall.

Rod ignored him. *Dirty Unworthy.*

'Hey, I know you,' the man continued over the murmurs of the newly erected Downtown stalls. The hot smell of his breath wafted in the humid, desert air. 'I've seen you here a few times.'

'You don't know me,' Rod mumbled, hitting the button again. He lost.

'You wanna try not hitting it so hard,' the man quipped.

'What did you say to me?' Rod wanted to lay a fist into his wobbling belly.

'Mate!' He held his hands up in jest. 'You need to try enhancers.'

Rod said nothing, only stared. *People like him are what's wrong with society.*

The man returned to his own machine, tapping the button calmly, letting the turnstiles whir and illuminate.

'I don't know why everyone is so angry all of a sudden.' He laughed, cynically. 'Life's been like this for years.'

'For you, yeah.' Rod traced his eyes down the Unworthy's body with obvious distaste.

'You think you're so high and mighty?' The man grunted. *You're treading a fine line.* Rod imagined wringing his neck in a side alley and spitting on his lifeless body.

'Thing is, though, we're the same. You and me.' The man sighed as his machine returned another bad result.

'We're not the same.' Rod boiled, tapping his Watch to his machine to cash in his small earnings. *I've had enough of this fool.*

'We are.' He looked at Rod playfully and shrugged. 'We're both here, ain't we? Both got something to escape from.' His red-speckled eyes shone in the night light as he coughed into a spluttering laugh.

Rod kept his nerve, pulling himself away and marching off in his anger, but it didn't take long for him to switch and turn back to the pop-up street casino, ready to knock that Unworthy through the wall. He seethed when he saw the fat idiot's chair was empty, but clenched his fists as he saw him plodding down a side-street. Rod swiftly followed him, embracing the darkness of the alley, illuminated only by a lantern on the wall, but full of the man's stench. After taking a breath, Rod bounded towards him, grabbing him by the neck of his sweaty vest. Ignoring his persistent grunts of discomfort, Rod repeatedly thrashed his fists into his stout chin, his escaping blood spreading over both their clothes and skin. The voices in Rod's head told him to stop, but the view of the man's face getting increasingly swollen and his eyes drooping under Rod's power was too inviting to refuse himself the victory now, and it wasn't long until the man went limp. Rod stood back with the taste of blood on his lips and stared up at the night sky peeking out between two rising buildings. He relished the relief that he'd finally found an outlet for his grief.

Personi Social Post

[video clip of protestor dropping a sign that reads 'Without Ambers in a cell, we're not safe and well' as they're tasered by drones]

Caption: Worthy citizens with a worthy cause. Is this how you treat us? Six weeks on from the new model and our streets don't feel any safer. Ambers and The Rogue are still out there.

400,228 loves

CHAPTER
SIXTEEN

It is her? Has she finally come?

A tapping echoed down the corridor beside his cell. Joon lifted his eyes to see her skinny body through the glass door, its reflection adding to the shine of her thin black hair. It had been months. Weeks of requesting to see her. He closed his eyes briefly and breathed, knowing it wasn't going to be easy. He could already feel the rage. *Why has she taken this long? She shouldn't look so smug.* Joon sat up on his concrete bench, anxious to make his demands.

'Oh, Joon,' Esabel tutted, sitting down on a padded chair an officer had wheeled in. 'You don't look well.' She removed her heels and stretched out her bare ankles. 'Do you like the colour?' she said, as Joon noticed the gold tips of her toes. He refocused and sat up straighter, holding her toying eyes.

'I need—' Joon started.

'Ah.' Esabel held her hand up. 'Me first. I thought I'd bring you this personally.' She forced a sympathetic look, taking a food package from the broad-shouldered officer. 'Here.' She handed it over and Joon took it, hot to the touch. 'You're looking ever so thin, Joon.'

'I want to talk to you about my wife,' Joon spat out croakily.

'Eat up.' She nodded towards the package.

She's delaying on purpose. She knows what I'm going to say. I could grab her. Make her listen. Joon controlled himself and humbly ripped open the package to find a steaming hot portion of pasta. He tentatively scooped the spoon into the sauce and took his first bite.

'I'd usually send you to my office, but I fancied stretching my legs.' Esabel exhaled, watching him eat. 'I've been stuck up there like a prisoner.'

Joon ignored the comment as he struggled to chew.

'I need to ask you something.' He swallowed, burning his throat.

'Me too. I've got a lot of questions.'

'I've already answered them.'

'Not all of them.' The eager blue of Esabel's eyes shone like lasers in the dim light. 'Did it hurt?'

'What?' Joon fixed his eyes on his own cracked, bare feet.

'When Ajay left.'

'Yes.'

'It didn't convince you to change?' She wiped her hands on the trousers of her black pantsuit. 'Even your own son leaving you behind?'

'No. Let my wife and her mother go.' Joon's shoulders fell. 'Please.'

'I remember how clever you were,' Esabel continued. 'You used to solve maths problems quicker than the teachers.' She leaned forward and lowered her tone. 'You had the potential for the best a Glorified could be.' She pursed her fake lips, leaning back again. 'But obviously, you went another way.'

He remembered how she once was. Her need to better him was once a desire to thrive with him. Her determination to taunt him was once a drive to uplift him. Her anger was once compassion. Their status as enemies was once friends. She changed as soon as his merit started to fall, leading to the day she left him alone on her doorstep.

'You turned your back on me,' Joon said bluntly.

'Well, you just got so angry all the time, Joon. It's no wonder you fell in merit.' She eyed his meal by his side. 'Are you not going to eat that?'

'I will.' He didn't move.

'While it's hot?' she demanded.

He picked up the box again, playing with the food and still thinking about Kelli and Karlane. *Ask her again.* But Esabel kept talking. He knew it was a tactic for her to stay in control. He had to accept the fact that she was.

'Do you remember when Davy Riley told you the wrong time for mindset class and you just flipped out?' Esabel smiled, shaking slightly with odd excitement. 'Poor Davy's probably still got that scar on his neck. Do you remember?'

Joon nodded, swirling the spoon around in the sauce. 'You consoled me afterwards.'

Esabel looked taken aback, as if he'd caught her off guard. *She clearly doesn't even remember the girl she was.*

'You told me to forget about it, that things would get better.' Joon blew on the spoon, eyeing Esabel's changing face. 'We went on one of our walks, down the mountain creek behind your parents' house?'

A strange silence filled the cell as Esabel's lips parted and she hesitated. The Command officer shifted uncomfortably, the noise of him adjusting his laser gun strap adding to the tension. Joon felt a sense of victory as he chewed on a hard piece of sauce-covered carrot. Had he caught her? Was the girl he once knew still in there, and was she screaming to get out?

CHAPTER
SEVENTEEN

Esabel didn't care for Joon trying to fool her with some overexaggerated memory. Yes, she had a strange streak as a child and into her teenage years where she was kind to people who didn't deserve it. But she was naïve, perhaps a little uneducated with the poor quality of the Education Centre curriculum back then. It didn't take long after her eighteenth birthday for her to realise that angry, lazy and unproductive people like Joon Blythefen were not the type of characters who would help her succeed. They wouldn't facilitate her return to the Quarters and they certainly wouldn't empower her to fulfil her family's legacy. She thought of the black banded tattoo on her wrist beneath her Watch. It was only right she cut people like him off. Swiftly, yes, brutally, perhaps, but necessary overall. *Those walks were splendid, though. Together under the dying of one day and the birth of another. Stop, stop, stop. Focus on the now.* He was testing her patience, not letting her have her fun and suggesting ridiculous notions. He had a nerve. It was decent of her to let him see her in the first place, and yet he was asking for more.

'Please, Esabel.' Joon breathed heavily. 'I know it's me you want to hurt, so I—'

'You were hoping you could take the punishment for them?' she barked, watching his insolent little face squirm. 'That's not how this works. You're all responsible for infecting our society.'

'But this is about Ajay, and I gave him that computer.' He stood then. 'It can't be about anything but that.'

Esabel laughed under her breath; he was becoming far too entitled. It was getting cold in the cell. *Let's get out of here. Tick, tick – time is running away.* She was becoming irritable. *No, no, no. I can't leave it with him having the last word.*

'Sit down.' She watched Joon slowly park himself back on the bench. 'Your little group is the very reason why I've got City productivity levels plateauing, or why it took an entire Watch remodelling to settle people's nerves. *Anyone* who is against the constitution is an enemy. Whether you blow things up or not.'

'By that principle, you've got to destroy most of the Side.'

'And don't you know I've been chipping away at that for years,' she bit, not letting him have the upper hand and relishing in his defeated body language. 'And don't think for a second we don't know about those within my City's walls. Like your daughter who distributed that material.'

Joon didn't look up.

'Oh, Joon, Joon.' She stood, her heels echoing around the cell as she placed a hand on his shoulder. 'Calm down now, honey, and don't worry about it. We don't discriminate – we'll get the rest of them. One by one.'

She casually tapped his cheek twice before moving over to the far wall, windowless and uninteresting. 'That's another trait you never really mastered.' She rolled her tongue across her top teeth. 'Patience.' Esabel turned back to Joon, who had now lifted his head; she ignored his sad eyes. 'A job done quickly is efficient, but there are some jobs that take years to perfect. Frustrating, I'll give you that.' She leaned against the frame of the glass door, giving the Command officer a telling glare. *We're almost done here.* 'But some of our best are Purified and converted and you know I don't like waste, so it's stubborn people like yourself who need to sleep lightly.' Esabel finished and clasped her hands together, beaming at Joon. 'Well, looks like we're done. There are more pressing matters at hand.' She turned, pleased with her work, before she was stopped short by more of his maddening voice.

'Why haven't you killed us yet?' he whispered.

She swivelled on her feet, eyebrows raised.

'There's no reason you can't. Nothing you couldn't make up for in the public eye. So why haven't you done it?' His eyes grew defiant, unrelenting. She hated that.

'How do you know your wife is still alive?'

'You'd have used it to hurt me already.'

'Oh, Joon . . .' She tutted. 'You don't know me like you think you do.' She flicked her fingers at the faceless Command officer, who tapped at his Watch. 'Just wait a little longer. Your time will come.'

The door closed behind her and the officer led her towards the elevator. As they walked, Esabel felt an unfamiliar anxiety crawling through her, like an unwanted parasite nibbling its way through a plant.

It's not because of his question. It's not. Nor was she saddened by the fear in his eyes when she implied that his precious wife was dead. She couldn't let anyone on to her indecision over what to do with them; her, him and that shrivelled woman in the hospital. Esabel breathed through the rising panic; she was probably just unnerved by the entire situation. *Killing him at the right time is best.* As the elevator zoomed towards her office, she thought about Joon's body being still, like stone, no words escaping from his mouth and his eyes were . . . *Stop.* Her mind took control. She didn't know why, but a pain somewhere deep inside shuddered at her imaginings, repressing them and forcing them shut. *That's not from me. I'm happy for him to die. He's only alive because the public might react. The popular opinion would be to send them back to the Side. That's right. Isn't it? Of course. Esabel Hevas doesn't doubt herself.*

but within moments, Mafi had made her way around and laid a firm hand on the activation pad of Genni's machine, shutting it down.

'Don't bother. I asked Tomm to start on it two hours ago.'

Genni's eyes danced over to Tomm's desk where he was busily flying numbers between screens. Nearer by, it wasn't a surprise to her that they had a listening audience; Genni glanced at her desk neighbour, who quickly turned her head as if she wasn't paying attention.

'It seems you've not met your daily targets or merit count for more than a week, Genni. And you logged out for more than three hours yesterday. Where were you?'

'Can we talk in your office?' Genni leaned closer.

Mafi shook her thin head. 'Just here is perfectly fine.'

Genni straightened up, almost in a plea to give her time to think. She could hardly say that she'd decided to spend the afternoon by Command, watching and waiting for the blacked-out vehicles spinning around the back of the building. It was, of course, a pointless exercise as her access stopped right by the back door, but it confirmed it was the quickest way to the Detention Centre. She could feel her breath thinning and her weight suddenly heavy in her knees, so she sat and rubbed her forehead.

'I wasn't feeling well,' Genni said quietly.

'Is it infectious?' Mafi didn't lower her voice and stood back.

'Oh no, nothing like that.' Genni put her hands up, conscious that being escorted out as infectious wasn't going to make this less embarrassing. 'Women stuff,' she lied under her breath.

'Are you not taking the meds?' Mafi narrowed her eyes at her, seeing right through her lie before sighing and flapping her hand. 'You know what, it doesn't matter, it won't change the outcome of this.'

Genni swallowed.

'You know how it works. You're suspended, with immediate effect.'

'But I haven't had a merit warning yet?' Genni protested.

'I don't care about your merit warning; I care about you submitting work on time.' Mafi's nostrils flared. 'That's something you haven't managed for a week. You have five minutes.'

Without another word, Mafi was gone, leaving only the echo of her heels behind. Genni sat frozen for a moment, unsure what to do. Did she just get up and leave? Or gather her small number of possessions from the drawers? Suspended wasn't forever, so maybe she could leave them there. She tapped the front of the drawer and scanned its contents as it slid open; she slipped an old drawing pad into her handbag, but the rest was insubstantial. Without giving herself the torture of seeing the disapproving eyes of colleagues or watching her picture fade into grey on the staff board, she left her chair strewn by the desk, and anxiously shuffled from the Dome.

Out into the humid air, she wanted to scream and was suddenly aware of the sweat forming on her neck beneath her hairline. Dropping her bag on the wall of the Plaza fountain, she tied her hair up and threw her arms back by her sides. It wasn't like she wanted to keep her job anyway. She'd wanted to leave as soon as she'd returned from the Side, but Reha had convinced her to stay with the system; one of the many things that conniving woman had told her that wasn't worth listening to. As soon as that thought skated across her mind, Genni's gut told her it wasn't wholly true, but that didn't stop her from believing it.

Reha and Lorcan and the rest of them had no place in her life anymore. She'd been back and forth with it. On the one hand, she'd enjoyed their community and their different way of life. But on the other hand, she couldn't stay around people who weren't willing to help their friends. So what if there wasn't a plan, why couldn't they make one? She couldn't continue living a life just doing the small things that were never enough.

She missed Caril, though, and as she sat on the fountain wall, she wondered who was taking her the bread. The Unworthy hadn't done anything wrong, other than being Unworthy in the first place, despite Genni sometimes believing it was through no fault of her own. She smiled as she remembered all the stories Caril told her about her earlier life, her family, before she was made redundant and she couldn't find another job. Maybe she should pop and see her, but that would mean risking bumping into Lorcan or any of the others, and she'd already made the decision to cut them out. She had to keep her integrity.

So, all of that landed her right back where she was before, living the life of merit-hunting, though she realised the suspension was a significant drainer on that plan. Determining not to dwell in self-pity, Genni jumped up but too quickly; her hip pushed her handbag into the fountain. She threw her hands into the water, scrambling to release it from the depths while shielding her face from the jets of spray. She knew people walking were watching her, but she decided she didn't care. They could watch, there were much crazier things happening in this City than a broken girl saving a handbag from drowning. But she'd failed at that too. It was completely sodden, as were her two drawing pads. She flicked through them, cursing out loud as she almost cried at the smudged pencil sketches from over the last year. They were like her journals, documenting all that she'd been feeling but on reflection, black smudgy messes weren't too far off. Whacking them back into her dripping bag, she vowed to herself she'd do better. She could live a merit-making life and slip under the radar and find a way to make a big difference in the Blythefens' or other people's lives who had been mistreated.

As she hurried towards the sky train, readying her wrist for authentication, she thought about how she just needed something normal to almost reset her brain. *Pearl and Mila.* She ignored the disgusted looks of others who stepped away from the drips her handbag was trailing behind her. Her friends. Not that they'd been friends much lately, but that was her fault, and she would make amends. She considered that felt like a good start to making things more normal and maybe then she would finally get her head straight.

CHAPTER
NINETEEN

Rod choked back the hurt as the *SkipSleep* needle retracted from his arm. He grabbed the sweaty ethanol bottle from the table beside him and chugged it back, sniffing up his frustration as he swallowed. He looked around his Glorified living room; the marble mantelpiece, the tall, freshly painted walls, the waiting drone swooping in and out on his every demand. *No, I couldn't lose it all. Could I? No one will know about the Unworthy in the alley. No one cares enough to investigate, but they might never give me my job back.* Rod rejected the weakness, breathing into the fact that his score was maintained, even though doing so was killing him physically. The ethanol was only an insurance policy to cover himself from the controlling nature of negative emotions. It gave him focus.

Taking another swig, he swiped his Watch to check in with his new regular pastime; *have they killed the Blythefens yet?* Not knowing always led him to the bottle again. *The project, they can't neglect the Side Eradication Project.* Rod dismissed all the news about protests declining and raving reviews of the new Watch model as he pulled himself from his chair, taking the steps of the large spiral staircase two at a time. The smiling face of Joon Blythefen came to mind and stopped him.

They haven't killed me because I've won. I've beaten you.

Rod put one hand on the wall, fighting a dizziness that swept over him. Stumbling back to his bedroom, he threw a shirt over his bare chest, heaving through his breathing. *It must be the heat.* Dressed, he stumbled downstairs again and strode through his double doors out into the light, having ordered his car to hover to the front of the winding driveway. He glanced up at the mountains and decided that he would find Jona, the idiot who got him fired. He'd force an update about the Blythefens to spill from his pathetic lips, but he realised he had to refrain from any physical violence. That felt difficult.

In the back seat, he imagined squeezing Jona's neck tighter. He squinted at the activation pad's green glow as it approved his Watch and he told the car to go. *Tighter. Tighter.* Until Jona was blue in the face. It would be satisfying. Empowering. Maybe then, if Jona was put in hospital, his spot vacant, they'd realise that job was Rod's. No, Rod checked himself. He couldn't do anything rash, acting on irrational instinct like when he attacked the repulsive Unworthy. He was lucky it was someone unimportant.

He watched the moving mountains, the car roaming towards Command as another face appeared in his head; Ajay's grandmother's drooped eyes held his attention.

I suppose you'll be no better than us soon. Unworthy.

The car silently halted and Rod stared blankly, not moving. *That old camel doesn't know a thing. Giving her whole life to deliver babies who never grew up to meet their potential, all because of an archaic device telling them to strive for nothing. Get out of the car. There's no time for this.*

He smacked the door control and dragged himself from the vehicle into Command's entrance, buttoning up his suit jacket and ignoring every passer-by as if nothing was untoward. No one knew of his decline, having not known his job in the first place; another advantage the prestige of undercover work had given him. *Had. Past tense.* Rod slammed down his thoughts as he sauntered into the Watch administration room, suddenly feeling jaded and questioning if the boost had even made a difference. *It's about attitude.* He'd sat too long at home, so decided on a double workout at the Tower later, after he'd dealt with Jona.

CHAPTER
TWENTY

It was funny how places could feel so unchanged despite how much life had moved on. Mansald Spas, owned by Genni's father, were such a place. Of course they'd had renovations, improved treatments, new beauty recommendations, updates to the dressing tables, but fundamentally they were the same as when her father first built them. A place to rest and recuperate while continuing to work. *Relax and Earn*, as the digital welcome screen boasted proudly above Genni's head as she nervously thought about meeting Pearl and Mila.

Scanning her Watch for entry, she kept her head down and made straight for the changing rooms. She dodged others as she closed herself into a cubicle and sat in front of the dressing table, following its instructions to reduce the puffiness around her eyes. Having the girls question why she'd been crying wasn't a conversation she wanted to have, not even with herself. It wasn't anything specific; it was only the natural order of things. Being suspended had given her a lot of time to think, and thinking led to tears, especially about the Blythefens and their fate. As she patted powder onto her cheeks, the last conversation she'd had with Reha rammed itself back into her mind.

'They wouldn't kill them publicly,' Reha had said, handing her a tissue.

'Why not? They're conspirators.' Genni had taken it, slightly embarrassed about breaking down in front of her and Lorcan.

'They've confirmed they're not part of The Rogue.' Reha sat opposite her in one of the armchairs, still holding a motherly gaze. 'Why they didn't lie about that to the public, I don't know.'

'It makes me nervous.' Lorcan had stared at his clasped hands. 'Like they have some sick, twisted plan coming.'

'But they could still do it?' Genni had said, her tears now dry.

Reha had nodded. 'But a lot of people wouldn't like it. There's not enough to warrant them dead, especially with the way the public feels towards Command. For now, that's working in our favour.'

Despite no raised voices or harsh words, Genni had barely said goodbye after that. Now back in the changing room, Genni squinted at the five columns of products the dressing table displayed on its mirror. She wasn't reading them; they all appeared to her a mesh of colours and patterns. It wasn't like the Blythefens were family, quite the opposite, but her frustration was for all the people like them being cheated and killed by a system that never saw them as people in the first place. Allowing them to suffer in the Detention Centre for no reason other than waiting to kill them quietly was barbaric. She shook herself, lobbed her make-up brushes back into her bag and yanked out her bathing costume. Holding the static fabric between her fingers, she rubbed the chip of paint on her right fingernail and considered again what she was doing there. Pearl and Mila wouldn't be expecting her to show; she'd flaked on them so many times since Ajay left.

She'd felt bad about her distance. There was so much going on in her head she seemed to have forgotten how to be a good friend. She knew Pearl would have noticed her lack of engagement and sharing on her channel; Genni had been staying off the socials, deciding they weren't particularly helpful for her state of mind. *Everyone has an opinion.* And Genni couldn't even think about Mila. On the few occasions they'd met up or chatted over a screen, Genni never asked what she was doing, and she couldn't remember the details of her new job in the Medical Centre. She was higher up – almost at M-497. She and Pearl were due to make Glorified around the same time if they met their targets. Genni was stagnant, staying solidly at M-411; her job, when they allowed her back, was the thing tying her down, but she'd managed to use personal development like exercise, healthy eating choices and educational movies so nothing would deteriorate at any great rate. If she couldn't help the Blythefens, and that was increasingly impossible, she needed something to control her frustration, and the triviality of a normal life might be just enough of a distraction.

Finally into her costume, she fell into the fresh, vanilla smell as she walked through the Treatment Centre, past several rooms where people lay on massage tables, their heads in the holes, working on screens beneath them. She glazed past the protocols on the doors to the rooms, detailing rules such as treatment time limits and the suggestion to request a break for any work calls. Hoisting her towel under her arm, Genni marched through the sliding glass doors into the swimming pool where several people were doing lengths, their Watches syncing to the merit counters at the end of each lane. She immediately spotted Pearl and Mila lounging on two pool chairs, both in costumes but swiping on multiple screens popping up from the chairs' integrated Watch-syncs.

Genni shuffled over in her flip flops, avoiding splashes from the pool.

'Hi,' she managed, laying her towel over the spare chair.

Both Pearl and Mila flicked down their screens excitedly and pulled their earphones out.

'Hi,' Mila smiled. 'You're here.'

Pearl said nothing but flipped her long locks behind her shoulders and rested on her side, her black, fitted swimsuit complementing her olive skin beautifully.

'Yeah. Sorry, I got a bit caught up.' Genni sighed as she sat on the chair, feeling the foam cushion moulding to her back. She could sense them looking at her as she logged in with her Watch, giving the pretence she wanted to do some work. Not that she had any to do currently.

'It's really good to see you,' Mila said softly, adjusting the rim of her green bikini before sipping the straw to an orange juice between her small lips.

'You too,' Genni said, not turning her head from her screens to avoid crying.

A sad silence fell between them. Genni wondered if the two of them were thinking about Ace, or The Rogue, or Ajay, or all three. Because she was. She never really stopped.

'Oh.' Mila drew her straw from her mouth. 'Jaxs wants you to see his new place.'

Genni widened her eyes. She immediately remembered seeing the invitation to Jaxson's Glorification celebration but had completely forgotten, never replied and definitely didn't show up. She was with Caril at the time, trying to encourage her to open a small food shack on the Outer-Ring streets.

'I completely missed his party. He probably thinks I'm awful, I should let him know that I—'

'It's OK.' Mila calmly placed her hand on Genni's wrist. 'He understood.'

'I should at least apologise. What's his place like?' As Genni asked the question, a calmness fell over her. It was the type of trivial conversation she needed.

'Oh, beautiful.' Mila nodded. 'He got it slightly cheaper, what with the property market near Command now.'

'Also not surprising with the size of the patio,' Pearl piped up, as she pursed her lips and took photos from her wrist.

'It's big enough,' Mila insisted. 'Before the attack, it would have gone for almost double.'

'I dunno, hun,' Pearl continued, 'his chairs come right to the edge of the pool. I might give him my designer's number.' Genni could see Pearl flicking through the photos she'd just taken, adjusting filters and saturation levels, particularly correcting the scar above her lip.

All three of them fell back to their screens for several moments, Genni scrolling through nothing in particular, and it wasn't long before Pearl took a call, joining many others who were yapping on their Watches across the swimmers in the pool.

'Hi, hun. Yeah, just at the spa. What we got?' It had been a while since Genni had heard Pearl's call voice; hyperbolically direct and authoritative. 'That's not going to work for me.' Pearl eyed the edges of her fingernails and sighed. 'I'll be back at the office in twenty. Positive vibes only, OK?' Pearl pulled her earphones out and shut down her screens. 'It's a real struggle for anyone to find anything positive to say,' she said, stretching her slender arms above her head.

'Not much material for it,' Mila said, eyes still on-screen.

'Hmm, at least *Personi* is pushing my stuff more.' Pearl flicked some fluff from her leg. 'The last thing I need is any more unfollows.'

Mila quickly presented concerned eyes and an awkwardness hung stagnant in the air.

'Why, what happened?' Genni asked, despite suspecting the answer was sensitive. She leaned forward in her chair, dismissing one of her screens.

'Nothing, really.' Mila shook her head lightly.

'Nothing? How can you say that?' Pearl sat up, her hair falling forward. 'I was abused.'

Mila gave Pearl a wide-eyed stare.

'Oh, come on, Mil. Don't look at me like that,' Pearl persisted, her eyes dancing between the two of them. 'Genni would have found out if she actually cared.'

'Pearl . . .' Mila flicked a screen away, just as a toned guy jumped from the pool and splashed the edge of their seats.

'What's that supposed to mean?' Genni narrowed her eyes, feeling her jaw tighten. The tone of confrontation made Genni's heart ricochet down to her belly, but her newfound confidence had forced her response to snap from her mouth.

'Just that while you've been AWOL, we've been dealing with stuff too, like my channel suffering because of my association with Ajay,' Pearl declared, moving closer and perching on the end of Mila's sun lounger.

'But it doesn't matter.' Mila gestured at Genni, all of her screens now gone. 'We know you've been hurting.'

'Yeah, like the rest of us.' Pearl clenched her own jaw.

'Pearl, stop it.' Mila tightened her upper lip.

'No, I've got to ask. Gen, where have you been lately? You ignore calls, you never see us and then you finally show up and expect us to forgive you.'

'I never asked for any forgiveness.' Genni could feel the emotion swelling in her throat and the cushions of her seat feeling more claustrophobic against her skin. 'You know what, I never should have come.' Genni unsynced her Watch, pulled her bathing suit straps onto her shoulders and threw her dress back over it.

'Gen, look, we're sorry—' Mila tried.

'So you're just going to walk away?' Pearl stood with Genni. 'Haven't you thought about how all this looks?'

'Excuse me?' Genni squinted at Pearl, her legs unsteady.

'You disappeared after what Ajay did; people might think you were in on it.'

'Alright, stop it.' Mila joined them standing, whispering to alert them to the listening ears around the pool.

'By people, you mean *you*?' Genni dropped her voice, anger still pulsing through her words.

After a slight pause, almost as if for consideration, Pearl said, 'I didn't say that.'

'Right,' Genni said quietly as her bottom lip trembled. She had nothing else to say so she didn't bother trying. Turning, she was back through the glass doors and out into the musty evening quicker than a drone delivering coffee. There was nowhere for her in this self-absorbed, disgusting City.

CHAPTER
TWENTY-ONE

Genni peered over the pan, letting the developing steam moisten her skin. She stared at the limp mint leaves floating on the surface of the water as she stirred it with a spoon and demanded the sugar to dissolve. Squinting at the screen from her Watch, she quickly focused back on the water; she did not want to burn it again. The recipe said to let it simmer for ten minutes but inevitably, that went by fast and she wasn't used to cooking. It was one of the first times she'd used the touch stove; the kitchen was mostly there for social gatherings or to heat up leftovers. She could have given up after the last attempt ruined a pan; she glanced over at the end of its pallid handle jutting out from the bin. But she needed the ethanol and she couldn't stomach it straight, nor would the drone service allow her to order any other ethanol-based drinks this week. So, her only option was to make a Tulo Tia herself. Glancing at her Watch screen, she swallowed as the work emails were stacking up into a high mountain of tasks she'd struggle to finish. She actually wished her suspension hadn't been lifted two weeks ago. There were times in the day when the sad reality of her situation weighed heavy on her mind and the only thing that loosened her up enough to distract herself was the small drop of ethanol in a Tulo Tia. Never ever more than that. She'd been down that road before.

With the sauce thickened, she whacked off the heat, leaving the syrup in the pan and turning to the fruit. *Add strawberries, blueberries and blackberries into a cocktail shaker and muddle to your desired consistency.*

'Damn,' she said as she swiped her screen away and brought up another, ordering the strawberries she'd forgotten.

It wasn't two minutes later when the drone arrived at her window. Scurrying over, she wiped her hand over the window unit and the glass slid open. She tapped her Watch to the drone's side with one hand and retrieved the strawberry box from its compartment with the other. Back in the kitchen, she lobbed all the berries into the cocktail shaker, wafting up the recipe again. A news alert swung into her screen which she briefly scanned: *New Metallic Range Cover for the new Watch model released in fifty-five different colours.* She flapped it away. Her heart had stopped jumping at every news alert in the fear or the hope that it was something about the Blythefens. In all her tactics, trying to save them, snooping around Command, trying to convince others to help her, even though she had no plan, the only way she seemed to barely function was by ignoring the issue completely and throwing herself into work and back into some sort of routine. But she knew she was kidding herself; she was just as miserable. If not more. At least with Reha, Lorcan and the others, she had friends. Unlike Pearl. Genni pressed hard with the muddler, smashing the fruit under its weight as she deciphered her scrambling thoughts.

Pearl had no right to say what she'd said about Ajay and even with two weeks passing, Genni still felt wounded by her cruelty. She pressed more firmly into the fruit, agonising over what happened. Over the years, she had disliked Pearl for many things; her melodrama, her obsession with correcting people, her inauthenticity on *Personi*, but she had never felt such deep-seated hatred towards her. The feeling sat uncomfortably on her chest, so intense she found herself needing to stop with the fruit and take a minute to breathe. *I should let this go. It's been long enough.* The intercom sounded. Genni moaned, not wanting to talk to anyone, especially if it was the protest groups again. It wouldn't take much to convince her to join if she didn't know it was futile. As her legs carried her to the door, she glanced back at the unopened bottle of ethanol on the kitchen table, not knowing whether her feelings towards it were healthy.

Clearing her throat, Genni pressed a soft finger to the door controls and mustered a word or two.

'Genni, it's me.'

Mila's calming voice bounced around the apartment as Genni stood back. She'd expected Mila to reach out but it had been weeks, so she'd thought she'd given up on her too. After inviting her in, she whizzed around the kitchen, turning off the stove, throwing dishes into the dishwasher, hiding the ethanol in a cupboard and placing the fruit-filled cocktail shaker in the sink. As Mila arrived, slipping her small frame through the sliding door, Genni was unsure whether a hug was appropriate but they both managed a light, sideways embrace.

'I've been meaning to come for ages,' Mila said as they let go. 'But you know, work.'

'Yeah, me too,' Genni said, offering her a seat on the sofa beneath her waterfall painting. Genni cast an eye over it, missing the feeling of a paintbrush between her fingers.

It was as if Mila could read her mind as she nodded towards the empty easel in the corner of the room.

'You're not painting much at the minute, then?' Her sad eyes fixed on it for a moment before they lifted towards Genni, who sat on the armchair opposite her.

Genni shook her head. 'I can't focus long enough without my mind drifting to things I don't want to think about. Work is better that way.'

Mila stroked her own hands, twisting her lip.

'I needed to come and tell you, Gen. That Pearl never meant what she said to you.'

'It sounded like she meant it.' Genni swallowed, glancing out the window as a billboard about dental health flickered.

'OK, maybe some of it,' Mila said, still anchored on Genni. 'Would you look at me?'

Genni complied, but not willingly. She fought back the tears.

'She would never believe you helped Ajay,' Mila said with such conviction, Genni felt her jaw loosen.

'Anyone will believe anything these days.' Genni choked on her words and struggled not to look away.

'She's just scared.' Mila's hands were poised on the lap of her dark-green skirt. 'Like most people.'

Mila's lip wobbled and Genni was drowning in a wave of sympathy. *Mila's scared too. It's never been only me. And I abandoned them.* The muggy air suddenly turned cool as Genni realised that this girl was her friend. She

QUIET ECHOES AT NIGHT

always had been and she'd let her down. Genni realised, despite being the one hurt the most, she managed to hurt others and little things, like picking up her Watch and saying 'hi' would have mattered. Little things like taking a loaf of bread to a woman who sometimes wouldn't eat otherwise.

'Mila, I'm sorry,' she said, as she retrieved two tissues from a nearby box. Using one to wipe her own eyes and offering another to Mila, she sat beside her on the sofa.

'Gen, I don't blame you—' Mila said, breathing heavily as she folded the tissue over to wipe her tears away carefully.

'But I've let you down, right?' Genni said, catching Mila in her ocean eyes. *They were green last time I saw her.*

'I'm not saying that, but . . .' Mila sighed quietly and choked, 'We all lost Ace too.'

Genni couldn't reply.

'I know you lost more,' Mila blew air through her circled lips. 'But Ajay was our friend and we've all had to deal with what he did in our own way.' She paused before lifting her head. 'But knowing you were OK would have helped.'

'I haven't been OK,' Genni admitted and fell back into the sofa. 'Right before you arrived I was trying to make a Tulo Tia because I've ordered too many this week.'

Mila laughed. 'You're not the only one to do that.'

'Yeah?' Genni smiled, breathing out in relief. 'Do you want one?'

Mila checked her Watch and said she'd love one but without too much ice. Genni pulled herself up from the sofa and they both made it to the kitchen. While she shook up the fruit, they talked about trivial matters, laughed about the destroyed pan in the bin and updated each other on their wardrobe's current suggestions, but as Genni strained the fruit into two glasses, Mila's voice turned somber again.

'You don't owe me anything, Gen,' she said as she watched the fruit mix fall. 'Especially not your time, but if you do need me, I am here for you.'

Suddenly, it was like Mila had lifted a filter from Genni's eyes, allowing the tears to fall through with no resistance, and her mouth produced little gasping breaths one after another in a rhythm of release. Genni held onto Mila, who hadn't hesitated to throw her arms around her, allowing Genni's head to rest on her shoulder as she began to cry too. Their sobbing lasted for several moments until Genni pulled away, and the two of them gave each other the same small smile, which then developed into panting laughs.

'Oh, man.' Genni wiped her eyes. 'I'm surprised I haven't dehydrated with the amount I'm crying at the moment.'

'There's no point holding it back.' Mila caught some tears on her chin, her rose-gold Watch cover bouncing the sun's light from the ceiling windows into Genni's face.

'I like your cover.' Genni nodded towards it.

'Oh, thanks.' Mila twisted her wrist. 'They finally released one I actually liked.'

'I saw there's a new metallic range,' Genni said, her breathing finally stabilising as she remembered glancing over the adverts for them earlier.

'I saw that.' Mila nodded. 'There's loads of them now, finally.'

'It seemed to take them long enough,' Genni agreed, enjoying its unimportance.

'I guess when enough people make a fuss,' Mila grabbed the syrup off the stove, 'anything can happen.'

Genni watched as Mila poured the perfectly prepared syrup into the glasses, but she only stared through its smooth symphony with the fruit as a concept settled on her like a warm, wrap-around blanket. She processed Mila's words before turning her head to her easel and painting equipment across the room. Excitement tingled through her legs and she felt an unfamiliar sense of peace, because something as pathetic as Watch covers could have just saved the Blythefens.

'They'll let them go,' Genni insisted as she addressed Reha and Lorcan, each occupying one half of Reha's sofa where her crumpled, drying clothes were draped over each end. 'I'm sure of it.'

Genni held her hands nervously on her lap, still catching her breath after issuing a soft apology. She had stood sheepishly by the door when Reha had let her in, enjoying the breeze of the fan after the hot outside air.

'I was wrong to cut you out when all you've both ever tried to do is help me,' she had said, fixing her gaze mostly on Lorcan. 'I was too frustrated that we couldn't do anything to help them, so I tried to ignore it and in turn, that meant ignoring you.' She had taken a step closer to Lorcan, almost as if she wanted to touch him, but she didn't and only stood watching him twist his lip. 'But what I won't apologise for is trying to get them out of there.' Genni had lifted her head higher. 'No one deserves to die for as little as buying a child a computer or believing something others don't.'

After some back-and-forth with Reha and Lorcan asking her not to do that again, Genni knew she was forgiven. The three of them had coffee together as Genni laid out her plan. Her argument was solid; she'd thought it over on the sky train as she whizzed around the City from her apartment, seeing Ace's face painted on the walls and overpasses. Genni wished she could read their minds as Lorcan looked at Reha, who returned the same concerned yet considerate look.

'OK, say you do this,' Reha said gruffly, leaning forward and scratching her birthmark. 'Have you got a plan to stay hidden?'

'Because they'll track you easily on *Personi*,' Lorcan added, also shuffling forward in his seat. 'You've seen the news of those arrests?'

Genni had and she'd also anticipated the question.

'I'll make it untraceable.' Genni stayed calm, despite the eagerness rising inside her. 'Not even use the socials, but paper.'

'Ink is expensive, Gen,' Lorcan said.

'I've got paint.' Genni shrugged her shoulders.

'So do I – at school, and I can replace them fine.' Reha nodded her head while stroking Alpha, the fox who had appeared and was resting its head on her lap. 'I think this could work.'

'OK.' Lorcan nodded. 'Then I'll help copy and distribute.' He threw Genni a look of admiration. 'Have you got a design?'

'Not yet, but I will.' Genni smiled, slowly processing their willingness to help after months of resistance.

It made sense. She realised that. Before she never had a plan; now that she did, they were not just listening but supporting. The answer had been around them all along. The power of public opinion and its ability to turn Command's hand.

Suddenly excitable, Genni leaned over the coffee table, grabbing her paints from her bag.

'Have you got any paper here?' she asked Reha, realising she should have brought a canvas from home.

'Here.' Reha stood, forcing Alpha to jump down from the sofa, and pulled a child's drawing down from her wall.

'Are you sure?' Genni said, eyebrows bent, knowing the drawings of her students must mean something to her if they're displayed around the house.

'Yes, of course.'

Genni briefly admired the shoddy crayon representation of the Social Sphere before flicking the page over to its plain side. It was a little thing, only a drawing, but enough little drawings would create a bigger picture, impossible to ignore. Like tiny echoes, repeating themselves, until Command had no where else to turn.

Steadying her hand, and embracing the unnatural thumping of her heart, she started to stroke out the words: 'Free the Blythefens'.

Personi Social Post

Vinxie Day – Personi – M-411 – W-51/Y2462 – 03:45

I wish people paid this much attention to me when I cry about Inspire's mascara going out of stock. #freethemascaras #getthemoutofstorage

12 loves

Nedd Tracor – Personi – M-385 – W-51/Y2462 – 03:47

Probably because you're a lowlife who only cares about superficial problems.

These are people's lives, not commodities.

1,842 loves

Vinxie Day – Personi – M-411 – W-51/Y2462 – 03:47

OK, sorry if you can't take a joke.

Nedd Tracor – Personi – M-385 – W-51/Y2462 – 03:48

I don't think Command holding innocent people captive is a joking matter, frankly.

Vinxie Day – Personi – M-411 – W-51/Y2462 – 03:48

There's no way they're totally innocent.

53 loves

Nedd Tracor – Personi – M-385 – W-51/Y2462 – 03:50

The interviews clearly showed they didn't know that he was part of The Rogue. Plus, there's loads of witnesses attesting to their characters. Have you seen this?

[attachment of a photo showing hundreds of signatures on a printed leaflet]

3,351 loves

CHAPTER
TWENTY-TWO

It was infuriating to be the only sane person living. Rod popped another 'Motivated' pill before combining it with a dose of 'Patience'. The advice was not to double-dose on Mood Enhancers but *what does anyone know?* When there were imbeciles spreading online and in the Outer-Rings crying for the Blythefens to be set free . . . If he wasn't sitting in The Skyhouse, surrounded by well-merited people, he'd let a loud rhythm of expletives tumble from his mouth.

We're going to get out. Free. Back to the Side. Back to our ways. We win. You lose.

Joon Blythefen's laugh rebounded around his head and Rod smacked the tall table he was sitting at, splashes of Tulo Ale spilling from his glass. He pushed out his chair, the scraping of its legs across the polished floor echoing around the bar and stealing people's focus from the skyline view to him storming out. He braced himself against the wall in the elevator, seething. *Command can't let them do this. Rod had failed to get any update from Jona but Esabel was clearly losing touch. If he was incompetent, then she was completely worthless.*

Out in the open night air, Rod was startled by the invasion of the City's bright illuminations, squinting to read a billboard above him, his vision blurring: *Invest in your future. Get your name on the list.*

The image of The Old Golden retirement home sparkled as he saw the shining snake of the sky train slither out from the station. He didn't know if it was the pills working their magic or in his very nature, but his bitter heart burned inside him like a fire that water couldn't put out. It was time for someone to put this right.

CHAPTER
TWENTY-THREE

Commuter time, around eight in the evening, was the best time to do it. Even better in the Inner-Rings, where the movement of rush existed in a flurry of swirling bodies with Watch screens glowing on ghostly, vacant faces. The billboards buzzed with coloured light, the air fresh with the smell of recent rain and the racket of scurrying footsteps.

It was the first time in four weeks they'd ventured this deep into the City to distribute. Genni caught sight of Lorcan as he disappeared into the crowd, his rucksack on, not full of Guiding Lights, but with leaflets painted by her hand. The new batch was the most striking yet; a portrait of the Blythefens behind bars with striking blue fonts and feathered outlines. She moved through the oblivious crowd and stuck posters all the way along a building's wall like a ricochet of laser shots. At the end, she peered back from beneath her lifted hood to see them; the cartoons of the Blythefens, one after another, causing people to move their eyes from their wrists. Genni was gone before anyone could spot her.

It was kind of exhilarating to be running against the law. She continued through the crowd, getting stalled by a street seller pawning off fake Watch covers. The woman made her reflect, momentarily. *How can the little merit from that job ever be worth it? Maybe she enjoys it.* Genni doubted it as she considered the woman's distraught face, ripped knee-high boots and scuffed bodycon dress. *She must be cold.* The post-storm air was icy. Genni wondered about offering her the jacket covering her own shoulders, but she had a long night ahead. Before taking any more time, she asked for her name and decided to tell Reha about her later. *She might be able to help.* With that, Genni was gone, moving through the blind crowd she was once part of, leaving more posters along walls and on pavements. She wouldn't stop. She couldn't. Not when it was working. When she went to sleep at night, knowing she was playing with fire, she slept soundly with the knowledge that what she was doing mattered. It mattered for the lives of three people who didn't deserve what they'd been given. It mattered, so she wouldn't stop.

'Hey, come on.' Lorcan had appeared again, grabbing her elbow and smiling, the black of his hoodie clear under the extensive street lighting. She didn't relent, chasing him down the side of a generic office building and watching him slip through a side door.

'What are you doing?' Genni followed him into a back-service elevator as someone emerged from it.

'The stars are always the clearest after a storm.' Lorcan swiped the button for the roof, ordering the elevator to quickly ascend.

'Are you kidding?' Genni stashed some posters back into her over-shoulder bag. 'We've still got three more rings to do.'

'There's time.' Lorcan rested his head on the wall and smirked at her.

Genni enjoyed that smile, one that convinced her that life was simple and stress was only a choice people made, and all of it could be fun. And he was right; the stars were clearest after a storm. She remembered from when she and Ajay used to watch them. The moon was seen best from this height too. 'Fine. Five minutes,' she eventually said, only gifting him a subtle smile back.

'Has anyone ever told you you're the most determined woman, nay, *person* in this City?' Lorcan raised an eyebrow.

'No.' Genni watched the elevator levels rise on the digital screen.

'I think you should take the title.'

Genni didn't respond as she felt his eyes on her turn to something more than friendly admiration. It wasn't that she didn't like the look, but she couldn't deal with it. There was too much at stake. For the last four weeks, she had been living every day posing as an M-411 citizen, when under the surface, she was the instigator of the latest round of unrest against Command. People like her had been arrested already, and who knew of their fate? Maybe that's what she'd do next. Use the public to free the Blythefens and then free everyone else who had been misrepresented. *One thing at a time, Genni.*

The elevator pinged to its stop and the two of them emerged out onto the rooftop.

Genni's breath got trapped as she craned her neck to see the plethora of bright desert stars beaming in a carpet of sparkles.

'Wow,' she whispered. 'Never gets old.'

Lorcan ran up to the roof edge and playfully sat down, legs dangling over, his eyes shooting straight up.

'It's the best, ain't it?' he sighed.

She agreed but stood still, considering how the last time she saw the stars so clearly was in the Blythefen's destroyed garden, when the planet Curtan was visible, and the stars surrounded it with the same stupendous splendour. As she stared, she could feel a tired weight on her eyes, their lids drooping with fatigue. She didn't think she'd ever worked so hard. It was like having a new job and she was desperate to make an impression and she wasn't sleeping well with the anxiety and needed *SkipSleep* to keep going. *This is why it's dangerous to stop. The tiredness catches up.* The Blythefens had been stuck for months, she could keep going for a few more weeks, and she shouldn't be stopping to gaze at the stars.

'OK, let's get back down.' She walked back to the elevator.

'That wasn't five minutes.' Lorcan laughed, lethargically pulling himself off the roof edge.

'We've got other jobs to do after this,' Genni reminded him, slamming the elevator screen as he ambled through its doors.

'Right.' Lorcan ordered it to descend. 'Something about tonight doesn't inspire me to fix car batteries.'

'We hopefully don't have to do this for much longer,' Genni said, thinking of their route through the next ring.

'I'll probably miss it. The thrill.' He widened his eyes, nudging Genni's arm and bringing his face closer to hers.

'Don't you always have that?' Genni smiled, pushing his face away with the flat of her hand. 'With what you do.' She had seen plenty of him planning his routes around the City to illegally deliver Guiding Lights.

'Yeah, course.' Lorcan nodded. 'But this feels a lot more peppery.'

'Peppery?' Genni raised an eyebrow.

'Yeah, you know, like, intense. Spicy.' He gestured with his hands as the elevator glided to the bottom. Genni shook her head at him, despite approving of his light-heartedness – but then a heaviness invaded her thoughts. *What will this mean for him?* If he got caught doing what she asked him to, that would be agonising. Her breathing grew weak, thinking more about being responsible for other people and the routes their lives might take. She was thankful that her wrist vibrated.

Until she wasn't.

Her panic tripled and Lorcan's laugh faded into silence with the look on her face.

Genni's hands started to shake and her Watch pinged again with her rising heart rate.

'Gen, what is it?' Lorcan placed a hand on her shoulder.

She gazed over the request from Command and then up at him, staring hard into his familiar, safe eyes.

'I think they've . . .' Genni breathed deeply, 'found me.'

'What?'

Genni zipped out into the night air, Lorcan scrambling after her. Everything was a blur and she could feel herself losing touch, not sure where to walk or even what to say.

'Genni?'

She walked quicker, the colours of the City a rainbow fuzz.

'Genni, stop.' Lorcan grabbed her arm, a touch she could only just feel as she turned, letting the crowds filter past as they slipped down another side street. She found comfort in his presence again.

'It's Command.' She closed her eyes and spoke slowly. 'They need me for questioning.'

Lorcan nodded, seeming to consider the danger of the situation. She stared down at some of her leaflets, wet on the ground after being blown in the storm. If they were caught, she'd never forgive herself for putting them all in danger. She should have done this alone.

'OK,' he said, too calmly. 'You don't know it's about this.'

'What else would it be about?' She pulled her hair back with one hand, feeling the sweat on her forehead.

Lorcan shrugged tensely. 'Ajay?'

'I've answered all their questions. It can't be that.'

'I don't know, Gen, but stay calm. If they knew it was you, they'd be here arresting you already.'

'Sure, OK.' Genni swallowed, knowing he was probably right, but it didn't stop her from realising that in a few short hours she, and everyone she'd dragged down with her, might never see the stars again.

CHAPTER
TWENTY-FOUR

There are things that can hurt people in ways unimagined. Actions that make them quake. Words that leave them sore. People in this City are like little leeches. Sucking its buildings, credit and merit dry. We have given them everything. Still, they take, take, take. And they vandalise. And they moan. And resist. They should all be exiled to the Side. They are worth nothing. But the masses always take control.

Esabel straightened her neck and inhaled slowly through her nose, letting her anger sit for a moment. Staring at one of the great pillars of the Command building, slathered in black paint, was doing nothing to calm her down. She clicked at the Command officer beside her, whose name she didn't care to know, beckoning him to step closer.

'Why,' she seethed quickly, 'is there no one here already getting this *filth* cleaned up?'

'Right,' the officer stuttered. 'Right away, Ms Hevas . . .' He started yapping into his Watch.

Esabel ordered him back. 'And get Salli down here.' She stared back at the black words trailing around the pillar. 'Now.'

As she waited, the fury merged with her emotion. These pillars had been standing there since the City was first built. They spoke of Tulo's history, her family's legacy of building the merit system and the paradisal life they all enjoyed. Yet ingrates had come along and marred it with black, oily paint. All for the lives of some Unworthies from the Side. Why would they care so much? Why did M-300 and below fools get so riled up over a few words online or a leaflet they found on the street? Esabel stroked her forehead, irritated by the heavy breathing of the officer who had failed to summon people quickly enough. She briefly glanced at the black band of her tattoo beneath her Watch. *I won't let my ancestors down.*

'Where,' Esabel whispered hotly, conscious of the public passing her in front of Command's grand entrance, 'is Salli?'

'Behind you.' The officer nodded.

Esabel swung around on her heels to find Salli, vice-chair to the Board, floundering towards her, panting and at risk of ripping her overly tight business suit as she ran.

'Sorry, Esabel, what is it?' Salli patted her eye to adjust her contact but quickly didn't need a response, her eyes widening on seeing the vandalised pillar. 'Oh.'

'Oh?' Esabel spoke over Salli's smaller stature. 'That's all you can say? Where are my leads for who's created this thing?' She could feel the rage escaping in her breath.

'We have a good one.' Salli put her arms out in defence. 'But we have to cross-check—'

'But?' Esabel longed to raise her voice. 'There should be no buts. You have everything you need; this *City*,' she paused, letting herself breathe slowly, 'this City has everything it needs to find whoever started this and yet it's been going on for weeks.'

'Well, if we started investigating sooner than last week,' Salli tapped at her wrist, 'instead of focusing on the other protests, then I might have seen results already.'

Esabel didn't flinch, despite feeling aghast at such a conniving and outrageous response. *Who does she think she is?* She stared down at her, pinching her lips together. Esabel waited long enough until Salli's eyes started to dart around her, squirming like a little worm.

'If *we* started?' Esabel asked before nodding her head in jest. 'Oh, OK. I see. You think *we* are on the same team.'

'I didn't mean, me and you, per se—'

'No, no, you're right. We are on the same side.' Esabel then shook her head. 'But we are not the same. See, you don't even understand what it means to be here. I suppose you probably think you were appointed to the Board to do a job. To coordinate teams and to get results. I adore those things, really I do.' She held a hand to her chest. 'But your tiny brain seemingly doesn't realise the sacrifices that have been made and the years of hard work that have got you to where you are standing today. Yet you think it's appropriate to discredit the memory of those who paved the way for you by questioning your superior.'

'That's not what I—'

'Ah, ah.' Esabel tutted, shaking a finger, bidding Salli's mouth shut. 'Just go.'

Salli nodded and turned away quickly in a feeble attempt to hide the tears welling in her contact-filled eyes.

'Oh, and Salli . . .' Esabel walked back towards her.

Salli froze and rotated slowly as Esabel sat her mouth right by her ear.

'Tell me when you find them, but don't wait to have them killed,' Esabel demanded.

She didn't bother watching Salli scuttle away, but clicked her fingers at the officers to escort her back to her office. She glanced at the cleaning team arriving and stopped herself from looking back at the work of the vandals. She wanted to be alone. To think. To straighten it all out. Command's highest, the Board, had said the leaflet thing could go south. She'd assured them it wouldn't catch on. *But I was wrong. I didn't think so many more would turn against me like this. Father never taught me how to deal with so much unrest. It's never happened before, but I cannot lose control. Esabel Hevas does not doubt herself.* Though she knew she had little choice. With the rallies over the Blythefens so close to Command and with all the public backing from the Outer-Rings and even some from the Inner sections, there was nothing else she could do. The public was already irritated enough about security, they couldn't risk another faction or group starting some sort of civil war.

Oh, Joon Blythefen. Someone out there must love you. But don't get too excited, they'll be dead by the end of the day.

CHAPTER
TWENTY-FIVE

The Command interrogation room felt like a box with enclosing walls. Forever moving in, like water rising, closer to her head until there was no more space to breathe. Genni sat on her clammy hands, waiting. It had been three minutes. The efficiency seemed lax. She wanted to close her eyes for a moment to compose herself, but she knew the drone floating beside her was recording her every move. She had to avoid looking nervous. It would give her away. Wouldn't it? She had no idea. All she knew was the banging of her heart, the sweat down her back, and the dry tunnel of her throat. *My Watch statistics. They have them. They'll know I'm nervous.* She held onto Reha's words from before. *It's hard not to worry, but try.* When she first said it, Genni couldn't have thought of anything more unhelpful, but in the moment, it was giving her focus. *Try. That's all you can do.* The door slid open and a man with one side of his shirt hanging from his trousers swooped in, tapping at his wrist.

'Miss Mansald.' He held her with tired eyes before sitting down across the table. 'I'm Detective Jona Jan.'

Genni nodded at him, discreetly taking deep breaths.

'There's something I want to show you,' he said, swiping at the air, a projector screen emerging from the drone behind them. 'It's a quick piece of surveillance footage.'

They've caught me. Genni lost her breath momentarily, waiting for a clip of her with Lorcan or Reha, nipping through the streets and distributing leaflets. *Was it last week in Downtown?* There were a lot of drones. It made life more difficult for them, but she thought they were careful. She'd have put more people in the Detention Centre than people she'd got out. It was reckless. All of it so reckless. They would never forgive her. She'd never forgive herself.

'Miss Mansald...' His gruff, dry voice echoed.

Genni's focus flew back into the room. She glanced up to see Ajay on the screen. *What?* He was standing in the street, by a sky train bridge, looking down at some Unworthy on the ground. *What is this?*

'Are you with me?' The detective grunted. Genni got hold of herself.

'Yes, sorry.' Genni looked back at Ajay, the first time she'd seen anything of him for a while. It hurt to see him. Still. She hated that.

The video started to play as Ajay bent down and hoisted the Unworthy up, helping him walk on an injured leg.

'Do you recognise the man he's with?' The detective spread his fingers over the screen, zooming in on the scruffy, bearded man with bruises around his cheeks and eyes.

'No.' Genni told the truth, which she hadn't expected to do. 'I've never seen him before.'

What was Ajay doing? When was this?

'Are you absolutely sure?'

'Yes,' Genni nodded. 'When was it?'

'Way before the attack. He takes him back to his apartment and the man stays the night. You're sure you've never met him?'

Genni stared at the table, confused, before shaking her head. The tape continued, and she watched the man emerge from Ajay's building on assisted crutches. Ajay had helped him. *Why?*

'I'm sorry,' Genni said instinctively after seeing the detective flop backwards in his chair.

He leaned forward. 'Miss Mansald, you're absolutely confident there is no connection between Ajay and this man? Did you have any idea of Ajay's connection to Unworthies or where he may have gone?'

'No.' Genni met his persistent gaze. 'I've already told you everything. All Ajay ever did was work. Like everyone else.'

He looked at a loss. 'You can go.'

Genni's instinct was to jump from her seat and run for the door with her unexpected freedom, but she controlled herself, moving slowly as if nothing was untoward. When she escaped and walked slowly down the corridor out into Command's foyer, she stopped by the large letters that spelt 'Progress is Strength' and leaned against the 'P'. Should she message Lorcan? He was probably binge-eating the biscuits in worry. No, that was dangerous. All their conversations since they started the campaign had been untraceable, she couldn't ruin that in her relief. Gathering herself, she stepped to leave but hesitated.

At least a dozen armed Command officers marched past her, surrounding a petite, black-haired woman with striking blue eyes. *Esabel Hevas?* She never came out in public. Genni glanced away, noticing others watching as Esabel disappeared into an elevator. Genni let her legs carry her outside. Donning her sunglasses as the sun fell over her, she glanced up at the cloudless sky, appreciating the smooth ascension of the pillars by Command's doors; the height of them, the majestic way they took precedence over the space. It was only a moment before she saw the vandalism; stark, bold words penned in black paint.

'Free the Blythefens' was snaking around the second pillar repeatedly, leaving work for the man spraying at it with a laser cleaner. Genni shuffled past him and couldn't help but smile.

CHAPTER
TWENTY-SIX

The elevator swooped into her office and the doors fell into the floor.

'Leave.' Esabel ordered the officers and the elevator to retreat downstairs. She hadn't taken two steps into her office before she realised her husband was sitting on one of the sofas with a glass in hand. 'What are you doing here?' She marched over to her desk and threw up her screens. 'There's plenty of work for you to be getting on with.'

'I thought you might want to talk,' Jamal said, placing his glass down on the table. His voice was tiring.

'No time for talking.'

'Esabel, you've got to make the right decision here.'

'Jam!' She fixed her eyes back on him. 'Don't you think I know the right answer? I always do.'

'Sure,' he nodded, standing and walking towards her, the noise of his feet making her tense. 'But there is the personal connection.'

She laughed. 'It's not personal with Joon Blythefen.'

'So you don't want him dead more than anyone else?'

Esabel didn't respond but continued tapping at her desk, opening the latest Rogue interview reports.

'The Side Eradication Project can get back up and running.' He leaned on her desk, looking pensive. 'Let him go now and we can get him back when people forget him.'

'You're wasting your breath, Jamal. I've just given the order.'

They stared at each other for a heated moment before Jamal nodded and sniffed, looking conciliated as he wandered back to the sofa. Esabel watched him, tracing his tall frame with her eyes. He sat again, sipping at his drink. *Why is he still in my office?*

'Your hair looks too grey,' Esabel said impulsively, tapping at her desk harder than usual.

'So, what now?' Jamal swirled his water in his glass, somewhat anxiously.

'You dye it.' Esabel stroked the air, enlarging a map of the forest, red circles pinpointed around suspected Rogue locations not far from the old base they'd discovered.

'Esabel . . .' Jamal's voice faded.

'We send in bombs.' The words were welcome on her tongue.

'What?' He placed his glass down and rose slowly.

'Blow them all up, like we should have done in the first place.' Esabel shrugged, her voice tart.

'Hang on,' Jamal moved forward again with defiance. 'That was never a consideration.'

'Yes, it was,' Esabel said curtly. 'It always has been.'

'No, Esabel. There are children in The Rogue camp.' Jamal's voice seemed to get caught in his throat. 'The Board and the Security Bureau have already decided it isn't an option.'

'The residents of the *City* are our children.' She didn't shift her eyes from his. 'And they're suffering. Sending drones in alone obviously hasn't worked.' She exhaled hard, the threat of the City falling too hard for her to bear. She needed to silence the public, she needed to silence The Rogue, she needed to be the only one with a voice. The merit system made a greater Tulo and she would never let her father's words fade away in vain.

'My great-grandfather created this City and left it to me,' she seethed, banging her finger to her chest, 'and the constitution *he* wrote clearly states that when the Board cannot fulfil their duty to uphold the progress of all of Tulo, then my family has the right to take ultimate control without needing their approval. The tattoo gives me that power.' She threw up her wrist, letting her Watch slide down to reveal the black band printed on her skin.

She watched Jamal, her insides churning as she considered him.

'What are you shaking your head at?' She pushed her weight through her wrists as she stood over her desk. 'We've given The Rogue chances.'

'You think a silly family tradition gives you the right to kill *children*?' Jamal put a shaking hand over his head. 'It's barbaric.'

Esabel squealed with rage for everything he'd just belittled. 'These Unworthies are destroying everything I've worked for. This is not a tradition; this is our legacy. The public will rest once we've dealt with them.'

'*Your* legacy?' Jamal shook his head and walked away, before hesitating at the elevator door. 'You know, you could at least call Arneld back.'

'I don't have time for his problems right now.' Esabel straightened her jacket and flattened a piece of stray hair on her head. 'You sort him out.'

'He needs you to let him stop.' Jamal swiped his Watch at the wall as the elevator doors swept open.

'He's got to keep going. He's got an image to improve.'

'There's only so much he can do. He's our son, not your show thing.'

'It was your idea in the first place.'

'Yes, and it's achieved what it needed to.'

'He doesn't understand hard work. The boy's merit makes my skin crawl.'

'He's Glorified, Esabel.'

'Barely.' She had the last word as more curt expressions flew back and forth, ending with Jamal disappearing behind the elevator doors.

She moaned into the high ceilings, wishing she'd thrown something at him. The story of the last thirty years. At least their merit had always given the impression of a strong marriage. They were a good match and that, fortunately, didn't change the more they disliked each other. It had started well and like most people through their history, she had adored the idea of being tied to another, but the more she thought about it, the more she realised it was a waste. It couldn't change; the public were suckers for tradition and they had power, a fact she was learning too well. Jamal wasn't Esabel's problem, though. It was Joon Blythefen.

Playing the moment over, when she swiped that button to tell them to release him, she wished she could reverse things. There must be another way to get the public back on her side, but there wasn't time. Always too little time. She flopped into her chair, feeling jaded. *That won't do.* She ripped back the cuff of her jacket and scanned her Watch against the port on the table. The *SkipSleep* needle was soon in her arm as she stared forward, thinking. Part of her felt confused. It was unsettling; she was always sure of what she wanted, but Joon Blythefen caused issues.

It wasn't that she didn't want him dead; she did.

She closed her eyes and saw the mountains of the Quarters, being with Joon, laughing. *Stop.* The feelings behind those memories were fabricated, the musings of a stupid teenage girl. He was nothing to her but a distraction, so she'd close the door to him. She'd moved on to what she needed to do.

Jamal was right; once they had sorted The Rogue, and the City returned to normal without lunatic M-300s moaning about everything they could to discredit them, the Blythefens could be killed. Quietly. Swiftly. Without all the complications.

She watched her daughter in the tank, the cord coming from her stomach. Could she really kill the children? Those poor, sweet children? *So beautiful. Children have gorgeous potential. It's not their fault their parents couldn't handle it. If they were mine, they would thrive.*

As the needle retracted from her arm, Esabel quietly laughed as she knew she'd hit on a good idea. A mega merit-making idea. *That's it. How has it taken me so long?* She'd lost sight. She had to give her children grace. Not those who repeatedly misbehaved and wouldn't comply, of course. But those who have been mistreated would be welcomed into her warm embrace. She would have to take them as her own and kill anyone who stood in her way.

As the thought settled peacefully, her Watch vibrated. Without hesitating, her fingers brushed the screen.

We've found the artist: Genni Mansald, daughter of businessman, Boris Mansald and sister of former compliance officer, Rod Mansald.

Her lips grew into a coy smile before blossoming into hot, hysterical laughter.

CHAPTER
TWENTY-SEVEN

There was nothing he could do to stop it. It was growing inside him. Fierce. Hungry. Untamed. Rod's heart had slammed shut. He was like a predatory desert animal prowling through the Glorified Gate, determined to eat. The news of the Blythefens' release had ripped through him with the speed and intensity of that needle slicing through Ace's arm. Swift, brutal and fatal. Command had them. They had them and all they had to do was finish the job. As he bounded through the Quarters, choosing a café on the main walkway, he readied himself to get what he wanted.

CHAPTER
TWENTY-EIGHT

Her euphoria distracted her from the stress of the last hour. Genni bounced into a seat on the sky train, and as the City whizzed by, she searched for more evidence that her campaign had grown. There were still loads of imprints of Ace's face over billboards, on walls, but *they* were there interweaved in among it all; the words she saw around Command's pillar, words she originally wrote on that leaflet.

Free the Blythefens

She sat back and smiled. It was crazy. All her life she had been on the same train as everyone else; living for the drug of impact, progress and success. Yet there had never been a moment where she felt as fulfilled as right then. *Was this what I was always meant to do?*

As she pondered on it more, and made awkward eye contact with a guy gripping a pole in the centre of the carriage, she realised that feeling had been there for weeks. Months, really. Since she started spending time with Reha and Lorcan, sure, but it was stronger with Unworthies, no, *people* like Caril. When she saw her cooking in Reha's kitchen, it was like something turned and everything felt warm inside. Until she'd had to return to the murk of the office and the rush of the Inner-Rings; all of it heavy and consuming.

Genni's focus wavered as she watched the repetition of Ace's face grow stronger. In some ways, it felt like it had been years without him. She realised she hadn't thought about him as much as she should have, especially with him becoming a City-wide symbol. Yet he was becoming less prominent, the drones lasering off his face in the Inner-Rings. After that, the only reminders of him would be in her memory. That fact was enough to knock her down from her previous high and tears bubbled back into her eyes.

She subtly wiped them as she noticed the guy from before again. He glanced up from his wrist in her direction before they both flicked their eyes away. Genni swiped at her own Watch, dismissing most things, but Ajay came back to mind. *Why did he help that man with the injured leg? What was he doing?* More secrets. She didn't know why she was surprised anymore. She wondered what she'd find out about him next; it didn't matter anyway. He didn't matter.

'You look like you've had a long day.'

Genni broke from her thoughts to see the guy now nestled in the seat between her and a skinny woman.

'No, not really.' Genni's eyes darted away from his chiselled jawline and shaved haircut.

'Well, that's good,' he nodded. 'I'm Harri.' He pulled his hand out which Genni shook feebly, saying nothing.

'Are you going to tell me your name?'

'I don't know you, sorry.'

'OK.' He fell back into his seat silently, letting a moment pass before he breathed more words over her. 'Has your profile picture been corrupted?'

'What?' Genni felt her eyebrows narrow.

'It's on the news. A load of people's identification pictures became blurry and distorted.' He tapped at his screen. 'Mine's still alright.'

Genni resisted the urge to check her own, as what did it matter?

'Do you know much about anti-procrastination techniques?' he said, without looking up.

Genni stared at him, considering how before, she wouldn't have questioned a stranger requesting to educate her. She never used to accept, mainly for a lack of social self-confidence and the little merit it gave her, but now, the very nature of its fabrication and inauthenticity tired her.

'I don't want to be educated, thank you,' she said simply, hoping he'd depart on the next stop as they were getting nearer to the Outer-Rings and he didn't look Unworthy enough.

'But you can educate me in return?' he argued. 'I thought you looked up to it.'

'Why?' she asked, whispering, not wanting to cause a scene for those around them. 'Because I look about your age, your score, and I'm busting every part of me to get as much merit as I can to be welcomed through that golden gate?'

'Isn't that what everyone's doing?' he asked, scratching his head awkwardly.

'That's exactly the problem.' Genni stood, spotting an empty seat at the other side of the carriage. He stood with her, trailing her as she walked down the carriage and whispering into her ear.

'Are you one of those protest types?' He sounded more curious than defiant, but still, Genni didn't respond and continued down the carriage. He didn't follow and as she sat, she watched him depart when the train stopped and he fell into the ignorant crowd without even looking back.

You need to be careful. She wasn't invincible and could get herself caught. Seeing the glisten of the Outer-Ring river come into view, she felt the tickle of a vibration on her wrist just as everyone in the carriage started to shuffle, all swiping or raising their Watches in similar motions. She popped out her screen to see the news alert spinning.

Her heart fluttered and all the saliva evaporated from her mouth.

The Blythefens were getting out.

CHAPTER
TWENTY-NINE

Trust is a complicated thing. So simple, yet so hard. Joon had faith they would get out, yet when it was happening, he questioned its integrity.

Esabel could be playing her awful games, sending officers down to his cell to escort him home. Kelli may not even be alive.

He'd been left in agony for months. The not knowing was the ultimate torment for him, and he guessed that's what Esabel was trying to achieve. The only thing that kept him sane was the hope she had been lying.

'Here.' A Command officer shoved a pair of sunglasses in Joon's free hands.

'Thank you,' he said instinctively, placing them on his face, readying his body for unfamiliar sunlight.

It was quiet in the corridor, only a few people filtered between rows of doors. Joon looked back, hoping to see Kelli with her own guarded convoy, but she wasn't there. He didn't know what to think. They said they would be transported back to the Side separately and he didn't ask questions, only wanting them to get on with it.

Insisting to see Kelli would have slowed things down entirely, but as he walked closer to the exit and he saw a hover vehicle swerve in front of the entrance, he readjusted. *How do I know she's coming home?* All the fear he'd bottled up after months of waiting suddenly invaded like a truck ramming through him.

He stopped still.

'Keep moving.' The officer jabbed him in the back with the butt of his laser gun.

'I want to see my wife.' He started walking again, slowly.

'You'll see her at home.' The officer in front, who took his last statement, scanned his Watch against the doorframe.

'How do I know that?' Joon stopped, his feet glued to the spot.

'Well, Unworthy, why don't you get in the van and you'll find out?' The officer lifted his visor, revealing his irritated eyes and stubbled, wide chin.

'No.' Joon breathed through the shake in his legs. 'I'm not leaving here without my wife.'

'She'll be along soon.' The officer drew out his words.

'I want her with me.'

'That's not our order.'

'I don't care.' He glanced at the open door to the black hover vehicle, leather seats ready inside. 'There's enough space for the two of us in there. So why not take us together? What aren't you telling me?'

The officer said nothing, but flicked his visor down and grunted at the other three under his command. 'Get him in the car.'

Joon resisted but the strength of three men took his body from the ground and threw it onto the leather upholstery of the backseat as two of the officers jumped into the front.

'Blueberry Bliss Lane, the Side,' one of them told the car and it swooped away silently.

'Take me back.' Joon smacked at the glass of the window.

'Just calm down, son, alright?' one of them said calmly. 'We've heard nothing of your wife getting hurt.'

'Eh, that's classified,' the other officer mumbled as Joon caught his breath.

'It'll shut him up,' the calmer officer quipped back.

Joon froze in the back seat, glancing up through his sunglasses at the panoramic roof to see the peaks of the mountains as the car drove through the Quarters. *Kelli might be safe. How can I believe that? They sounded sincere, but they could have staged that whole act.*

Joon clutched at his chest; he wasn't as fit as he used to be.

OK, what next? I'll get home. I'll wait for her, but if she doesn't arrive within an hour, I can come straight back. I'll walk if I must. Or I could escape from the car now.

Joon tried to release the door quietly. Double-locked. *Of course. Just stay calm.* He closed his eyes. *Please let her be safe. Please.*

He glanced out the window at the swirl of people walking within the Quarters' golden walls, in and out of the small exclusive shops, restaurants and spas. He noticed the delicate blooms of an upcoming hanging basket outside one of the cafés.

It's OK. It's OK. She'll come home. She will—

Joon's thoughts scrambled as the car window shattered.

CHAPTER
THIRTY

Rod felt the reassuring heat from the laser pistol seep into his palms.

Returning it to the inside pocket of his light jacket, he twisted his nose at the pollen budding from the overly bright flowers in the basket above him. He vacated his seat at the café and swiftly marched down an alley, leaving his untouched smoothie behind.

He listened to the crowds of panicked people cowering by the still vehicle with the ruined window and congratulated himself on always being an excellent shot.

CHAPTER
THIRTY-ONE

Esabel flicked down the screen before Salli could hang up.

The distortion of her profile picture, all pixelated like smashed make-up powder, didn't even upset her nerves. She sat there, still, staring into the office.

There was a complicated feeling. A sadness, so strong she couldn't bat it away.

She stood and walked slowly over to her daughter in the tank. Placing a hand on the glass, she felt nothing but love as she watched the little body bob within the fluid.

This is what I wanted: Joon, dead.

Isn't it? It's the waste. It must be the waste.

'You're a good girl, aren't you?' she whispered, peering closer to the tank. 'So if Mummy told you a secret, you wouldn't tell anybody.' She shook her head. 'No, you wouldn't.'

She breathed and noticed a small shake in her hands against the glass. *Don't be weak. Tick, tick. Time is moving. Focus. There's the Mansald girl, Rod and The Rogue. I can't. I need a moment. Just a moment with my girl.*

'The truth is, Mummy was scared.' The words felt dirty on her tongue. 'Scared because she didn't understand what she was feeling. She wanted to kill Joon Blythefen.'

She paused, glancing down at her black heels against the white marble floor. 'But also, she didn't. Because there was a time when she loved him, or thought that she did. But she didn't know love then.' She kissed the glass and watched it steam up from the heat of her mouth. 'You'll be ready soon, my child. This world is mean sometimes but Mummy will protect you. I must.'

Esabel continued whispering to herself, trying to process the news of Joon's death. *It's fantastic news. Brilliant, even. No one can know the sad part. Hide it. Bury it. Deep within the back of your mind. Gone. Forever. That's it.*

Esabel held her head up and breathed, striding her way back to her desk. Her head felt foggy. Falling into her seat, she swiped at her drawer, it gracefully sliding open to reveal her Mood Enhancer stash. She used her nails to select 'Calm' and popped the pill into her mouth. She felt out of control. Of course it was right Joon Blythefen was dead, and it was a relief he was. Even more so, she wasn't the one to have to do it. It was obvious to her that Rod had pulled the trigger. There was no one else more unstable. The situation with his sister should be her priority, alongside The Rogue and taking their children, so she shouldn't be getting caught up with the fact Joon's body would soon be in a metal chamber.

He had so much potential.

'Such a waste,' Esabel tutted, and it wasn't until an involuntary sniff escaped that she realised the tears on her cheeks.

She hurried for a tissue, flicking up her Watch screen and dabbing at her eyes in the mirror mode. *A moment of weakness. No one can see. It's OK, Esabel. Progress is*

Strength, and Joon Blythefen did not live for progress, so why should he live at all? Keep focused, keep the constitution, protect your daughter and this City.

She could feel the enhancer doing its work as a wave of contentment moved over her; she synced her Watch to her desk. She glanced out at the Quarters, and then even further into the City where clouds were uniting in the desert sky.

There's always more work to be done.

She stroked the rim of the tattoo under her Watch. *I can't let them down.*

So, first things first, who needs to be fired for the broken profile pictures? And if they haven't already killed Genni Mansald, I've got just the person for the job.

CHAPTER
THIRTY-TWO

Running from the sky train, Genni barged past people and took no notice of a cursing street seller as she ran through his product screens and his newest customer.

She took a shortcut down an alley and soon sprinted into the blanket of the sun, over an Inner-Ring bridge, the blue of the river painted in the reflection on Command boats. Taking a sharp left, she could see the entrance to the River House, where she knew Reha would be, as she wasn't at home in the Outer-Ring.

Maybe Lorcan would be there too and they could all celebrate together. She wondered what the plan would be – would they travel over to the Side to welcome the Blythefens home? Or would they wait it out a little? Let them get settled in before bothering them? She didn't know, but she was elated.

The air was humid and close, but that didn't stop her pace. A small wind was taking hold, gathering up stray protest leaflets into her path.

Do they already know? They must do. What if they don't? How can I tell them? I should slow down so I'm not exhausted.

She lessened her pace as she grew nearer to the small house on the side of the river. She hurried through the door, taking her time on the small ladder down to the River House's industrial steel doors. They were open, meaning people were already there. She made her way quickly down the sloped steps under the dim lights, smiling as she went, trying to contain herself. She could hear voices. Genni skipped through the doors to see the back of Reha, Lorcan and the others, all gathered around the sofas and chairs.

'Have you seen . . . the news?' Genni was breathless, speaking loudly as she bounced into the room. They all turned to look at her, Lorcan's eyes protective above a soaked T-shirt that clung to his chest. *He's soaking wet. Why?* Her eyes jumped to Reha, who also appeared uncomfortable.

There was a short silence until Genni's eyes locked on the man sitting in the furthest armchair.

He sat forward, arms on his knees. He was also drenched, his clothes ripped and stretched. His hair had grown longer, bedraggled, and he had some bushy scruff around his jawline, showing he hadn't shaved in months.

The beard didn't suit him.

She stared.

His hair was long, tied back.

She hated that too.

Everything felt ice cold.

She didn't know how long passed before she swallowed and managed to speak.

'You're here.' Genni glared at Ajay longer, the pain pulsing through her body keeping her frozen.

Ajay had stood up by this point, as if out of respect, but he had barely looked her in the eyes. Genni glanced away, trying to look at anything but him. He said nothing in response, as Reha came and touched Genni's arm.

'Ajay has come back to tell us about The Rogue.' Reha's words came out slow, muffled and sensitive. 'They're planning something.'

Genni blinked at him, tears sitting under her eyes. No one knew what to do. Everyone was as still as the two of them. Ajay eventually sat back down, eyes flicking back awkwardly on Genni, whose stomach was flipping.

How is he here?

Why are they with him?

Do they trust him?

He. Killed. Ace.

Genni should have launched herself at him. To make him hurt. To make him pay. But she couldn't move.

'OK...' Trixy finally gave Genni a caring look, adjusted her glasses and stood with her back to Ajay. 'We should all talk.'

The group agreed, taking themselves off to another corner of the room, leaving Ajay alone in the chair. Genni glanced at him, but he didn't look back, his eyes fixed on the palms of his grubby hands. She couldn't process it. There was nothing she could say. Months without him, healing from the mess he left behind, and he just walked back into the life she'd made for herself as if nothing had happened?

That was not happening.

These were *her* friends. He would have nothing to do with them. He couldn't. That wasn't fair. She should turn him in. That's when she noticed an activated Guiding

Light device beside him and she could have sworn the whole device had moved by itself.

But she wouldn't give him the respect to care. *The guy is scum. I hate him. His parents are free and no one cares because he is here.*

'Genni.' Lorcan was standing in front of her, blurry. 'Come on,' he whispered, leading her over to the group with a damp hand. *Why are they both so wet?*

She stroked her arms, feeling the strong threat of a breakdown as her lip quivered slightly. The group seemed restless but Trixy took control, her short hair sitting serenely above her shoulders.

'Let's take this calmly.' She gestured. 'Genni, are you OK?'

'I ...' Genni's mouth went dry. 'How is he here?'

'He contacted me earlier today.' Genni took in Reha's apologetic tone. *She knew he was coming. And she didn't warn me.* A storm of betrayal blew inside her.

'It's all a bad idea.' Yarin frantically pulled a hand over his skinny head. Genni tried to conceal her hurt by concentrating on him.

'Yarin ...' Trixy pleaded with him.

'The guy's a criminal,' Yarin insisted, eyebrows drawn inwards fiercely. 'He can't be here.'

'OK,' Reha responded. Genni couldn't look at her. 'But the information he has is important. We have to let Command know.'

'How do you know he's telling the truth?' Yarin crossed his arms over his thin chest.

Genni glanced back at Ajay, who had his head turned towards the glowing figure of The Guiding Light. *Please, go away.* She had been so ready for something good.

'Just give Genni a minute, mate,' Lorcan piped up, his kind eyes fixed on her. 'This is a shock.'

'Don't act so righteous. You're the one who pulled him out,' Yarin remarked, regret instantly apparent in his eyes.

'Don't be an idiot.' Lorcan stared him down.

Pulled him out of where? Lorcan knew Ajay was coming too?

A second knife to the heart.

Genni didn't stay to hear anything else. Needing some air, she took a few paces backwards before retreating up the steps.

She found herself back by the side of the river, climbing down some steps to watch the water flow gracefully through its current. It was there again. The pain. Seeing Ajay was bringing it all back; the person she had become in the last couple of months was fading and the broken mess was invading.

This isn't fair. He was gone. I can only move on if he's gone.

For months, the concept of him had stayed; in the news, in people's talk, with his family, but him, the real him, the tangible him who she could see, smell, *touch* was sitting in that chair. The same man who told her things no one had before, and maybe no one would again. The same man she had devoted everything to and the same man who smashed her heart apart. He was the same man, only different. There was a different aura about him. Something she couldn't quite place.

It doesn't even matter. The man I knew was a lie. All of it was lies. Everything about Tulo is a lie. There is nothing in life that is solely good.

Closing her eyes, she dismissed that final thought, knowing it wasn't the truth. There was good all around her, she only had to look for it. Wiping her face, she sniffed back the tears.

Genni glanced down the edge of the river and found Caril sitting with her broken trolley, swinging her feet just above the water. She smiled, thinking of how much that woman had grown since she'd met her. The fact she was confident enough to travel to the Inner-Ring was testament to that; Caril was once an Unworthy, until she became a person who cooked for others, who could ride the sky train alone, and who could meet more people than she thought possible.

Genni wondered if that had something to do with her.

She wanted to forget about Ajay and Reha and Lorcan. So, she wandered down the river to see Caril's grin welcoming her. Genni knew she'd need to go back inside and face all that, but not yet – she would sit with Caril and talk about the three best ways to cut a carrot, that Caril's feet were too dry, how she was allergic to spinach, and whatever else. Because that's what Caril enjoyed and Genni liked it too.

It was only minutes after she'd sat that her Watch vibrated. She noticed an anxiety in the crowds around them; people running, gathering, all seemingly comparing their wrists.

'Oh dear.' Caril spluttered a laugh through a mouthful of cake.

'What?' Genni asked half-heartedly, one eye on two badly dressed girls gasping at their wrists and then at each other fearfully.

'Has yours gone funny too?'

'I haven't checked.' Genni turned back to the ripples in the river lapping over each other. She didn't care if her profile picture was blurry. But Caril quickly shuffled closer and forced her food-splattered Watch in Genni's face.

She pulled her wrist back and blinked at the screen. *The score.*

'That's impossible.' Genni frantically tapped at her own device and saw the same thing.

'Impossible or not,' Caril peeled back the wrapper of another strawberry sponge, 'we're about to have some fun.'

PART TWO

THE DESERT

Tulo Country

ROGUE
BASE
CAMP

CHAPTER
ONE

His twenty-seventh birthday wasn't supposed to be like this.

Usually, he wouldn't care that it was his birthday at all. They were never important in the place where every moment was precious, the City where the lights and billboards sparkled against a dark desert sky and people stayed awake to maintain their repetitious lives.

Work – merit, run – merit, talk – merit, *SkipSleep* – merit.

No one would waste time on celebrating *them* on an annual basis. If anything, birthdays were embarrassing, a sign of failure – another year passing without hitting M-500. Another year not being able to brag about a house in the mountains of the Glorified Quarters. So, Ajay Ambers considered, his twenty-seventh birthday *should* have merely been another 'happy merit-making day'.

Instead, his throat was dry, with every muscle and limb fatigued. His eyes stung in their sockets as his ripped, damp clothing constricted around his skin. Dragging his heavy, bony legs forward, he craned his neck and begged the trees on the edge of the forest to cover him.

Happy birthday, Ajay.

At least he thought it was his birthday.

Time, that precious commodity he used to protect, had blurred. He'd managed to keep a rough calculation of when the sun had dropped and pulled itself back up again. It was probably about three weeks since Callum and The Rogue shoved him into that van. *Three? Four? Does it matter?*

He had no food.

No water.

He was dying, probably.

He was alone, definitely.

That would never change; he'd done everything right to be labelled Unworthy and friendless. Even The Rogue, literally the enemies of society, didn't like him. When the storm broke out and he lost himself in the forest, part of him thought Charlene and Haro would come to find him. But life should have taught him already – the best of people is rarely seen. They live for themselves and when it came to The Rogue, they existed to destroy Command. They would fail; their current symbol of hope was a tin of peaches from a drop-off.

It was only right. Charlene had nothing to gain by searching the forest for him. It was the same with Ace, he supposed. When he found out Ajay was illegally living in the City after hacking his way in, Ace would have lost everything if he didn't report him. That was before Ajay lost control and took everything from Ace anyway. A pain in Ajay's chest stole his breath; the same stabbing feeling lived constantly within him, twisting and tightening.

'You're going the wrong way.' Its voice bounced up the smooth trunks of the trees as it pulled Ajay out from his insular, solemn walk. He ignored it and kept staggering onwards, grief growing heavier with every step.

'You need to take the south-western route.'

Ajay glared down at the device in his hands; the hologram of its faceless figure crossed its sparkling arms.

He stopped, his words straining through his teeth. 'I'm not going to the tree.'

'OK,' it said, and disappeared back into its case.

Ajay, although relieved, grew more irritated. The Guiding Light had never done this before. He thought it was an audio playback device, not something capable of conscious communication or having the ability to turn itself off.

I could try to break it again. It might work this time.

Am I sure it's even real?

When he'd found it in the sand an hour earlier, he'd gone from disbelieving to infuriated. He'd laughed at first when he uncovered it. Hysterically. In what he thought would be his final moments, his brain had decided to send him what he hated the most. But he'd decided he was completely delusional, especially when the thing started talking, saying something like, 'Don't be scared, I'm real, I can help you.'

To that, Ajay responded that he was imagining things, sparking a short dialogue that flew back and forth into the waking dawn until Ajay swiped at the device to turn it off.

Its holographic body hadn't moved. It didn't even flinch.

'What?' Ajay had hauled it up to examine its model.

It was identical to the devices he'd seen before. Oblong in shape, black, smooth all over with the strange symbol on its surface.

'Why aren't you turning off?' he had said, confusion rife.

'I can decide not to,' it had said, so casually.

'You can't make decisions,' Ajay had spat, still sat in the dirt.

Confusion wasn't something Ajay enjoyed. It was for people of lower intellect. When he learned something new, it didn't take him long to understand, but still, this had him stumped. He knew The Guiding Light; he understood its interface and its resource allocation; it was no way near powerful enough for artificial intelligence.

All it held were sets of recordings – those stories it would tell. It shouldn't have been able to decide anything independently. City androids or drones weren't that advanced yet.

It had then even been sarcastic with him, joking that blood was rushing to its head as Ajay held it upside down.

'You can't do that,' he yelled into its light before battling to silence it.

But he couldn't. Even throwing it at a rock had failed. Eventually, he'd given up and let it lecture him that he needed food and water. He told it it was a genius. The sarcasm seemed contagious. But Ajay couldn't bring himself to leave it behind. He always knew his curiosity over technology would kill him one day. He needed answers over its new intricacies, but that didn't mean he had to take its suggestions.

He now strained his neck and glanced at the rounded tips of the fruit in the trees above him. If only he hadn't lost his rope in the storm, he could climb to get those and then he wouldn't have to go anywhere.

I could survive here. Make this clearing my base.

The Rogue had given him enough practice. Admittedly, he didn't have the pits to hide him from Command's patrolling drones or any Country storms, but he could muddle through. Then, perhaps, history would move on. The Rogue would be dissolved after Command finally dealt with them and he would be known as the Wild Forest Man. Or the Forest Legend. Or The Legend of the Wild Forest Man. His story could be told to children before they went to sleep, or maybe by then they would have developed *SkipSleep* for kids. Regardless, he could be Tulo famous. One man, against all the odds, survives alone in the harsh reality of Tulo Country and becomes one with the forest. That would be quite a status. Did that mean they'd forget all the other stuff he'd done? And with that impossibility, Ajay cursed into the hot air.

Small whizzing birds fluttered above him. *Maybe I could catch you now. No.* He'd already had this debate with himself. The energy to catch one of those tiny, brown bodies would be enough to kill him off. Nor was it worth it. There was more meat on a leftover kebab stick. *Maybe I could get up one of these trees.* He knew how to do it, having spent weeks climbing them in The Rogue. But, with no ropes? *Could I use my sack somehow?* He pulled it down from his shoulder and felt the material, knowing it would be too slippery to hold him. Plus, he wouldn't have the stamina to hold himself up.

He swore again.

It said to go to the largest Baffle tree. I could listen to it. He corrected himself. *That would get me nowhere.* When he'd lost The Rogue in the storm, he was ready to die.

Now though, he was back to where he'd been before – remembering that he didn't deserve that simplicity. He'd killed his best friend, destroyed people's lives and maybe he couldn't just die; he had to struggle through living.

And he had to do it alone.

CHAPTER
TWO

This is bad.

The trees around him were swirling in a wheel of colours, spinning in and out of focus and stealing his balance. Ajay took a huge breath, clinging to the nearest tree, his legs fumbling beneath him. But once he shuffled his back down the trunk, he managed to find his breathing.

OK, OK. I'm OK. Think.

He couldn't stay here. His body was screaming with exhaustion and dehydration and whatever else, but lying under the beating sun in his climbing suit wasn't going to improve his chances.

I won't make it to the tree.

He'd only been walking fifteen minutes and it was impossible to calculate his fluid loss from the last couple of hours, but more had come out than in. He cursed. *What can I do?*

'Ditch the suit.'

Ajay hadn't even noticed the Light pop up from its case beside him. It spoke softly, mirroring the low tweets of the birds in the branches above him.

'No.' Ajay closed his eyes. 'I need it.'

'It's causing you to sweat.'

'I don't care. It'll protect me.' Ajay knew he wasn't making sense. He didn't want it to be right. Again.

'In combination with all the other factors causing your dehydration, it'll kill you.' With that, The Guiding Light said nothing else.

Ajay kept his eyes tightly shut, grinding his teeth. He didn't need the suit; he was far from The Rogue camp, and their infrared technology only worked at night anyway. He'd keep it in his sack for when he needed it.

He said nothing, not giving the device any satisfaction.

Rolling over, he pulled the suit off his bruised legs, revealing his trousers beneath. Shoving the suit into his sack, he considered ditching the balaclava too. *Don't, your head.* He squinted at the white sun dappling through the trees, shielding his eyes with his hand.

He staggered to his feet, feeling cooler and able to stand straight again. Maybe it was a warning from his body before. *But I've got to get food and water soon, like now.* It felt hopeless. He wouldn't drink his own urine. The educational movie specifically said not to do that; there's a reason why the kidneys work to expel all the bad stuff bodies don't want. Was there anything around him that could harbour water? The flowers? Fo Doktrin? Also a no-go. Without boiling that down, his stomach wouldn't thank him – even greater dehydration. Could he make a fire to cook the leaves? He had no bowl to put it in. His sack would melt. It's not like he could use The Guiding Light as a pan. Stretching his neck, the inside of his throat felt like stale bread. Even the lukewarm water from a Side tap would be good enough. He groaned at the Light, shining of its own accord.

'We could try going for the tree again. I promise you there's food there,' the Guide repeated.

The irritation was back. Hot and sharp.

Ajay didn't respond but fell to the sandy dirt and cursed, trying to resist tears as he soothed the healing bump on his forehead. He remembered waking up, delirious, after he'd run into a tree during the storm. *If only it had killed me.*

'You won't achieve anything by sitting there,' the Light said.

Ajay delivered a quick, hard stomp to its hardware. He felt the pain tingle into his ankle. 'What makes you think I'll listen to you? Do you even have a map?'

Ajay felt a small sense of satisfaction as it didn't respond, but its glow ebbed softly through its silence. 'I didn't think so,' he said.

As he stared numbly forward through the dwindling foliage, he noticed something sticking out from the ground. It looked metal. It looked hopeful.

Stumbling to his feet, shoving the Guide under his arm, he approached what seemed to be some sort of door from a vehicle – hard to know what kind with its rusted exterior, but it didn't look like a door to a hover car or Command van. Those had much bigger window insets. This didn't have a space for a window at all.

Several species of plant had colonised across its surface, painting it a sort of brown-green colour. Dropping the device, he mustered the energy to lift the door upwards. It wasn't as heavy as he expected; flecks of rust chipped off as he threw the door backwards onto its other side. He jumped back as small insects burst out across the dirt. Its underlay was also decayed, although he could make out some white, painted letters along its rim. *N-4. Maybe a 7, or a 0. Then another n, or could it be an m?* He tilted his head, trying to decipher more before concluding it was probably an old resource cart and it didn't provide him with anything to eat or drink.

Come on, come on. There must be something.

Ajay lumbered on for another half an hour, not talking to The Guiding Light, when he saw it trickling down a tree trunk. A wobbly, wet line, like a finger smudge on a condensed glass. *Water? Is that water?*

Tripping over in his desperate excitement, Ajay fell against the tree and saw how the substance was thicker and cloudier than water. More like an opaque gel or syrup. His eyes danced up the tree to see where it was bleeding; the thick liquid was dripping from a hole about 3 metres up. *Is it safe? Only one way to find out.* Ajay hesitated, stroking his head and scanning the dirt. Was that how he wanted to go? He was probably ten minutes from the tallest tree, which apparently, would solve all his problems. He flipped the Guide over in his hands before placing it down with urgency. He pushed a log against the tree, the arch of his back tight with strain before he jumped up and reached for the liquid. His index finger got immediately covered. It was stickier than expected and with one graze across his nostrils, it was immediately off the menu. Coughing from the stench, Ajay floundered off the log, holding back vomit. He felt a light tickle on his hand. Turning it over, he found a small insect, with a ballooned bum and six long, stringy legs, crawling between the crevasses of his fingers.

Ajay whacked it against his trousers before glancing back at the hole in the tree where he could see he'd disturbed a colony. Hundreds of them ran across the trunk's surface, blackening it with their colour. Quickly grabbing the Guide, he retreated and after the adrenaline subsided, Ajay was aware of his thirst again.

'That was close,' the Guide's voice boomed.

Ajay, startled, swore at it.

'They were Coktres. Their bite causes a skin infection.'

'Oh.' Ajay glanced at the splattered insect remains on his right trouser leg, thankful it hadn't decided to get its pincers into his skin. 'Can I eat it?'

'Not if you want to live. You should be more careful.'

Ajay huffed. Why did he even ask for its opinion?

'We're getting closer to the edge too,' the Guide continued, glowing from the ground. 'And the creatures in the desert work by their own rules.'

Ajay subtly swallowed his anxiety. *That's a fair point, but an obvious one.*

'We're not far from the tree, by the way.' The Guide twisted its body of light back towards the sun-kissed trees, a repetitive wave of green.

'Would you shut up about the tree?' Ajay massaged his forehead, defeated, before sliding down the nearest trunk. 'How do you even know where it is?'

'I know the forest well,' it said. 'But you don't have to listen to me.'

He watched the Light fade back into its case and embraced the cumbersome tweets of the birds, briefly thinking about how everything it said made no sense. *It knows the forest. What? There's nothing I can do to understand. Or survive.* He scratched at the dry dirt, feeling it between his cracked fingers. *Now do I die?* He scrunched his eyes tight, the pounding of his dehydration loud. The minutes dripped by, while he contemplated his limited options, until he groaned – realising there was no use not trying something, just to save his pride.

'Hey,' he moaned at the case. Nothing came back.

'Hey.' He kicked it with his boot. The Light appeared. 'How far away is the tree?' He turned his face away, his jaw tight.

'About twenty minutes south-west.' Its smooth voice grated against him.

'And how will I get the fruit?' Ajay stared at a bird fluttering from one tree to another.

'You just need to cause a vibration on its trunk. Trust me, the fruit will drop.'

'That doesn't make any sense.' He turned to it, its Light flooding into his maddened eyes.

'Does it have to?' its tone seemed to shrug.

Ajay didn't bother to reply but put his head in his hands.

'We can start walking and find some plants too.'

'I can't have the Fo Doktrin.' He snapped his hands from his face. *And there's no 'we' in this situation.*

'I know. But there's always the Duskdrops.'

Callum ate those in The Rogue.

'They do have some nutritious value, but not enough to sustain you long-term. There'll be some on the way, if you want to go.'

Ajay tried to fight back his frustration.

How does it know all this? It's showing levels of advancement I've never even read about, even beyond the X-Level Technology Command has been working on, but that's in its early stages and has nowhere near this level of artificial intelligence, and this thing is meant to be hundreds of years old. Maybe I did die when I ran into the tree and this is some afterlife where I'm tortured with a lack of understanding forever.

He relented and stood up. Saying nothing, he grabbed at the Light and walked. Welcoming the quiet, soft breeze that tampered with the desert's close, sticky air, he watched the Guide's glow silently ebb as they continued to move through the trees.

After fifteen minutes of distracting himself with the crunch of dry leaves beneath his feet, Ajay stumbled when he saw a trail of Duskdrop flowers around the trunk of a tree.

He hurried, pulling them from their stems.

'They taste of nothing.' He chewed, the feeling of eating still good enough.

'Yeah, they're not the best,' the Light said from his feet. 'We're here now anyway.'

Ajay turned his head and choked on the flower. The tallest Baffle tree, wider and greater than all the others, towered above him like the City's tallest skyscrapers; so dominant and majestic, like it was the only thing that mattered.

CHAPTER
THREE

Ajay reckoned he was five years old when they'd had the conversation.

He and his grandma were sitting on top of the hill, staring towards the City's skyline against a typical lilac sky. The moon encased half-built skyscrapers in its shine. If it wasn't for the flicker of a breaking billboard in the Side, the scene would have been completely tranquil. Ajay played with the sand, grabbing fistfuls and trickling it over his knees, giggling at the sensation. His grandma seemed to be relaxing, hands on her lap, eyes closed. His finger became a hover vehicle and zoomed around the sand, leaving its track behind it. As he spun on his knees with his finger's motion, he stopped when he saw the forest. He'd seen it before, that tree – huge, foreboding, and towering over all the rest.

'Why is that tree taller, Grandma?' he remembered asking, finally intrigued by its difference.

'There are trees of all different shapes and sizes.' His grandma's eyes remained closed as she exhaled deeply. 'A bit like people.'

'Its branches are super-big.'

'Yes, you're right.' Grandma slowly spun to look towards the forest too. 'It probably wants to give the rest of the trees a big hug.'

Ajay, more than two decades on, could almost feel her warmth as he remembered her arms surrounding his tiny body. Seeing the tree from a distance was deceptive – it had always blended in, a silent constant. Other than featuring in an occasional childhood fantasy, or a messy crayon sketch of the forest, it was always just the hugging tree.

A large, forgettable, everyday tree.

But from where Ajay stood, it was impossible to ignore. He knew the tree was big, *but this big...?* Walking around it slowly, twigs snapping under his step, he reckoned its surface area was three times the size of the other Baffle trees. He caught his breath and wondered how deep its roots went into the dry desert earth and how the other trees around it had managed to survive against its dominance. Placing the Guide down, Ajay moved closer and clambered over its surfacing roots, placing a hand on the thick, smooth trunk. It was warm to the touch and dust stuck to his palm. Looking up, he finally admired the way its fat body protruded into the sky, higher and higher, bursting into the life of its wide, welcoming branches that gave birth to elegant, green leaves. Ajay felt blank. It was like the first time he'd seen the City for real. Or the first time he went to the shopping centre. As if the very fabric of his surroundings were too much to process – wiping his mind completely. Yet, unlike the others, it was over something quite simple. One beautiful piece of nature, seemingly untouched and uncomplicated. No drones buzzed overhead, only small chirping birds. No people barged past him or through him, he was alone, in tranquillity. No business, no rush, no anxiety. Only the tree and its ethereal power, strong enough to hold him in the moment.

Until Ajay noticed its imperfections. He saw one above his head and didn't dare place his finger in it. A deep trenched crack in the trunk, splintering from the ground to about midway along its surface. Walking around it again, Ajay noticed more splits in the bark, almost as if the tree had been squashed from above. *How could that happen?* The only answer he had was a rapid change in temperature, like a sudden freeze overnight, causing it to expand and split. Yet the cracks were deep and repetitious, like they'd been there for a long time. *Curious.* Trailing his eyes further down the trunk, he followed the line of its emerging roots, and spotted something in the dirt beneath them.

The object was covered in dry, black moss and small sprouting buds, but Ajay could see an exposed, sharp corner of hardware. He pulled it from its spot, battling against smaller roots as he seized the object from nature's arms. Wiping away the dirt and moss, he uncovered an archaic device; a flat screen, just bigger than a Watch face cuddled in a chunky black casing. Tapping at it, and turning it over, Ajay knew it was dead. *Figures.*

The pang in his stomach forced him to refocus; the Duskdrops had done nothing to satisfy him. He instinctively dropped the broken device into his trouser pocket and gazed upwards. *The fruit. I can't even see it; I can barely see the branches, it's that high. There's nothing I can use to get up there, either. So, I'm supposed to cause a vibration?*

'Shall we get you something to eat?' the Guide asked, and as Ajay looked down at it, he felt as if its illumination had got bigger, like the surface area of its light was covering more than before.

'What kind of question is that? Isn't the answer obvious?' Ajay stared blankly forward through the trees that led to the wide expanse of desert.

'All you need to do is knock on the tree.' The Guide's voice was almost tender.

Ajay glanced back at the Guide, seeing small glowing flickers coming off it, like wingsparks, bugs soon to emerge with the setting sun.

'Knock on it?' Ajay bent his eyebrows.

The Light nodded its faceless head. 'Right.'

Am I sure this isn't all in my mind? No. No, I'm not.

Ajay swore, laughter muffling with the words. 'This is ridiculous.' He reached over his head and knocked on the tree three times. It went silent.

Brilliant.

With so little energy left, he slumped down the tree trunk and scanned the edge of the forest. He could just make out buildings through the waves of evening heat bubbling in the air. *The Side.* If he could get there, then he might survive. But he'd be caught by Command instantly, if his name was still on the wanted list like the insiders from The Rogue had reported. That was assuming he'd survive the trip there which, given his beaten condition, he wouldn't. *Maybe I could lay a trap or do some tracking. See if any animals—*

A loud crack came from above, like the snapping of multiple branches at once.

He didn't move before hearing a thud on the other side of the tree.

Two more thuds came. *It could be an animal. One I could catch, or one that could catch me.* He cursed again. Another thud. *Or, it couldn't be, could it?* Standing slowly, he figured he'd better defend himself in case the enigmatic tree hadn't dropped fruit. He grimaced as some leaves crunched beneath his feet. *Alright, just stay calm. Get that rock.* Ajay spotted a boulder next to him, a poor weapon for silencing a felkar or a ginel. *Slowly. Slowly.* He edged around the tree trunk, his arms wide against its sides. The thuds had stopped, leaving only a nervous silence. Ajay held his breath. He reached the other side and stepped out quickly. He stopped cold and dropped the boulder in disbelief.

There on the ground were four large pieces of fruit. Ajay looked up, seeing the distant leaves still ruffling. *You've got to be joking. What? How?* He stared at the fruit; their hard shells decorated in several shades of orange. *A joke. I'm playing a joke on myself. I need to get my head straight. None of this is real, The Guiding Light isn't talking to me and this fruit did not fall as it said it would. Nope. Not believing that. But, if it is there . . .* Ajay bent his body back around the tree, watching the Guide as it continued to sit and glow. *If it is there, it's food.*

Hesitantly, Ajay hauled a couple up, knowing he'd have to come back for the others. They were heavier and richer in colour than the Kakafruit from the other trees. Ajay returned to his spot by the Light, falling to the ground, and stared at it suspiciously. It didn't seem to react so Ajay said nothing. *Is it safe to eat? How do I know? Oh, screw it.* He smashed the fruit against a boulder repeatedly and then broke into it with his cracked, dirty hands.

CHAPTER
FOUR

Ajay was utterly absorbed. The present struggle of life momentarily faded like a wisp of wind passing; his only focus was the sweet nourishment bursting between his teeth.

It was the greatest thing he'd ever tasted. Ripping into it, he buried his head in its shell, trying to compare it to something. Its juice was a bit like coconut, but more refreshing. Its flesh like a mango, but tastier. Its succulence was more delicious than a camel burger.

'How is it?' the Guide asked lightly.

'It's . . .' Ajay grunted as he tore off another bite. 'Good.'

He examined its bright, pink glistening flesh in the glow of The Guiding Light beside him and saw he'd barely made a dent; there was an excess left and he was almost full. Night had drawn in and he hadn't even noticed. The trees had grown ominous as dark shadows had crept under the yellow light of the moon and the rich, radiant spots of wingsparks' wings. *Beautiful.*

As he chewed through his remaining bites, a recurring thought returned.

Survival isn't what I deserve. His part in the death of his best friend didn't entitle him to anything, not even life. *It's not all my fault, though, is it?*

He considered, as he picked fruit from his teeth, that Callum and The Rogue were right about one thing; the merit system was flawed – how was it that Side children could only be welcomed into the City by suffering through Purification, when they'd never had the choice over what they believed? The status of being Unworthy was written for him before he was born. *So much for hope.*

Although . . . this thing . . . he stared at the Light, thinking *. . . is doing things it's never done before. How?* Ajay wiped the juice around his mouth.

'What do you think it tastes like?' the Guide asked, taking the liberty to continue the conversation.

'I dunno.' Ajay moved the fruit to the side and lay down. 'A coconut, a bit,' he mumbled, hands behind his head, eyes darting up the giant tree.

'It is similar to a coconut tree.' The Guiding Light grew quieter over the sound of the nightlife. 'But they are much thinner and wouldn't survive here, not against the dominance of the Baffles and how much water they take from the ground.'

Ajay, his fatigue making things blurry, didn't respond despite being confused. He'd never thought coconuts grew on trees. They were genetically engineered in the City, at Command's Foodex Centre in the Retail District, like most things. He slithered into a foetal position, grabbing the four pieces of fruit and cradling them to protect them from anything that might take them away.

It was strange. The desire to survive. Especially when he wasn't sure what he was surviving for. *A coconut tree? How much more am I missing?*

'How do you know so much about the forest?' Ajay asked, yawning, the weight of the day heavy.

'That device you found,' the Guide said. 'It'll tell you more about me, if you want to know.'

Lethargically retrieving it from his pocket, Ajay gave it a lazy look, stroking his dirty hands over its small, cracked, aged exterior. Without another thought, his eyes drooped and the hardware fell on his chest as he was overcome by sleep.

CHAPTER

FIVE

Trickles of rain splashed over the damaged pores of his skin, slipping through the crevasses of his facial scars.

He kept his eyes closed and breathed deeply. He needed stillness with the turbulence swirling around inside him. His life was full of it. So, Callum savoured the tranquillity of nothing: when there was only him, the serene swaying of the trees, and the cool stroke of a post-storm breeze. He knew once he opened his eyes, he wouldn't stop for days. He knew once he walked back into camp, he couldn't lose his focus. He knew once tonight was over, they'd have to find a way out. All this meant this moment was important, to recentre and brace himself for what could be coming. He took one last, deep breath and let it linger in the damp, humid air; it whistled as it slowly escaped his quivering mouth. His eyes drifted open and he let the green-topped trees steal his attention over the stark cries of children beyond them.

What are we going to do now? We've never done this before.

Callum snatched up another quick breath as he saw a blue-speckled toxlizard scuttle furiously between the foliage. He froze and watched the smaller lizards following it. Their combined colours lit up the dark ground before they disappeared between bushes of Fo Doktrin and left behind the same barren dirt.

I should get a tox to bite me. It wouldn't take long for me to die. That would be easier. Cleaner.

Cursing out loud, he didn't let himself entertain the thought. Instead, Callum glanced down at the red, muddied headband between his fingers, letting the dirt of its fabric crawl underneath his chewed, blackened fingernails. Reaching behind his back, he grabbed his water bottle from the side-pocket of his rucksack, and poured a tiny drop over the headband carefully.

The kids need to go first. In case.

Having returned the bottle to his bag, he pushed the slightly damp cloth through his sweaty hair. He shivered.

The drones were always going to come.

Callum glanced down at the red flashing Alert Band vibrating on his wrist. The moment Sid, one of the Spotters, had sent the alarm, Callum's chest burned. The pain of knowing they'd be attacked stole his ability to do anything. They'd prepared for this, but the reality of it happening was almost too much to process. Even if The Rogue community hid in the underground pits, their presence was obvious; pots lying strewn by solar hobs, chairs placed in neat social circles, spare sacks and Climbers' ropes hanging off hooks on trees. He continued to stare at his wrist, pulsing with dangerous colour.

It's been five minutes. Command will be here soon. We will lose people tonight.

'Cal?' The voice through the trees was hurried. Ki then stumbled between two trunks, bracing himself against them, his bloodshot eyes frantic. 'Come on.'

A moment of peace was always just that. A moment. With no hesitation, Callum followed Ki and heard them before he saw them – the red shots of drones splintering through the trees.

The snap-hiss of a laser skimmed by his ear and his body was thrown to the ground, his hands protecting his head. Laser shots suffocated the clearing between the trees, bouncing off littered pots and tattooing the trees with their scorch. Callum's eyes were tightly shut. He heard a child's scream. His head flicked up to the battle in the rising sunlight. Drones swooped in between the trees, The Rogue were floundering, calling for loved ones before darting in various directions. Callum could feel his heartbeat in his throat as he sprinted towards a boy in stained, grey overalls, crying out from the middle of the massacre, seeing the bodies of adults falling around him. Callum mirrored the distressed tears of the boy, just as shocked, just as traumatised. *They're not tasering. They're killing. Weaponised. The boy. Get the boy.* Callum lost a breath, seeing a drone swoop towards the child from behind, emerging from the depths of the forest beyond. *Don't you dare.* Callum ran faster, the burning in his legs only spurring him on, even when he realised he was too late. The drone was already there.

'No!' Callum roared, reaching towards the child, despite being metres away. It was as if the chaos around him didn't matter. He barely noticed as Rogue men and women emerged with weapons of their own and drones started to fall with the bodies. It was only about the boy, who was too little.

'Stop!' Callum shouted with the beat of his hammering run. He screamed at Maze, his large physique dominant as he shot another drone, which fire-balled into a tree, sending its branches ablaze.

Maze then spun towards the boy and aimed at the drone going for him. He hesitated. Callum stopped. The drone didn't touch the boy. It lowered its guns as if in the moment, when it got close enough, it had a change of heart. That decision meant Maze could shoot it into the ground, its weight scraping and crashing along the dirt, before Maze descended back into the chaos, crying at others with guns and directing those without to run.

Callum made a beeline for the child, reaching him and scooping him under his arms.

'Mum!' the boy spluttered. 'My mum, no, no, no.'

Callum hissed as the kid's bite pinched his side and caused him to let up his grip. The kid ran back into the thick of it, screaming for his mother. Callum wouldn't be the man who let a child run through a warzone surrounded by blazing trees. It was soon going to be hard to escape. *No dead children, not today.* Callum took a split second to catch on to a few other kids cowering over bodies and herding together like scared desert mice into pits. *The fire will catch. They can't stay there.* He made after the boy, thinking about being his age and how a drone's taser imprinted the mark that lived on his face. *Not today.* Callum didn't take his eyes off him as the kid flapped between drones, bodies and pits, looking for who he'd lost. Speaking into his Watch, Callum didn't stop running.

'Ki, Maze, anyone.' He coughed. 'The kids are in the pits. Repeat, the kids are in the pits. They're not shooting them but the fire will catch the foliage. Get them out.'

Callum's words hit quicker than the laser shots as other adults with guns gestured to delegate people to gather children from the pits, where they'd usually sleep peacefully beneath the ground. Callum caught up with the boy, grabbing his small shoulders and lifting him up.

'No, no, stop, please!' the boy screamed, cutting through Callum.

'I'm sorry. We have to go.' He hoisted the kid over his shoulder this time, painfully ignoring his repeated slaps against his back.

'No, stop, Mum!' The kid struggled between words. 'I can't leave her, I can't leave, take me back!'

'I'm sorry,' Callum couldn't help but repeat. He ran towards a group of children who had been retrieved from the pits as drones continued to ignore them and shoot at the adults. Garcia, a Spotter, saw Callum and shouted between her shots at more oncoming drones.

'Cal!' she squawked. 'Come with me.' She shouted commands at the children, telling them all to hold hands and follow her. 'Or Cal!' She pointed straight at him when he arrived. 'Don't leave me or Cal, OK?'

He turned to run as another explosion sent them all ducking to the ground and a deafening sound erupted.

'Garcia!' Callum roared at seeing it; a blown-up drone descending upon the running group of children.

'Move!' Garcia threw children's bodies sideways as she allowed the flaming machine to become one with her, its weight hitting her head and its flames overpowering her body. The moment was still and shattering as the children's wails were sharp pins in his ears.

'Go, keep going. This way.' Callum hoisted the crying, struggling boy further over his shoulder, not letting go. He swallowed the innocence of the small girl in a nightgown holding a hand-sewn toy with one hand and her friend with the other. *They shouldn't have to see this.* He stopped thinking. *Just get them out.*

'Run, keep running.' The patting of their little feet and their worried whispers were the music of heartbreak. Callum whispered a curse word as a fresh line of drones flew towards them through the drizzle of the post-storm air.

'This way!' he shouted, directing the children down a sideline of trees. *How can I track them all, to make sure I get them all somewhere safe? It's too far to run all the way to the new camp now. I need help. There are too many.* He turned around, unable to count accurately, but there were at least ten children with him, running through the forest. But he noticed the drones, that had clearly seen them, weren't following. *For the same reason they didn't shoot the boy? They're children.*

'Don't stop, come on, keep going!' he encouraged the kids. Despite being desperate to put the boy down, he was too much of a flight risk, so Callum endured with the pain of his back. He breathed into his wrist. 'It's the kids. They won't hurt the kids,' he panted. 'Get the rest of them out, and others, run!'

'Cal?' Ki's voice spluttered through the Watch. 'Cal, where are you? Where do we go?'

'Ki!' Callum rushed. 'Get the rest of the kids out, destroy as many drones as you can and encourage people to run in different directions. Disperse them across the forest.'

'But where's the new camp? How do we get to the new camp?' Ki whimpered.

'What, do you . . .?' Callum's breath failed as he slowed down, noting that the sound of the battle was waning and any drone activity was gone. He stopped the children, not registering their teary faces. 'Ki, where are you now?' Callum gritted his teeth. *He's supposed to be leading us and he can't remember how to access the map? He's out of his depth. A coward.*

'I just need to know . . . where . . .'

Juley, a Runner, burst through the line. 'Callum, we're running west, a load of drones following. I'm with Maze.'

'No, don't run west.' Callum felt hollow. 'That's too close to the edge.'

'Other drones are going east. It should leave each drone pack thin enough so people make it.'

'How many are there?'

Silence came back.

'Juley, how many are there?' Callum spat on the Watch. The continuing quiet told him all he needed to know. *There's no way they'll outrun or outshoot them.*

'It's OK, scar boy.' Maze's gruff voice took Callum by surprise. Something usually loaded with cynicism was riddled with compassion.

'Maze, turn back.'

'I ain't backing down.' Maze was panting between cursing. 'Do one thing for me; don't let the scum win.'

'No, both of you, turn back—'

227

'This is the only way, Cal. That's us, over and out.' Juley cut the line.

Callum fell to his knees, letting the boy – who didn't run – fall to the ground. He joined the others as Callum attempted to squeeze back his tears. He couldn't speak. *After everything we've been through, they're gone.*

Don't let the scum win.

We'll try.

Ki's voice exploded from his Watch.

'Cal, where are we going?'

Callum numbly lifted his wrist. His voice cracked.

'The map's in the file "Nothing Pillow".'

'I'll see you there.' Ki's voice faded out, suddenly authoritative again. 'Get the children there, safe.'

Callum nodded, absorbing the responsibility for the broken children around him and all the light of the new morning returning to him dark. An older girl, maybe twelve, offered Callum her hand. He looked up into her eyes, so marred by trauma, but strong and fierce.

'We have to go,' she whispered, flicking her eyes to the smallest of them, the girl with the ragged toy.

Catching himself then, he clasped his hand into hers and rose up over them, patting the hair of the headstrong girl. He turned to the motherless boy who was still trying to catch his breath.

'Come with us. I don't know where your mother is, but I must make sure you're safe.' Callum took in his scared expression, but watched the boy nod between gasps for air. 'Let's go.' He addressed them all; the girl with the toy, the defiant twelve-year-old, a scrawny boy with numerous freckles, another with none; a child with frayed plaits, holding the hand of a sibling with the same, plump nose, and then he noticed her. Jessy. *Simonee's daughter. Where was Simonee?* Her face was dirty and her blonde hair infested with dry leaves. 'Don't let go of anyone's hand and we walk slowly, OK?'

'Don't we need to run?' Jessy's sweet but urgent voice played with Callum's emotions.

'Not now,' he choked. 'They're not coming this way, I promise.' He offered her his hand as they stepped cautiously through the trees.

Walking through his discomfort, he hated himself for making a promise he didn't know he could keep, but these children were his responsibility. The calmer he could encourage them to be, the easier it would be to keep them safe.

CHAPTER

SIX

Ajay flinched awake, alarmed, instantly aware of his vulnerability.

He watched the dark mesh of trees, The Guiding Light illuminating only a few metres in front of him. *There's nothing there. I'd hear anything approaching. I think. Don't think about it. You'll never sleep if you do.* His eyelids softened again.

Then he heard it. His eyes sprang open.

The beeping. The mechanical swoop. The sound of every office floor. The background of every City street. Usually it was welcome, accompanied by a coffee, meal or anticipated delivery, but like a restless hour of sleep, that was all in the past.

With all his fears about the wildlife, he'd forgotten about the man-made monsters. It was only a slight hum, still a distance off, and as Ajay sat up, he could see the red blinking lights hovering between the gloomy trunks. *It could be coming this way. It's surely time to move.* He glanced to the west, the desert spanning out into a sea of black. *Do I go out there? Absolutely not.* The darkness was so impenetrable, he would be walking blind, not to mention the unknown beasts that could be waiting for food. Though he did have the Guide for some visibility. Ajay clenched his fists, feeling the scratchy soil of the ground. *Or I could just let them catch me.*

He spotted the drone's light again, slightly brighter than before. He'd always known the moderate freedom he had in the forest was a lie; he would one day face the consequences of what he'd done, whatever Command decided they would be. If he was labelled as one of The Rogue, an Unworthy, he was certain it could only be one thing. He reconsidered. *I am living with the consequences of my actions. Aren't I?* It was hardly an existence worth fighting for, being alone and broken. He turned back to the dark desert.

'What are you doing?' The Guide appeared dimly, whispering.

'Thinking.' Ajay squinted into the black expanse. *I'd never survive; there's the heat, no shelter, the predators. But I can't stay in the forest, not with drones still searching for The Rogue. I never thought they'd be out this far.*

'We should move, it's coming this way.' The Light had never been so quiet, even with its volume on its lowest level.

'I know, I'm just working out—' Ajay paused, listening again for the drone. It was definitely drawing in, the hum starker. *What should I do? The desert. Surely, I can't.*

'Haven't you ever wondered what's out there?' The Guide said, as if reading his mind. 'What more there is to see?'

'No,' Ajay stuttered, one eye on the forest. 'I've never needed it, or wanted to.' He sat up straighter, moving to find the drone.

'Well, now is as good a time as ever.'

'There's no way.' Ajay's attention drew back to the reappearing flashing light. *If I'm going to go, I need to go now.* 'I can't – it wouldn't work. You said it yourself, the desert's dangerous.'

'Yes, but what is there to lose?' the Guide asked.

'Other than my life?' Ajay breathed, not able to ignore the increasing volume of the drone's mechanical approach.

Ajay stared down at the Light, its faceless, tiny head seemingly staring back at him.

Ace would think I'm a coward.

I am a coward.

Ace would always push himself to go further, to go beyond what he'd already achieved. A memory jumped at Ajay, stark and detailed. He and Ace were sitting in the Skyhouse after his interview for the Quarters' retirement village.

'So, I don't know what to do,' Ajay had said, removing his tie.

'There's a lot to learn from old biddies.' Ace probably took a swig of Tulo Ale. 'Especially when they're high calibre.'

'Most of them aren't up for educating people. They made that *very* clear.'

'They have been doing it for years.'

'I guess,' Ajay shrugged, checking his Watch for his rest timer.

'They deserve to be looked after till the end,' Ace explained. 'The ruthless side of me would say get rid. But you know I'm a softie. So, I think you should go and help them go to the toilet when they just can't hold on.' Ace smirked, before taking another swig. 'It's better than your other option. You won't learn half as much packing delivery boxes.'

'It would be easier, though.' Ajay would have preferred to mindlessly pack boxes to help with the supply and demand issues at that time. Especially because working with older people would have reminded him of Grandma and how he'd left the Side, for a life without her in it.

'Nothing easy produces real results.' Ace raised his eyebrows. 'Come on, Jay. Have an adventure for once.'

Those words were so loud in Ajay's mind that he almost couldn't hear the drone edging closer. He stood, sliding up the big tree's trunk. *OK, I'll go.* He swung his fruit-filled sack around his shoulders and picked up the Guide, saying nothing but holding it out in front of him, its glow lighting his way as he started off west.

Into the unknown.

Ajay rarely looked at the stars. In The Rogue, they only peeked through the trees. In the City, the billboards and skyscrapers drowned them out. At the Side, he was never interested enough to look up, only across at the City's more appealing skyline. But out in the desert, they were intrusive. The Guiding Light was brighter than Ajay had ever seen it, brightening a good stretch of land around them where he'd decided to lie down until morning.

The first initial moments in the desert were terrifying. He'd stepped tentatively into the black, flinching at every whistle of night breeze or the snap of twigs beneath his heavy feet. Yet as they got further from the forest, the Light grew brighter in his hands and the desert expanded around him. A never-ending sand. *That's a song.* Ajay remembered as he stared at the stars, twizzling the small device he'd found at the tree in one hand. It was curious. *So, this tells me more about how you do what you do?* He eyed the Light. *Except the thing is dead, so its only use is a fidget toy.* He continued to muse on his knowledge of the stars. Shining, burning through their thermonuclear fusion of hydrogen into helium, releasing all that energy out into the vastness of space. Thousands of them, thousands of miles away. Light-years away. They had been so irrelevant to his life. Merely existing and ageing along with him. His only interaction was the odd occasion he and Genni watched them from a roof. There was no merit in understanding more about them; so much information he'd yet to attain because it wasn't worth it. There was no knowledge for knowledge's sake. As he watched them sparkle, it was the first time he considered – how did people originally know what they were? The insight of why they shone like they did. That would require research beyond merit. Perhaps there was more acceptance for this sort of research earlier in their history, before the Revolution, when progress in life was a side-point, not a necessity.

Ajay realised that was the type of question he would ask her. He couldn't believe he never had. Grandma knew more than she let on to other people. A lot of what he knew came from her, filling in the gaps the school couldn't. About endangered species, Tulo's infrastructure; the City regimes, Command and camel farms. How food came, how food went, what she learned about babies and family and the intricacies of human behaviour. *She never mentioned a coconut tree, though.* Everything she knew was passed down from her parents and their parents before her. *Maybe they'd never seen coconut trees, either.* There were some things he ignored, some he absorbed, but she was always the one he asked. Even in the City, when questions arose, he remembered being in bed with her sitting on a wicker stool, gracing him with a story or an explanation.

In his lost existence, exhausted from the walking of the previous day, he whispered, 'Grandma, who first found out about the stars?'

The silence of response was oddly comforting. He didn't know where she was, or if she was even alive. Not knowing was enough to give him hope. If she wasn't here with him, the likelihood was she was somewhere better. He hoped Callum had told the truth, back in the camp, when he said she was safe. But anything could have happened to her and his parents since he'd gone to check on them. Even if she was in a Command prison cell – and that thought was like a laser shot through his chest – at least she'd have more than he did: shelter. That was the right way round. He didn't deserve nearly as much as she did. They were both paying the price for their Unworthiness. She'd always embraced being Unworthy, never even thinking about Purification. It was a life she chose and she was happy. Ajay chose a different way and he was never happy. Not really. Even those moments laced by joy with Ace and Genni were interwoven with threads of paranoia and dread. At least he was free from that feeling, and he could just exist with the beautiful, natural, star-illuminated sky. *And yet, you selfish idiot, if she is in Command, you have the freedom she should have.*

Ajay couldn't bear to think any more about it and flinched as a cooing travelled towards him. When nothing came close, he breathed slowly, conscious of the dangers he was exposed to out in the open. He considered, though, if it wasn't for The Guiding Light, he'd have been as good as dead already. He would have certainly felt the starting effects of extreme hypothermia. That was another thing Grandma taught him; the temperature dropped in the desert at night because the sand couldn't retain the heat the sun had given during the day. He was effectively lying on beds of cold rock, and with no trees for shelter around, it was no surprise he could see his breath smoking out into the air. And yet, just hours earlier, the device that disrupted his life saved it again. It was another aggravating moment of confusion and overwhelming curiosity when the device started to emit heat as well as light. It was like sleeping next to a hot steel pan. Shuffling, Ajay tried to snuggle in closer to it as he held on to his sack.

Staring into the Light, he whispered, 'Seriously, what are you?'

CHAPTER
SEVEN

For ten years Callum had called that old stretch of forest home.

There weren't many of them when he arrived and The Rogue, its name and its purpose, hadn't existed – it was more of an unspoken concept back then. They slept rougher, no pits, no electricity, no plane interceptions for a steady food and water supply. If Callum was honest, all they had was each other.

Callum thought about those days as he distributed small tins of corn to a line of hungry, sleep-deprived, broken people. Those days were simpler. *We lived better.*

'Cheers, Cal,' Tori said quietly, taking a tin from him with one hand and struggling to keep her daughter balanced on her hip with the other. The light was low but Callum returned her smile, warmed by the sight of Lolo sleeping, her face nestled into her mother's shoulder.

You made it back here. Both of you.

Callum nodded at her, his lip twitching when she stroked his arm as she left.

The wave of emotion when he and the children arrived was just that, a wave. The relief rose as parents emerged from the trees and ran to their lost children, joy rippling through the diminished crowd with force before it crashed into excruciating pain. Small feet of other children, most of them bare, walked through the centre of the clearing with no one left to claim them. Callum was thankful the boy he'd battled with wasn't one of them. His cry for his mother as he fell headfirst into her arms, her tears joining with his, stole Callum's filter. The tears ran freely. Many people had taken the lost children in as their own, but they could never be a replacement. Callum knew that more than anyone.

He continued to hand out the tins, anger bubbling inside him. *We need to focus.*

It couldn't just be about survival, but justice, and if not about justice, change.

How can we get the City to change? This is their fault. The ones who attacked on Liberation Day – they should have stuck to the plan. Command only, no citizens.

Since then, things had got worse; the lessening drop-offs, slow uptake in recruits, the discontentment in camp, the inability to form a plan through Ki's poor leadership and Ajay causing contention. *He isn't back yet. Where are the Climbers? They'll have got caught in the storm, but they should have found the new camp by now.* His brain felt fried.

It shouldn't have happened like this. He was never supposed to be grieving over orphans and handing out expired corn to the hungry. *We were always meant to bring change.* He thought of the old base; the upturned hover van functioning as his induction shack and his pit personalised by a drawing of his mother and inscriptions of poems he had chiselled into its walls. It was familiar, almost comfortable, and it grew as he and the other

Recruiters got better at their jobs. There was hope to bring Command down and abolish the merit system. There was hope for a different future. *This was never what we wanted. There's no hope. Recruitment is over. Fletch could have the motive but no one, no matter how angry they are with Command, will risk joining us now.*

He thought more about Fletch, the Command Watch engineer he'd met in the City last month, who had grievances with management. *I should stop wasting my time with him. He'll never be one of us.* He was pulled from his thoughts as he offered a tin to a man with soiled fingers. The man lingered, fixing his gaze on Callum, his palm still out in front of him.

'Sorry, there's only one each.' Callum moved towards the next in line.

'Are you kidding me, bud? I've been digging all night.'

'Sorry.' Callum met his persistent eyes. 'That's all there is.'

'But I'm wrecked. I need more,' the man continued, his knuckles tightening around the small, yellow-labelled tin.

'Well, there isn't any more. There's another twenty people waiting, at least,' Callum sniffed, allowing the woman behind the man to come forward and take her tin.

'I've done my job, making this camp for months so these lots' children are safe and I can't even have an extra one.' The man laughed cynically. 'Nah, bud.' The man violently plunged his spare hand into the plastic box, pulling out three or four tins between his fingers. Callum flinched, grabbing the man's wrist and knocking the tins; they scattered across the dirt.

Callum pulled the man closer, speaking calmly but with gritted teeth. 'That's all there is.'

The man shoved Callum off his arm before marching away from the small crowd of startled, watchful eyes. Callum breathed, his head shaking as he continued with the tins, gazing past people.

We're divided.

No hope.

He began to pick up the tins from the ground. An image came to mind fleetingly; him sitting with a group of close friends playing a round of cards, Curzo or a simple numbers game. He used to play with Ajay for hours, back in the Side. It stopped him worrying about the mental state of his mother at home. They just played. He considered how there were hours over the last ten years where a game of cards would have been entirely possible between the trees. But there was never anyone to play with. *They are all so angry.* He had his baggage, but he'd never argue about getting more food when it was scarce.

'I've done my job.' Yeah, we all have, mate. Are people here any better than out there? Maze said to not let the scum win. In that case, could anyone win at all?

Not like the attack. He realised the whole plan was an error in judgement. Next time it needed to be clean and it needed to be different.

As the last few dregs of people collected their tins, and Callum took the last one for himself, Ajay's voice popped into his head with the words he'd spoken the week before. Words which had been haunting Callum ever since.

'Doing the same thing will only give the same result.'

As he moved the empty box from the table to the ground in between water barrels and other equipment, he snapped his head towards a squawking sound. It was a woman crying uncontrollably. He jogged through the trees with Fo Doktrin and other plants nipping at his ankles. He made it out to the clearing to find the Climbers had returned.

The distraught woman was one of the Spotters who must have been off shift. She was being comforted by a Climber. Callum knew the problem instantly. He wasn't there. Trav, the father of her children and long-term partner, hadn't returned from the climb. That only meant one thing. Another one gone. Callum closed his eyes before glancing at Charlene who was standing pensively on the edge of the scene, eyes sad and tired. *Did it happen during the storm? Or had they made it back to the old camp and got caught in the chaos?* Everything had happened so fast; he'd forgotten how nervous he'd felt when they'd decided to head out in the storm. *Did they even get any of the Kakafruit we are so desperate for?* Looking at the Climbers' sacks, he got his answer. The trip wasn't worth a death. *It never should be.*

Swallowing the clog in his throat, Callum instinctively started collecting the sacks and rolling them up, knowing they had to act soon.

We need a different result; Ajay might have had an idea when he said that. I could ask him.

That's when he stopped, realising. Trav wasn't the only one missing. Ajay was gone too.

CHAPTER
EIGHT

'What happened?' Callum asked Charlene, who was squatting at the edge of her new pit.

'The storm.' She didn't look up, her mouth as unsteady as a forest path. 'These holes are smaller than the others.' She struggled with words, pulling a hairbrush from her bag.

'What happened to Trav?' Callum moved closer.

She sighed, her arms on her knees, face down. 'The tree he was in got hit and he fell, the ropes caught him all wrong.' Her words caught in her throat. 'He was just swaying there.'

A moment of silence passed between them as she wiped her eyes subtly. 'I said we shouldn't have gone out in that; we didn't have the equipment or the experience.'

Callum breathed, not letting himself imagine Trav hanging lifeless from a tree, flames engulfing his body.

'What are we going to do about the pits? People are way too nervous to sleep outside now, and these things won't fit even two of us. I'll be completely cramped.' Charlene stood and glanced down at her long legs.

'We must make do, Charl. They didn't have a lot of time,' Callum said, referring to the Diggers who had prepared a back-up camp; he then scratched at his scars, anxious to ask about Ajay, but Charlene beat him to it.

'Ajay told me, you know.'

'Told you what?'

'About you and him, when you were kids.' She sat again, nodding at his face, sympathy hot in her blue eyes. 'That it was his fault, your scar.'

'Oh.' Callum sat down too, peering into her pit, empty other than an old blanket, its pilling dotted like raindrops on the sand.

Charlene cursed about Ajay as she cradled her neck.

'Where is he?' Callum almost whispered. 'I need to speak to him.'

She shrugged, saying he got himself lost, as she fidgeted with the teeth of the hairbrush. Callum wondered if his mental state could take any more disappointment.

'Did you try to look for him?'

Charlene shook her head as she restlessly untied her hair. 'The storm was too strong . . .' She struggled as the brush hit a knot. 'Haro called for him, but I just kept running.' She flung the brush into the pit. 'Anyway, Ajay is not my responsibility. He never was and he didn't want to be here. He'll have seen his opportunity and taken it.'

'He won't survive out there.' Callum focused on her angry face. 'I think he'd have known that. He wouldn't have chosen to run.'

Charlene seemed to stumble over her breath as she jumped down into her pit, bringing her large bag with her. 'Well, at least he got what he deserved.' She patted the dust from the trousers of her climbing suit.

'I'm not sure you mean that.' Callum spotted the sudden quiver of Charlene's lip as she kept her eyes on the floor.

'I'm tired.' She reached up for the handle on her pit door, forcing Callum to stand. 'Tell Ki about the size of the pits. It's not going to work.' With that, she banged her pit shut and disappeared beneath the ground, leaving Callum and its camouflaged roof in her wake.

He pulled his own rucksack tighter to his back as he walked back through the new camp. Despite the insignificant nature of her request, Charlene was right – the pits were tighter. He grimaced as he saw a man settling down to sleep on the ground while his partner and two kids squeezed into the small pit beside him. It was the best the Diggers could do in the time they had; it was imperative they had a new camp ready, just in case. Without the pits and the suits, where were they going to hide?

Callum nodded at more tired faces as he made his way deeper through the trees to find a pit alone in the corner. It was a small, untidy hole, big enough to hold him if he slept curled up like a snake. He glanced around, making sure there were no other takers before dropping his bag and himself into it. He breathed out a ton of air and felt the grease of his brown, tatty hair.

It was never meant to be like this.

He felt hollow again with the vision of Trav dead in the trees. Ajay had been claimed by the forest, and they'd lost so many more. Like Tayler. The growing pain of his absence was unwanted; his memory of the only mentor he'd ever known was tainted by the bad decisions they eventually made. Callum couldn't help but remember Tayler's compassionate eyes and the way small wrinkles used to dance around them under strong, bushy eyebrows. The day he met Tayler on the Outer-Ring felt like the day he finally got a father. When he and Ajay, as trespassing Unworthies, got caught in the City's shopping centre, it was Tayler, with a firm hand on his teenage shoulder, who had told him the truth.

'The merit system only takes, it never gives.'

Callum hadn't fully understood that, when he stood by the Outer-Ring river, cold, shaken and beaten by Command. At first, Callum's anger at Ajay fuelled him, before it turned to a general distaste for City people, because that's all Ajay was. It was all he wanted. So obsessed with the idea of Glorification that Callum was thrown aside. That wasn't what angered him anymore, though. Ajay was merely a product of the system. Despite disliking him enough not to renew their friendship while he was in camp, Callum didn't hate Ajay.

As he unpacked his rucksack, he asked himself the same question he'd asked thousands of times. If the roles were reversed, would he, Callum, have left Ajay to the drones in the shopping centre? He would hope not, but then he didn't know, having never been in that position. As he thought about the last time he and Ajay spoke, he flung down a few random items into an old cardboard box; a leaking shampoo bottle, a battered comb and a few hair ties.

Callum had gone to the Side to check on his family as Ajay had requested last week, and all he found was a dark, empty house with blown-out windows and a garden covered in ash. Command had been there and had left nothing behind. But Callum, for whatever reason, found some empathy deep inside of himself to keep that hurt from Ajay. Why give the guy more to stress about when he was deeply grieving and clearly confused about his loyalties and his actions? It felt right to keep quiet.

Having filled the cardboard box with his food tin and a few dead Watches that hadn't been programmed for communication, Callum pulled a hooded cloak from his rucksack. He turned the deep-green fabric over in his hands, its synthetic shine coming out strong in the sun. He eyed the gold symbol on its back, a silhouette of a lizard. He couldn't remember whose stupid idea that was, but it was one of the traitors who shot at the public. He quickly shoved the cloak back into his bag, not wanting someone to wander by his pit and see it. The attack was the first and last time he ever wore it. After what happened, the cloaks and the symbol were never mentioned, much like those who invented it. *It could have been Tayler's idea.*

Staring lifelessly into his pit, he remembered coming back to the forest after the attack; the pain of the betrayal sent them backwards for months, until Ki took up the leadership and the new committee was formed, trying to piece things back together, but failing. Still, the principle remained the same. *Maybe that's why I won't get rid of the cloak.*

'The merit system only takes, it never gives,' he whispered to himself in affirmation before pulling down the top of his pit and plunging himself into darkness.

CHAPTER
NINE

The morning air was fresh and welcome, the lilac brush of the sky smudging over the darkness of night. Ajay stood, noting a herd of slow-moving camels on the horizon, and Ace was heavy on his mind. He'd been so distracted recently, but as soon as he'd escaped the forest, the cloud of grief came back, swirling all around him and squeezing the air from his body. *Please stop.* Ajay sobbed instantly, cradling his head under the morning sun. *Distraction.* He breathed deeply, craning his neck and letting the rays baste his skin as he summoned back the tears. *Don't think. Not about him. You can't start a day like this. Come on. Think: how long can I survive out here?*

He looked through the glaze of his tears at the fruit in his sack. *I've had half but I could have stretched it further.* He groaned at the loss of a steady food supply from the tree. *I can't be too greedy. There's enough for, maybe, two and a half weeks, that is, if I don't catch any desert mouse or whatever out here. Water. If I don't find water, the fruit won't even matter. I'll be dead anyway.* He spun on his feet, focusing instead on the stretch of desert he'd already crossed, the forest no longer there. He reckoned he'd walked about ten miles. In two and a half weeks, he would be almost 200 miles from where he began. *Am I crazy?* There was no guarantee he would find any more food, so death was most likely inevitable. At least he was doing something. *Distraction.*

Ignoring everything else, he gathered his things, pulled his balaclava over his sun-kissed face and powered on, the sore ache in his thighs now increasingly familiar. Although, he was pleasantly surprised at how fresh he felt; despite the obvious emotion, he had plenty of energy. Striving forward, he moved his sack round to protect one arm at a time from the sun, and considered how barren the desert really was. There'd been little out there so far, other than the camels and a few flocks of large birds. Ajay had held his breath, terrified they could have an affinity for flesh like his. There were also some desert rodents that would burrow into the sand too quickly for him to catch among dry bushes, random pieces of fabric, steel from old buildings and stray rocks. The old railway couldn't have been too far away, presumably running parallel to his direction. *That's hopeful.* The planes went north for resources, so there must be something vaguely useful out there. *The planes could see me. It's a risk. I'm still wanted by Command. So, what?* There was no point in worrying about things like that, not anymore. *I'll deal with it if it happens. At least going north gives me some sort of purpose.*

Ajay slung his sack around his front, prising out some fruit and slurping at its juice as he walked. The Guiding Light was shining through the fabric on his sack, almost invisible as it caught the sun.

His body felt strong as he strode, thinking he hadn't felt so energised since before the Liberation Day attack.

Before his whole life went up in smoke, and before . . . Ace. *Please go away. Ace, I love you, mate, and I'm sorry, but please go away.* He focused on the beautiful white of the sky ahead to see a wisping cloud. *It looks like a shovel. Or an upside down road sign. Or one of those walking –*

His thoughts broke as his body jolted.

His sack fell from his back.

Its weight pulled him down, his hands slamming the sand.

My foot.

My damn foot.

A drag had grasped his ankle, sucking him in, and his left foot was going too, both legs being pulled backwards, the sack's straps twizzling and getting uncomfortably tighter around his shoulders.

Ajay groaned, disbelieving his rapid descent into the ground, realising it was quicksand. It was up to his knees as he pressed down, feeling the grains seeping into his trousers, scratching his legs. Moving the sack from his back, he pushed his weight into it to try to pull himself out, but the grains' grip on him was too fast and too tight.

He was going.

Quickly.

His breathing grew erratic.

He cried out into the empty desert.

His heart felt like a rock in his chest, its vibrations beating up his body and pulsing into his ears. He grunted out in desperation as he pushed with all his strength on his sack to free his legs from talons in the ground. *Is this it? Is this how I'm going to die?* His Unworthy status fluttered past his thoughts, stark and painful.

'Come on,' Ajay huffed. 'Come on!' He cried louder, sweat falling beneath his balaclava, the muscles in his arms at full strain before he noticed. *Wait.* Ajay gasped.

A strong force against his legs – a sharp, powerful pinch.

Ajay tried to twist his body; it was still sliding lower into the ground and he couldn't see what was attacking him, its pinching repeating several times across his legs.

Sharp.

Fast.

Constant.

Ajay squirmed, whimpering at the increasing potential that he was about to be eaten, or his legs were being trimmed like a well-groomed bush in the Quarters. He tried to kick out but nothing happened; he was at the mercy of whatever monster was beneath.

Until the pinching slowed down, and became intermittent, and eventually faded away, along with the sucking of the sand, and then everything was still.

Ajay breathed, relieved. *What was that?*

Glancing down at his invisible legs, glued beneath the sand, he wondered if they were even still there. He couldn't feel them, jammed between thousands of tightly packed grains, but Ajay let the optimist inside him win. *My legs are there. They're there. They're tingling – that's a good sign.* He exhaled again, scanning around the unchanged desert, the sun beating down, the sand stretching for miles. Starting to think straighter, he examined the sand around his body and stuck his forefinger into it. Wet, almost sticky. *A trap for prey. Just this spot.*

Scanning around, he saw he was in the middle of a wet circle. *What happens now? The sand dries and I'm free?*

Or will it set around me and I die here? Wiggling his legs didn't seem to help; he tried to lie backwards, but his legs were already too deep.

Ajay threw off his balaclava to get some air to his face and wiped his tired eyes, trying to think. He grabbed some fruit from the sack, grunting with its refreshment.

He glanced at the dormant Guiding Light, fruit between his teeth. He turned away from it, still relishing the fruit, almost to distract himself from his impending death, stuck in sand. Or he could, ask it. *No, not doing that. How could it help me? It can't. Yeah, it knows things about the desert or whatever, but it can't help me here.*

Ajay finished the fruit and pushed up on the sack again, trying to release his legs, but it was as if the sand was setting around him and his upper-arm strength wasn't enough to break him free. He felt, suddenly, quite weak. *Ace might have been strong enough.* He was back again. Ajay closed his eyes, but out of nowhere, vomit shot up his throat and out of his mouth, firing into the sand. Spluttering, Ajay was sick again, gasping for air. *Help, I need help.*

Ajay spat out a curse word, not thinking anymore, but desperate.

The Light shot out – its figure more translucent in the bright sun.

'I'm...' Ajay heaved, '...stuck.'

'That's a sandfish hole.' The Guiding Light seemed to inspect the circle of wet sand around Ajay's body.

'I think I've been bitten.' Ajay exhaled slowly, before vomiting again. His breathing faltered and things started to spin. Angered and impatient, he mustered some strength to push up onto his sack again.

'Struggling like that won't work.' The Guide spoke plainly. 'Hold on to me.'

Ajay paused, momentarily focusing.

'Hold on to the sides of my case, I'll pull you out.'

Ajay didn't respond and returned to grappling with the sack, holding back the nausea, and only thinking about the possible poison that might be making its way to his heart and other organs.

'I can counter your weight, trust me. Just hold on.'

'Counter my weight?' Ajay sneered. 'Are you kidding?'

'Trust me.'

'I can't. You're just a hologra—' Ajay caught his breath. 'I can't . . . it's not . . . I . . .' He gasped again, the Guide fading in and out of his dizzying vision.

'Ajay, hold on.'

Exhausted and helpless, Ajay flopped his hands either side of the surprisingly cool device. With his head hanging, he considered how long the poison would take to kill him. Then something changed. In his daze, he could see his arms lifting, and as his vision cleared slightly, he marvelled as he watched The Guiding Light. *Nah, no, nope. That's not real. I'm hallucinating.*

It was floating. Levitating several millimetres off the ground, going higher, taking his arms with it. Slowly, it moved backwards and he felt the resistance of its pull. First it was his waist, followed by his hips, until his legs and feet were dragged free. Ajay flopped onto his stomach, The Guiding Light setting itself down by his head.

'What . . .' Ajay panted. 'You can't . . .' His speech slurred and everything faded to black.

CHAPTER
TEN

Waking up was like breathing. It happened without the need to think. Light slid into Ajay's eyes, his body giving him the command.

Can't be asleep. How late, how late? Grandma? No, Genni. Can't be late. Better get dressed. Mustard tie or salmon tie? Salmon. Blue. Blue.

He saw nothing but a white sky.

Paint on the ceiling. New. White, white.

His fingers clawed slowly at the sand.

Soft. Soft bed covers. No, no, no. No sleep. Shouldn't sleep. Merit. Merit, dropping.

He sat up with urgency, his head rushing and screaming.

'Ah,' he hissed.

Where am I? Where? Too white.

He slammed his eyes shut.

'Take it easy, lie down,' the soft voice encouraged. Ajay obeyed.

The Guiding Light. It's here. The Side? No, too white. Too hot. Hot. Desert. Sand.

Grimacing through the muddled head throb, the memory returned to him.

Legs. Poison. The Guiding Light. Flying. No. I'll be late. Genni, can't be late. Ace too. Pain, pain. It hurts.

'My head.' Ajay drew in a breath, his left hand resting on his forehead.

'It's OK, take your time.' The Light sounded close but far away.

'I better tell Genni I'm ill,' Ajay mumbled.

'Genni isn't here, you're confused,' its voice boomed.

Ajay lost speech, pressing his head harder.

Genni, not here. Where is Genni? Where is Ace? Where is anyone? Sand. Desert. Ace, dead. The Guiding Light, flying.

'Where am I?'

'You fell into a sandfish hole. You've been dealing with the effects of its poison for about twelve hours,' the Light bellowed. 'It'll take some time to adjust.'

Sandfish. Hole. Stuck. Escaped.

'You're too loud.' He kicked out his legs.

'OK, take your time.'

Only the silence of the desert returned to him as he forced himself to breathe slowly, letting several minutes pass. *Inhale, exhale.* During those moments, everything came back. *OK, OK. You are in the desert. You got lost in The Rogue, got fruit from the tree, came out here with The Guiding Light, stood in that sandfish hole, and then it got you out. You weren't strong enough, but it was.* Ajay, still lying down, twisted his head sideways, watching The Guiding Light silently sitting on the sand beside him. In his delusion, its light looked bigger than ever, spreading out across the length of Ajay's body like some sort of shield. As soon as he noticed, the light sucked back into its usual figure, swirling on top of the device as always.

'You got me out.' He rested his hands on his belly. 'How did you get me out?'

'I pulled you using—'

'No, no,' Ajay interrupted, hoisting himself up to sitting. 'I know literally what you did, but how? I've seen your code, *multiple times*, and there was no functionality remotely like that. So how?'

'You couldn't see what you weren't looking for.' The Guide ebbed in its movements, a wisp of wind throwing sand over its hardware.

'Wait. So, I've been carrying you around on my back, and all this time you could . . .' Ajay stopped with the heaviness of his headache as he tried to remember his teenage investigation of the Guide. Surely he would have seen something.

You couldn't see what you weren't looking for.

He was obsessed with seeing its similarities to the Watch's top-level programming interface; that's all he cared about – a way to hack into the City and get the merit-worthy life he believed he deserved. *So, this could be a technology beyond the X-Level developments? Something Command couldn't even program yet?*

The hot tingle down his legs stole his attention back.

He rushed to roll up his trousers and panicked at his legs boasting sore, red and ballooning bites. Ajay cursed, feeling heat pulsate across his body.

'Yeah, they're nasty,' the Guide said as Ajay could see more clearly. They were full of fluid, throbbing and sensitive as he hovered his shaky fingers over them.

'How long until it wears off?' Ajay asked, wheezing.

'The headache should be gone soon. Have some fruit.' The Guiding Light floated towards the sack. *It's doing it again.* Ajay murmured sounds as he moved towards it. 'The blisters may take a few days, but you'll be able to walk fine.'

'Seriously, how do you know this?' He rustled through the sack, straining from his torso, before finding fruit and slurping at it. *Sweet Tulo. That's good.*

'I've been through it myself,' it said, causing Ajay to choke.

'You ... what?'

'I got bitten once.' It spoke with the tone of shrugging shoulders. 'A long time ago.'

'You got bitten?'

'Yes.' It lowered itself to the ground gracefully. 'We can talk more about that, but for now, you need to get your strength back.'

With that, the light fell back into its case.

Ajay didn't think more of it as he didn't want to talk. He did just want to lie there and sleep. *Hang on.* He patted his cheeks. They didn't feel sore. *How am I not completely sunburnt? The light. It was bigger, across my whole body. Did it protect me? No, that's not ... is it? And it said it had been bitten. How? Was it a person?* Ajay looked at it again, the lifeless oval device beaming in the sun's reflection. *I need to know everything, but then ... then I would have to talk to it. Like, properly.* He swallowed, feeling uncomfortable. How could he tolerate something he'd hated for so long?

But one thing was obvious, he wasn't good at surviving alone.

If it wasn't for a welcome breeze causing it to waft, Ajay wouldn't have seen it; the beige colour of its fabric masking its presence as it peeked out of the buff grains. Ajay stooped down towards it, his knees clicking through the holes in his trousers. He stroked it with his fingers. *Some sort of synthetic polyester.* He pulled it upwards and more of it kept coming; sand showered down as it emerged from the desert's grip. *A jumpsuit. Like a resource worker or Command officer would wear.* It had a brass zip down its front, rusty with teeth missing, and Ajay expected to see the Command logo above the right ripped pocket but instead, there were two words. One read 'Scalen' and the other had faded into something unreadable. Its typography was bold yet calligraphic and it had a symbol, like a shooting star, striking across the back of the letters. He hadn't heard of the brand 'Scalen', nor could he imagine what they did. The jumpsuit was crusty, too, adding to its ancient feel. Despite questioning its age, it was comforting. It was evidence he wasn't the only one to have been out in the desert long enough to lose something.

Did someone die in this jumpsuit? Ajay rejected the thought and was thankful for the provision of a change of clothes. Lifting it up higher, its beige colour disagreeing with him, he realised it would never fit him. Way too small. Still, it would protect the skin of his neck as he walked, or could be extra coverage at night. He rolled it up, threw it around his neck and marched on.

The Guiding Light had been right when it said the blisters wouldn't take long to settle down. It had been a few days of sleeping and other than the odd itch, and the obvious scarring on his legs, Ajay wouldn't have known they were there anymore. The whole experience had convinced him that he was too exposed. So, knowing there were mountains towards the west, it made sense for him to head that way. Shelter. Water. And probably more food. *Though the fruit seems good enough.*

He'd been intermittently slurping at its juice to keep hydrated, but he hadn't thought about eating since his last rest, at least three miles back. If in some dream life he was accepted back in the City, there was no doubt about what he'd do. It was the ultimate business proposition. There should be experiments on the fruit from that tree, to compare its energy-enhancement against Fo Doktrin. After all, that was the main ingredient for *SkipSleep*, and he would endeavour to say the fruit's effects were stronger. While it didn't seem to negate the need for rest, the times he'd spent awake felt more alive since he'd been eating it. In another life, he could have sold it for credit and merit. But what was the point of thinking of another life? *This is the one I've got.*

As he walked, he continued to watch his step, seeing sandfish holes where the sand was slightly darker in colour. He grimaced at one as a rodent was sucked beneath the sand. He turned away, addressing the Light, which was floating beside him.

'So, you can also shield me from the sun?'

'Are you feeling the heat?' the Guide asked.

'No,' Ajay stuttered. 'All the time while I was asleep. I woke up once and there was a sort of cast over me.'

'I didn't want you to get burnt.'

Ajay shook himself. *It has compassion?*

'You said I need to listen to that thing,' he nodded back to his sack, referring to the device he found by the tree. 'To find out more about you. I assume it's an audio player.' Ajay went on to say that it was useless – broken.

'Why have you assumed it's broken?'

Ajay realised the validity of the Guide's question, and after a moment of giving it some proper thought, he berated himself further. *Idiot.* He dropped his sack and fished it out. Flipping it over in his hands, he looked over its clunky casing and saw no ports around its battered edges, which determined it was new enough to be solar-powered. Its mini panels were probably embedded into its screen, just like a Watch. He said nothing, almost embarrassed for his thoughtlessness but instead, he simply noted the position of the sun. He tied the device, through a gap in its hardware, with the loop on top of his sack and left it hanging from its top, soaking in the rays. *Maybe soon I'll get some answers.*

'This way to the mountains?' he asked, looking to the west.

CHAPTER
ELEVEN

It was only when Ajay stopped for some fruit that he realised.

'It's charged.' Ajay untangled the old device from the top of his sack. 'Thirty-two per cent.'

'OK.' The Guide seemed to dim, floating beside him. 'That gives us some time.'

Ajay stood, tapping at the screen. 'Wait, there's not much on here. It's only one application.' Ajay flicked into the air. 'No pop-out screen, either.' He held the chunk of its casing, examining the interface and scrolling down a list of dated files.

'They're all recordings from Year minus-1.' Ajay forgot about the fruit and threw his sack back over his shoulder. 'The year before the Revolution.' He scrolled back to the top. 'Oh, no, the first is from minus-6.'

'Start there,' the Guide muttered quietly.

Static vibrated from the device until a soft, high voice superseded it. A child.

'My name is Deva Hevas and I am seven years old and this is my life. I live in a place called Tulo. It's a big city with a big, big desert that goes on for miles and mil—' Ajay hit the pause button.

'What . . .' He squinted at it, thinking. 'This is a diary.' The device's screen light competed with the reflection of the sun. 'A *Hevas'* diary.' Ajay assumed the Light wasn't ignorant about its significance.

'It is,' the Light confirmed.

Ajay hit the pause button but didn't stop walking. He took in the sands ahead, letting up in his pace to allow a family of large lizards to fade into the distance. Everything was sticky – the air, his sweat – and the information he'd heard over the last half an hour was equally as unpleasant. *There was so much wrong.* He sipped from a shard of fruit in his other hand, remembering Deva's horrific retelling of the baby mortality rate before the Revolution. *Her baby brother never saw his first birthday. So wrong.* It wasn't the first time over the last few hours that Ajay felt the weight of his little gratitude. Back then, water was so scarce that babies were born too soon, and he used to complain about the warm water from the Side taps.

'Why didn't they go to the mountains? Like Command does?' He turned to the Guide, its light battling against the sun.

'They didn't have the resources or infrastructure to travel that far yet.'

'Shouldn't that have been a priority?' Ajay argued, discarding the fruit. 'The government had enough to do it, surely.'

'They didn't see it like that.'

'Why not?' Ajay said instinctively. He dropped his shoulders and cursed.

Deva's words came back, his thoughts mimicking her soft, excitable voice.

Did I tell you about the water towers? They stand tall and strong in front of where the buildings get higher. There are four of them. This is where any collected water goes from rainfall or if the resource workers get any from the trees. Then it is, as Mother says, 'rationed' between everyone. But the government people get the biggest part.

All Ajay could think about was Liberation Day. It was hard to isolate its concept from the attack; the bombs and being shot among the balloons and the decadent stalls. But it was so highly celebrated because of what society escaped through the Revolution – the life Deva Hevas had lived. He'd never truly understood that before, despite seeing the promo video repeatedly, but it didn't communicate the terror and the injustice like she did.

'I don't understand, though.' Ajay swallowed any emotion. 'What does this tell me about your technology?' He stopped and turned towards the south, pulling the beige jacket around his mouth as wind wisped sand up.

'It has everything to do with it, if we continue to listen.' The Guide's words were muffled with the breeze as Ajay squinted at something in the distance.

'Can you see that?' He pointed.

It was dark, box-like, not much bigger than a hover vehicle.

It can't be.

It *was* a hover vehicle. Or at least some mode of transportation. *An old carriage from a railway line? But the lines were built much further south. Still, one could have made it here somehow over the years.* Tulo storms had moved bigger things. Jogging unsteadily across the sand, he confirmed it – a hover vehicle.

'No way!' Ajay hurried, dropping the diary inside his sack, which he hoisted back over his shoulder.

He wasn't excited at the prospect that it might work, as that was highly unlikely, but it had parts. Old pieces of machinery he could use. Ki and The Rogue had managed to make use of old, abandoned vehicles. Why couldn't he? For weapons, or cooking tools, or something that would aid his survival to get to the mountains, or even shelter for the night. He bounded towards the abandoned car, his heart rate increasing. Even before reaching it, he could see it was in rough shape. Most of its surrounding bumper was torn, exposing the silver metal beneath its dented and misshapen exterior. Close enough to see, Ajay guessed it was probably about forty or fifty years old, by the look of the model. It still had a manual steering wheel in place and the seats were arranged two front, two back, rather than in the modern sofa style. He wasn't sure whether he needed to be cautious. There was no knowing what manner of wild animal could be resting in there. Maybe he shouldn't bother investigating. It was unlikely an old Command vehicle, branded by the faded symbol on its side, would have anything useful inside it. Then again, he didn't know the circumstances in which it had been abandoned; it could be dangerous, but Ajay was too curious. He always had been.

CHAPTER
TWELVE

Looking around for a weapon in case of a threat inside the vehicle, he twisted his lip at only sand and dry, withered sticks, presumably dropped by birds. Neither would be particularly effective against a felkar. Dropping his sack, he grabbed The Guiding Light from the air. It had been robust enough when he'd tried to destroy it, so it would no doubt survive a few bashes on a predator's head.

Tiptoeing forward, Ajay continuously scanned around the car, flat on its bumper, its fans buried in the sand. He peered through the back smashed window to see very little. Some of the seats' fabric had gone, the work of desert mites, he guessed, and there was nothing on the floor but a few mouldy food packets. That couldn't be what was causing the nasty stench that forced Ajay to hold his nose with his spare hand. He did well not to heave.

Moving on, he rammed The Guiding Light through the front window to get a better view. Scraping away the glass, he stuck his head in again, holding The Guiding Light out for defence. He soon relaxed. There was nothing in there but a sand-encrusted control panel and a small, printed photograph above the steering wheel. It was surprising for someone working at Command not to have a digital screen for a photograph, but then again, it was old. The fact that the wheel was out of its compartment suggested to Ajay that something had gone wrong with the driverless function on its last voyage. In the photograph, he could make out a large family; two parents and five children. He couldn't tell if there was another child or a fox due to the strong fading in the bottom corner. That's when he spotted the glove compartment in front of the other seat. Ignoring the smell, he dropped The Guiding Light inside the car and clambered in after it, trying to be light in his movement to avoid cutting himself on any broken glass.

Pulling open the drawer, he grimaced as a plethora of sweet wrappers fell out onto his lap. The majority were empty but there was still one browned, crystallised sweet left. Hurriedly, he struggled to pull the melted candy away from its wrapper but quickly noticed the tiny insects enjoying themselves on its aged toffee surface. Throwing it into the desert, Ajay then recovered the main contents of the drawer; a bulky, paper manual in a plastic cover. A Driverless C-867. Made in Y-2414. He flipped it over and read the blurb through the plastic.

The purpose of this comprehensive manual is to aid any user in the unlikely event of a malfunction where the vehicle's digital assistant becomes unavailable. If the digital operations are functional, the assistant will cater for the specific problem you are facing and will provide a more accurate diagnosis.

Turning the book over and back again, Ajay returned it to the glove compartment but not before noticing the remaining items: small transparent bags full of withered, brown plant leaves. *Fo Doktrin? A dodgy dealer?* Ajay scoffed. Even back then, Command officers were thugs. Throwing the old leaves back into the compartment, he sat back on the seat, breathing in another strong wave of the stench.

'What is that?' he moaned, struggling with the door handle and making it out of the vehicle. His fingers pressed to his nose, he staggered around to the boot to find it dented and partially open. Peering down, he saw a small, unmoving foot inside. He didn't give himself time to think, but pulled the boot open, and immediately threw both hands back over his face.

Looking at it was almost as bad as smelling it. What was left of the animal was barely distinguishable. Ajay thought he knew which side was the head, but he couldn't be sure. He guessed it was once about the size of a drone, with a round body and black fur, though curiously, he could see dotted blue lines running between its hairs. The amount of worms and other insects buzzing around it took away anything else conclusive. Ajay, hands over his mouth and nose, moved his eyes away, squirming at the death invading his reality. His thoughts turned to Ace. Invasive, sudden. *I can never run from what I did. And there's also no way I can sleep in this car tonight.*

He slammed the lid of the boot and clonked his body on the sand.

'What are you doing?' The Light appeared slowly, its voice soft and figure stark in the approaching evening.

'Nothing,' Ajay stuttered, having forgotten all about it. 'Resting.'

'Why?' Its voice travelled casually through the desert air. 'Haven't you just discovered something?'

Silence invaded as Ajay didn't waste time on its stupid questions. He closed his eyes, leaning his head back towards the descending sun.

'The car is probably solar-powered too.' The Guiding Light floated over the car's boot and the carcass inside it.

'What?' Ajay grunted, frustrated at several things – The Guiding Light talking and telling him something he already knew, and that it disrupted a moment of peace while he tried to process the disappointment of the vehicle, the sight of death in the boot, and the thoughts of Ace it had stabbed through him.

'We could fix it.' It spoke without any air of doubt, like the suggestion wasn't ludicrous.

Ajay sprang up, leaving the car and the Light behind.

'You can figure out what's broken.' It followed him through the buzzing desert air.

'I'm not listening to you.' Ajay stared at the desert, the mountain peaks still feeling out of reach.

'It's worth a go. I'll help you.' The Guiding Light floated towards him. Ajay gritted his teeth and held back on the outburst brewing under his tongue. 'I don't see a reason why you can't.' The Guiding Light flew slightly higher, hovering above Ajay's head, its compassionate and excited sound falling over him with a chill. 'You've been travelling across the desert for days now. What are the chances of coming across a *hover car*?'

'Why does that matter?'

'You would have thought it was pretty impossible, in all this sand, to find a car, but you did.'

'It's much less probable I'll be able to fix it.' Ajay squinted at The Guiding Light before glancing at the car wreckage. 'I suppose there is a manual.'

'Good. That should be a light read.'

'I was joking.'

'So was I.'

Ajay stayed silent, processing a quick, grunting laugh as it fell from the Guide. *It can't find things funny.* He wiped his face, scrunching it up like paper into a ball, convincing himself the Guide wasn't capable of being happy, or angry, or sad, or offended. Ajay felt a tension run across his back as his mouth went dry. *Am I considering this? It's been right about everything so far.* He glanced back at the car and let a four-letter word fall from his lips.

CHAPTER
THIRTEEN

Are you crazy? Why are you listening? Because what else is there? It could get me to the mountains quicker. To water quicker. To shelter quicker, or back to Grandma quicker.

It's impossible; only another way to fail.

Does that matter?

Yes, all failures stop progress, and Progress is Strength.

Strength for what?

Meaning something. Being someone.

That's gone now; I'm Unworthy.

Yes, you are.

Shutting off his mind, Ajay cumbersomely climbed back through the car window and settled in the front seat; he begrudgingly opened the glove compartment again, sifting through the wrappers and cables with one hand, while the other pressed his nostrils shut. He found the bulky paper manual enclosed in its cellophane cover. The Guiding Light floated through the opposite window and placed itself down on the seat beside him.

Without a word, he retreated from the car to escape the smell and returned to a spot on the sand, thankful for the cooler air of dusk. He simply ripped the manual open, releasing a fresh smell of paper which had been locked in for so long. He focused on the cover photo of happy passengers with electric smiles and wavy letters spelling 'Fly Freely'. Flicking straight to the next page, he trailed his finger down the extensive contents: occupant protection, fingerprint locking system, alarm, steering wheel back-up, wipers and washers, *blah blah*. The other entries were a blur until he reached 'fans and propellers' (*they're properly broken*), then 'vehicle care' (*a bit late for that*), before stopping at 'vehicle battery' (*feels like a decent place to start*). Ajay flipped the pages over, giving himself a paper cut, not having handled paper in a while. Sucking the blood from his finger, he scanned the key details, resting the book on his crossed legs.

The batteries are located centrally beneath the vehicle.

Ajay returned to the car and peered through the window to the back seats, scanning the two of them separately before squinting at the floor and envisioning the batteries beneath. *I'll need to see how they're connected to the solar panels on the roof, which are probably just as wrecked.* He stroked his hand across the roof, feeling the tickle from the small grooves between each concealed panel. *How do I fix damaged solar panels? And the whole thing is flat on the sand, its fans' propellers not having spun in years. And even if I did manage to fix the batteries and the panels and whatever else, there's still the motor. Dad used to talk about it; all the reasons for a motor to pack it in. Its insulation is surely degraded, or overheated, or contaminated with foreign objects by now. Slow down.* He had a headache, but returned to the list.

- Watch Synchronisation
- Navigation System
- Maintenance
- Driverless Functions

That's all meaningless unless I get the batteries charged or the motor working. I could start there. No, no, the batteries are what powers the motor. But what if I . . . then I could . . . but that wouldn't . . . Ajay slammed the manual shut with a snap.

'This is never gonna work.' Ajay dropped the book to the sand.

'You can't give up already. Where's your stamina?' The Guiding Light asked, floating around like an over-the-top chandelier. 'It's only a problem to solve like all the others.'

Momentarily, Ajay did feel inspired to remember how many obstacles he'd overcome before. Hacking into the City had once felt impossible, but he did it.

'I can't do it anymore.' Ajay closed his eyes softly.

'It's worth a try.'

'You don't know what this feels like.'

'What *what* feels like?'

Ajay couldn't say: *to feel broken and ashamed. To feel like not one thing in your life is worth redeeming. That nothing you ever do will be Worthy, that everything you try falls flat, that you fought so hard for people to see your value but you only ended up hurting the ones you cared about most.*

He wasn't about to pour himself out to a machine, even if it did seem to have more personable qualities than he'd ever given it credit for. Instead, he just responded, 'I can't look at this now. I'll think about it tomorrow.'

The manual went back where it came from as one day drifted off and another replaced it with a fresh vigour.

The colours of the soft, humid morning layered over each other in cushioned red waves. Ajay was thinking about his father as he let himself take in the shades of the sky. He had watched him as a kid in the Side restoring many recycled vehicles from the City. That was probably the only thing he and his father bonded over, and it was also only the beginning of his father's talents, ones never used for merit, or progress, or ambition. Whenever Ajay pondered on that, grief strangled him with all the ferocity of the colours in the sky. Grief that his whole family had so much to give, and they never did. Not on the level they could have. And grief that he didn't know if he'd ever see them again, or even where they were now. *So much to give.*

For all that wastage, though, his dad had taught him a thing or two about hover vehicles, particularly that whenever they'd broken down and their parking fans packed up, there was a mechanism for lifting the car and accessing the batteries and propellers beneath it. He made his way to the car and felt a new energy as his boots dented the sand. Crouching down, he traced his fingers along the bottom edge of the car frame, taking little notice of the Light floating after him.

'Morning,' it said.

Ajay didn't respond but only thought out loud: 'There should be . . . somewhere.'

Dusting away sand from the car's exterior, he placed his dry fingers down the grooves and curled them around the latch he was looking for. 'Gotcha.'

He straightened himself slowly, mirroring the motion of the metal legs emerging from beneath the car, lifting the vehicle up steadily onto one side. It was no surprise the electronic assistance wasn't working, but the legs were taking most of the car's weight as Ajay willed them up. They stopped and fell abruptly, throwing Ajay forward and driving his knee into the side door.

'Youch.' Ajay grabbed his kneecap and took a moment to let the sting subside, mumbling curse words beneath his breath. Once he'd recovered, he didn't hesitate to try the latch again, and watched the legs slip through the sand and fall once more, the sand running around the legs' tiny, rubber wheels like water.

'Come on, come on.' Ajay exhaled as he tried again and The Guiding Light drifted in closer.

'The wheels are slipping.'

Ajay didn't thank it for its obvious statement but managed to wedge his shoulder under the car to stabilise the legs as they rose.

'Ajay, it's not going to hold.'

'I don't . . . remember asking for your opinion,' Ajay huffed, seizing as he straightened up.

'Maybe a rock could hold it, but you should let go.'

'Do you . . . see . . .' Ajay panted, 'any rocks?'

His legs swiftly buckled, he let go and rolled to the side; the car made a pop as it hit the sand again. Ajay exhaled with his arms over his knees and spent too many minutes blinking at the deflated car.

'Don't say anything. I'm trying to think,' Ajay commanded the Light who sat beside him. 'I could try to get it on its back.'

'The whole thing?' Its amused doubt didn't go unnoticed.

If it had a face, Ajay might have punched it.

Ajay clenched his jaw and tightly tied his left shoelace. 'If I could get the legs up for long enough, I could push it over.'

'Could we work from the inside?'

'No.' He grimaced and crisply retied his other lace while he was at it. 'The battery pack is underneath and I need to check for damage.'

'I think . . . ' The Guiding Light paused before hovering further off the sand, 'you could try from above to see—'

'I'd have to pull everything out,' Ajay interrupted sharply, throwing a hand towards the car, 'and get through a sheet of metal.' He fiercely pulled down the cuff of his trousers over his boots. 'It's easier to access from underneath.'

'Not if you can't get there.'

'I'm going from underneath.'

'What about if you tried taking the seats—'

'I'm going from underneath!'

Ajay battled through a churning stomach as the heat of the sun torched his skin. *It's getting too hot to work. Brilliant, and I've got nowhere.* He walked awkwardly towards the car and grew tense at the mechanical noise of the Light following him.

'What if, as you say, I could walk to find a couple of rocks . . .' Ajay scanned the area, seeing nothing but orange stretching out before him; the withered bushes had disappeared, leaving only plain, far-reaching sand.

'Is that a good idea?' The Guiding Light climbed the air.
'You just said to use a rock!'

'No, I said a rock may be able to hold it. That's different,'
it commented, hovering at Ajay's eyeline, the light over
his face.

Ajay instantly turned his back on it, staring hard at the
car again.

'There's got to be a way to get under there,' he almost
whispered, trying to ignore the Light completely.

'Why do you need to?'

Ajay groaned, pulling a shard of fruit from his sack
on the ground. He tried to eat through his irritation, but
he instantly snapped his body back towards the Light,
unmoved from its spot in the air.

'You know, there is such a thing as listening.' Ajay
waited for a response but nothing came; the Light
just ebbed in its usual annoying way, with an air of
disciplinary authority, the way a parent would look at a
child and not have to say anything at all. 'Don't act like
that. I've told you the battery pack could be degraded or
damaged, so there's no more questions . . .' He bit into
the fruit again, looking away. 'I've got to get under it.'

The Light still said nothing and Ajay subtly shook
his head, tracing the back of his teeth with his tongue.
*Getting to the mountains quicker would be helpful, but I
may still survive without the water . . . but then I'll never
know about Grandma, I can't walk that far and the vehicle
may not even work. It is just . . .*

At that moment, his eyes were taken captive by a
beautiful creature piercing the air with the graceful
stroke of its wings. It was unlike any bird he'd seen;
almost gold in colour, but long and skinny in stature,

its beak almost the length of its body steering it towards the west. Ajay followed the magnificent bird, its wings spanning the horizon, stilling the moment so Ajay was very aware of his breath; caught short in amazement.

'Wow,' he whispered instinctively as the great bird eventually disappeared.

'Have you ever seen one up close?' the Guide said softly, its tone complementing the stillness.

'I don't . . .' Ajay paused, eyes transfixed at the space in the sky where it had flown. 'I don't know what it is.' He swallowed.

'It's a gazzen. They rarely leave their nests in the mountains, only when they're in need of a new food source.'

Ajay raised his eyebrows.

'I happened upon one once,' it said, its hologram facing out into the desert. 'I was on a walk and there it was, right in front of me, digging its beak into the sand. For a moment, we held eye contact before it flew away.' The Light spun itself back to face Ajay. 'They're very private creatures.' It smoothly moved past him towards the car.

Instantly and with urgency, Ajay followed it.

'You walked? Just like you got bitten by a sandfish?'

'Once, yes.' It sat down on the car bonnet. 'I walked a lot.'

'But you can't have,' Ajay growled, leaning against the window frame.

'Why not?' it asked.

'Because . . .' Ajay took a breath. 'Because you're a . . . recordings, a transcript.'

'Where do you think they came from?'

'Well, sure, they came from *someone* . . . back then. It wasn't Deva Hevas.' Ajay stared at the Light harder. 'But you, yourself, whatever you are, can't be *real*. We don't have that kind of technology yet.'

'Well, I guess we should keep listening,' it said, moving over to the sack, slumped on the front seat, where the diary sat waiting.

'What about the car?'

'We've got time. I thought you wanted answers?'

Another half-hour had drifted away as Ajay slapped at the pause button.

'That's you?' He turned to The Guiding Light. 'You're the guy with no shoes?' His words got caught; he absorbed Deva's description of a man walking barefoot in the rain. 'You were real . . . a man . . . and a little girl saw you from her window.'

'I had walked a long way.' It seemed to breathe deeply. 'To find them.'

Ajay looked at his own bare feet, cracked and dry, even after the protection of boots.

'Who are you?' He suddenly felt a sort of unexplainable fear, like he was in the presence of someone he shouldn't be. 'Who are you *really*?'

'I'm help.'

Ajay let out an instinctive, grunting laugh before recognising how much it *had* helped him the last few days. But he still remembered the rest of it; his whole life it had felt intrusive and restrictive, and never valuable.

Yet he couldn't shake the idea of it being connected to a once-living consciousness. *That* transcended everything he ever thought or understood about the device. *But this might not be the truth.* Slowly, he decided he didn't have the energy to debate it, and accepted its uncertainty. It was like steam releasing from his shoulders, making him feel somewhat lighter. He wanted to press the play button to further question its validity, but as he scanned the desert, his attention was stolen by the problem of the car. *There must be a way.* After what felt like hours, Ajay raised his head at the Light, which seemed to be shining on his face expectantly.

'I don't think I believe all this, but . . .' Ajay shook his head and swallowed, the gravitas building in his voice. 'I think I want to fix this car.' *For survival and for Grandma.*

'OK. We can do that.'

'And you might be right about starting from the inside,' Ajay admitted, hot pain in his words.

'Sure, OK. You could start with the seats and try to access the wiring, up to the panels on the roof.'

'Yeah.' Ajay exhaled, exhausted, thinking about the bird, and Deva and The Guiding Light walking, seeing and experiencing, like he or any other person would. 'OK.'

'But Ajay . . .' The Guiding Light stopped Ajay in his tracks as his mind started whirring. 'You might want to get rid of the body in the boot first.'

CHAPTER
FOURTEEN

Ajay heaved both at the smell on his hands and the small, snapped leg he'd dropped to the ground. Breathing over the boot, he steadied himself.

He counted to three and without hesitating, he jammed his arms under the weight of the creature. Despite being small, it packed some serious pounds; he stumbled as he threw its load to the ground. The thing tumbled, its black fur and blue-lined decoration more vibrant against the orange sand. Once he'd dragged it away, he braced himself against his knees, ordering the vomit back.

'You doing OK?' The Light floated by his head, its tone jovial.

'That's not funny,' Ajay huffed. 'My hands stink of it.'

'Use the juice from your finished fruit skins,' the Light suggested as it set itself down by his feet. 'It has antibacterial properties.'

Moments later, Ajay breathed out a laugh over how quickly the fruit juice seemed to dissipate any scent of death on his fingers. After another twenty minutes, he was high from the productivity; he hadn't hesitated to wipe the inside of the car and boot with the fruit too, and he'd managed to tip the back seats forward, but he was soon caught in a problem.

Get a grip.

You're getting upset about a bolt.

A bolt.

He stared lifelessly at the two large hexagonal bolts that clamped the seats to the floorboards – as rusted as some of the car itself.

If I can't get the seats out, I can't get to the batteries.

I could try to make something to wrap around it.

Thinking noises escaped from his tongue as he glanced at The Guiding Light, which was sitting quietly on the neighbouring car seat. *Get some leverage to shift the bolt.* As soon as Ajay thought about it, he eyed the seatbelt hanging on the side of the seat. *I could use that fabric to make a kind of thin rope, wrap it around the bolt tightly. Use it to pull the bolt like you would with a spanner.* Another thought inspired him to action. He jumped from the car and returned to the front windscreen where the left wiper was broken, its jagged end pointing up to the sky. Taking care, he snapped it off before cradling his neck under the heat of the midday sun. *That looks sharp enough.* Ajay, back at the window, felt that rush; one step closer to a problem solved. Once the seats were out, he'd be able to access the underfloor wiring going directly from the packs into the solar panels on the roof. It was a start and it felt good.

As he climbed through the back window, he ordered The Guiding Light to hover over to the opposite seat. Ajay's growing warmth towards it was uncomfortable, resentment still burning furiously inside, but he'd decided it would do as an outlet for at least some of his stewing thoughts.

Having bent the sharp end of the wiper up, he took it to the seatbelt on the opposite seat and started slowly cutting through the fabric, its ripping sound filling the car.

'I'm craving kale chips,' he said as he imagined their satisfying crunch.

'Kale chips?' The Guide spun around, zooming back into the main compartment of the car. 'Of all things, you want kale chips?'

'Have you ever tried them?' Ajay scoffed.

'No, but I know what they taste like.'

'How can you, when you've never tried them?' Ajay asked blankly, holding his gaze at the figure's head.

'I know from other people's experiences,' it said curtly. 'They're dry and lack flavour. That's the majority opinion.'

'Your sources are biased.' Ajay exhaled as he got to the edge of the seatbelt, snapping it apart horizontally. 'Only based on a small population of the market.'

'You're saying my data is from people in the Side.' The Guide moved closer, setting itself back down on the seat beside Ajay, lighting up the seatbelt he was pulling out from its clasps next to the headrest.

'Exactly. I'm guessing . . .' He paused, growing distracted by feeding the belt through the loop of the clasp. 'Ah, you . . .' Ajay shifted the belt as it got jammed before it ran freely through the clasp and out the other side. 'Yeah, so,' Ajay continued, pulling the belt apart, '*they* told you what *they* thought about kale chips.'

'That's correct.' The Guide spoke over the intermittent shredding sounds.

'So, most of your feedback on their taste and satisfaction would be from people who make their own potato chips and freely add salt.' Ajay paused as he remembered how delicately salted and carefully prepared his mother's potato chips were. 'Or the high-merit deducting indulgent stuff in the ration.' Ajay grunted as he hit a more resistant part of the belt, using more force to get through it. 'Side people are bound to describe kale chips as dry when they only have the fatty, salty stuff to compare it to.' He exhaled as he found the end of the belt, pleased with two thin strips of fabric. 'I, on the other hand, quite like them and would love a packet right now.'

'I'm just surprised that from anything you could crave, it would be kale chips. If you want a change from the fruit, you could go and find a burrow mouse or a micro-boar,' it suggested.

'Seems like a waste of energy to me,' Ajay muttered, knowing that the fruit was lasting him and it was still delicious.

'There used to be a lot more life. You wouldn't have needed to go so far,' it explained. 'It's like my father used to say: once one species dominates, all others are forced to bow.'

It had a father? Well, if it was a real person, then yeah, I suppose it makes sense for it to have had a dad. So, it had a mother too. But do I even believe that someone's consciousness is inside this thing? The only way that could work would be if we had an understanding of how you could test whether something is sentient, and we don't. Even if it was possible, how do you make that sentient thing have the same properties as a specific person, who knows it is their identity? And the collected information becomes their memories? And how would they even make decisions based on those memories? I guess you could make different models that react to those pieces of information, but how do you make a model that's reflective of that person? No idea.

'That's it.' He threw the tattered seatbelt on The Guiding Light and grabbed the diary from the front seat. 'I can't wait any longer.'

I must prove to myself that this isn't real.

CHAPTER
FIFTEEN

The year minus-4. Deva was nine years old and Ajay could picture her planting tomatoes in the garden as she recalled eavesdropping on her gossiping neighbours from the adjacent house. They described the man with no shoes as 'impoverished' and yet they also said, 'his skin glows' and 'he looks well hydrated for a beggar'.

The Guiding Light, or as Ajay imagined, a man with dark, styled hair – *wait, it wouldn't be styled, he probably couldn't afford to have it cut* – Ajay glanced at The Guiding Light. *What did you look like?* The man had started to knock on people's doors, offering melons and cans of water, leading to a lot of speculation over whether he'd stolen it from the government's water towers or from people's houses, but everything was accounted for. Ajay, though keen for the story to move on, understood the suspicion it caused; Deva described the twitching curtains as he passed by, plus the whispers and gossip in the streets.

A twist. He has strawberry-blond hair. And wide, mesmerising eyes. Two eyes but different colours. One bright blue, the other a mix of blue and yellow. Olive skin, but healthier than everyone else's. Ajay struggled to adjust the way he'd originally imagined the man, just as Deva revealed his name.

'That's your name?' He paused the recording and turned to the Light, still sat in the neighbouring car seat. 'Osgar?'

'Yes.'

'I've never heard that before.'

'Well, it's not Tuloian.'

Ajay scrunched his eyes. 'What?'

'It's complicated.' The Light opened its glowing arms.

'So, you came all that way from wherever, just to sit with people in the desert. Why? And what does it have to do with your technology?' Ajay recalled Deva's description:

I watched them all from my window. They carry fold-up chairs and sit together by the allotments. I wanted to go but Mummy wouldn't let me.

'Because I wanted to be with them,' the Light said simply. 'I'd been on my own for a long time.'

I can relate to that. Ajay flicked at a long insect with five or six transparent wings as it bounced into the car.

'What does it mean?' Ajay asked as the insect fluttered away into the moving day. 'Your name?'

'A warrior,' the Light affirmed. 'My mother chose it.'

'Did you like it?'

'Do you like yours?'

'I guess.' Ajay shrugged. He explained his name was given to him by Lillie; he'd never questioned it because it gave him the life he'd always dreamed about.

'What about the one you were born with?'

'I dunno.' Ajay enjoyed the headrest. 'I just had to change it.'

'Are you glad you did?'

Ajay searched for a way to sweep away the question, because really, it was asking: are you glad you left the Side? Are you pleased you traded Karle for Ajay? And that was so loaded, because mostly, he was. But in another way, he realised it could have been the worst decision of his life.

'Where are your parents now?' he asked, digging for a distraction.

'Gone.'

Ajay nodded, swallowing back the sincerity of the Light's voice. *Maybe this is real.* Without understanding the internal workings of its artificial intelligence, he had nothing to believe otherwise. His brain was exploding. The technological advancement was incredible. *Grandma never mentioned it could do so much more. That's assuming she spoke to it in the same way.* Ajay sat bolt upright.

'Does Grandma talk to you like this?'

'Yes,' the Light said plainly.

And she never told me.

'So, you can talk to her now?' Ajay pressed in desperately on the device. 'Where is she? Is she safe? Alive? Can I speak to her?'

'Calm down.' It didn't move despite Ajay practically being on top of it, feeling the warmth of the device on his leg. 'You can't speak to her, but I can tell you, she's alive.'

'Why not?' Ajay insisted, thinking deeply. 'Surely if you can communicate in real time and your light can protect me from the heat of the sun, you can connect to other Guiding Light devices and I could speak to her, like through a Watch.'

'That would work, yes.'

'Seriously?' Ajay gasped. *I should have seen this sooner.* 'OK, put me through to her.'

'Ajay, I told you. I can't. She has no devices near her right now.'

Ajay slumped in his seat, coming down from the euphoria of possibility before his heart ached over the realisation.

'Hang on.' His mouth went dry. 'That means she's not at home.' He remembered every room was often blanketed in the glow of its light. 'Then, where is she?' Fear was crippling him, despite knowing the threat of Command taking her.

'Would it help you to know all the details right now?' the Guide asked.

'Maybe I could do something.'

'The best thing you can do for her right now is focus on this car.'

'How will that help?'

'To get back to her, when the time is right.'

'When is that?'

'Ajay.' The Light softened. 'Just take one thing at a time.'

Ajay picked up the seatbelt and twisted it around his hand, his stomach filling with angst. He just sat in the feeling of not knowing what to feel. From the moment he left Ace at his apartment to run and get to his grandma, he had been looking for ways to protect her, through Callum and his first failed escape from The Rogue. But truly, the heartbreaking reality was there was nothing he could do. He was totally and utterly powerless. To protect

CHAPTER
SIXTEEN

It had been a week since they lost Ajay and nothing had changed. Callum stared numbly at the base of the tree.

'Is that all you got?' Haro grunted, his stumpy stature just visible through Callum's goggles as he scaled down the Baffle tree, a small sack of fruit in his hand.

'There ain't much up there that's not black,' Callum retorted, reminding himself to swap his gloves after touching some fruit contaminated by poisonous toxlizard saliva.

'Must be more than that.' Haro's ropes were still around his solid waist as he riffled through Callum's limited pick.

'My arms got tired, alright?'

Haro seemed to grunt in acceptance of his poor performance. Callum was better at recruitment; he had the ability to spot any 'Unworthies' with unusual or unjust circumstances, but he mainly failed when it came to physical activities and stamina. Anyway, there was always something wrong with him, according to others. He was either too slow, or too weak, or too quiet. His father never rated him on anything; he never thought Callum was worth it. Not that Callum should care. *Not after what he did, leaving Mum and letting me, a ten-year-old kid, deal with his mess.*

Callum gathered up his fruit and transferred them to another bag. He tugged at the rope around his waist, before swapping his gloves.

'You don't have to go again.' Haro steadied his legs on a tree a few metres away.

'I do,' Callum responded, double-checking the rope.

'We need to find a compromise, Cal,' Haro said, still holding his weight against the tree. 'Otherwise we'll never have a plan.'

Callum looked around nervously, watching the other Climbers; some original, others desperate replacements like himself.

'You think they don't know?' Haro's familiar frown was visible enough through the night-vision goggles over Callum's balaclava. 'They know we're not in control.'

Callum didn't respond. He reeled inside at how little progress they and the others on The Rogue Committee had made earlier that day.

'Don't you dare take this away from me!' Ki was angered when Callum suggested not using explosives on Command.

'Away from you?' Callum lost his patience. 'This is about all of us, Ki.'

Ki breathed through his flaring nostrils.

'Look,' Callum had addressed the three of them – Ki, Haro and Marta. 'The other month, when we asked Ajay to be involved, he said something that I couldn't get out of my head.' Callum had felt a new awkwardness with the mention of Ajay's name, his refusal to comply still causing a sting. 'He said that us doing the same thing will only reap the same result.' He had watched Ki's legs wobbling, mirrored in his own voice. 'Just killing those at the top isn't going to change anything. If it's the system that's the problem, we must *show* people why.'

'How?' Marta asked, blowing her growing hair from her face.

'I don't know yet,' Callum had answered honestly, which in hindsight was bound to lead to a blow-out.

Ki barked out some aggressive, sarcastic comment.

'And how much closer are you with your plan?' Haro had interjected.

'At least I know we need to kill Command.'

'That's not knowing any more than Callum does.'

'I've basically got the explosives ready.'

'Well, fantastic, why don't you fly over there and smoke them up on your own?' Haro had started to boil.

'We're missing something here.' Marta's face was taut. 'What about the children? They're starving. Maybe it's best we turn ourselves in.'

'What?' All three men stared.

'I'd happily sacrifice myself so kids wouldn't die.' Marta's voice didn't waver; Callum knew she meant it. The community was her home. She was born into them and so she'd die for them.

'We're not at that point yet, Marta,' Ki snarled. 'Don't be so overdramatic.'

'Overdramatic? It won't be long until we're dealing with extreme malnourishment and I'm not willing to watch that happen. So, without a proper plan, I don't see another option.' Marta was right in Ki's face.

Callum had got between them at that point, reminding them that others in the camp were bound to hear their raised voices. The four of them then took a moment to breathe before Ki couldn't help but fill the silence.

'Maze would have agreed with me.' His jaw was tight.

Marta let out a noise of disgust.

'Maze is gone, he doesn't get a vote.' Haro gestured wildly.

'Right, well,' Ki fumbled, 'what are we supposed to do?'

Callum had frustratingly thought: *Aren't you supposed to answer that question, leader?* Instead, Callum invited them all to sit on the ground again, the air feeling more accommodating.

'I have some promising leads in the City,' Callum lied, 'including a Watch engineer whose information might be helpful to us in some way. So, give me some time with that.'

Callum hated deception; Fletch, the engineer, didn't know Callum was with The Rogue and so was no more use than a snapped climbing rope. Yet something in his gut kept him going back to his new friend.

'We need to talk about what happens after, too,' Haro had cut in.

'After what?' Ki sighed.

'If we win. We always said we'd take over, but how?' Haro stood and paced. 'The public isn't going to let us scrap the system or have any empathy with us, despite us doing our best to show them why we've done what we have.'

'That's why if we can avoid killing—' Callum tried.

'No. You don't understand. I must—' Ki had paused, frustrated tears welling in his small eyes before he'd quickly excused himself and walked away.

Haro's voice was muffled to Callum as he faded back into the present, the rope around his waist constricting his breathing. Haro didn't lower his voice as he cursed with every other word. 'Our indecision is why everyone is so freaking on edge.'

'Do you think anyone will try to take the lead?' Callum whispered, loosening his rope slightly.

'I wish,' Haro grunted. 'We're all as helpless as each other.'

'We don't have to be.' Callum scraped mud off his right boot.

'No, but people shouldn't starve, either.' Haro coughed as if the severity of the situation was playing even with his cold emotions. 'Let's find a compromise. No one is going to blame us for a bit of violence, Cal. Given the circumstances.' A new confidence was weaving into his tone.

Losing energy for it, Callum nodded, despite the anxiety sitting on his chest. *We can't do the same thing. Killing can't be the solution, because nothing good could come after.*

Haro seemed to hesitate before thudding his strong legs back on the ground. Leaving the rope tied around the tree, he moved towards Callum, his body pulling back as the rope around his waist grew taut. He took a breath, twisting his hands around the rope. 'Charl told me you asked about Ajay.'

Callum didn't respond, trying to understand why that even mattered.

'I couldn't do nothing,' Haro said, downcast. 'He was gone in the storm before I realised.'

'He wasn't going to help us anyway.' Callum shrugged his tense shoulders, trying to keep his voice steady.

'I wasn't talking about that.' Haro cleared his throat. 'You were both given a bad run.'

Callum almost laughed. *Haro always knows.* He knew that deep down, Callum cared about Ajay. His sadness over Ajay's disappearance wasn't about the plan, or survival, even though they kidnapped him for those reasons. *He was your first-ever friend, not your enemy.*

'Isn't that what we've all had?' Callum asked, swallowing any emotion and edging closer to the tree he was about to climb. 'A bad run?'

'Yeah.' Haro stepped back. 'But some worse than others.'

'You lost your family, what's worse than that?' Callum strained to pull a knot tighter and readjusted his goggles.

'Losing yourself,' Haro affirmed, as if the answer had been ready for a while. 'That kid stopped being himself way before he ended up here.'

Haro didn't say anything else, and Callum didn't watch as he heard the scuttling of Haro's little feet hurrying him up the tree. He stared at the smooth, dark outline of the trunk in front of him, hoping Haro was talking about Ajay and not him. *I never stopped being myself, not like Ajay did. He changed his name. He rejected his childhood. He abandoned his family for his obsession with merit and Glorification. I was never that selfish. Me leaving my mother to be here was not the same. I'd been through it and Command mistreated me. I couldn't merely exist in the Side after that. But, maybe, on some level, I owed it to my mother to let her know I was alive.* Callum closed his eyes, trying to banish the thought that always returned. The guilt of not going back and leaving her to stew in the unknown. *That was selfish, too. It felt easier. She would have begged me to come home but I belonged here. Trying to make a difference so no one would ever feel how they made me feel.*

Callum glanced up the tree. *There must be more than this. It can't all be questions, starvation, regrets, fires, death and unequal handouts of merit and power.* He fixed his feet on the trunk and strained to take himself up the tree.

'Please,' he whispered up wishfully at the stars as the ground got further away. 'Someone show me a plan.'

CHAPTER
SEVENTEEN

'Wow, that's slow.' Ajay's initial high of seeing the car's charging light faded with the day. 'That's going to take hours, probably all day tomorrow.' He pulled his balaclava from his face as the sun splintered its final rays into the vehicle and The Guiding Light sat on the dashboard.

'Well, it could be worse, given the circumstances.'

Ajay didn't waste energy on a reply, despite knowing it was right. The car was unlikely to charge quickly. It wasn't like the solar panels were in top condition. He'd even read it in the manual.

All solar panels degrade over time, microcracks form in their cells due to adverse weather and temperatures so it is advised to get your vehicle checked annually to ensure maximum performance.

And still, he let his hopes get carried away, somehow believing it would kick in with its normal unparalleled charging speed. He pulled himself from the car and grimaced at the long, skinny carcass on the ground. He crouched, wiping his tired eyes and lecturing himself to stop feeling depressed. *It's a miracle it's working at all.*

Ajay pulled the carcass of the silocat towards him. He considered the creature's face and closed its bead-like eyes. He grabbed its fist-sized head, cupping his hands over its tiny ears, held his breath and twisted. Hard. Ajay refused to think of the pain; he had little option with the fruit running out, and when it had tottered towards the car an hour earlier, he'd done it quickly. Kindly.

'Why are you disappointed?' the Light asked.

'I'm not.' Ajay didn't look up but discarded the head and flicked out the sharp wiper blade from his pocket. 'I'm just being impatient.'

After two dull days of twisting together frayed and damaged wires inside and outside the vehicle, he'd been hoping for some excitement. He pressed his thumbs into the exposed flesh of the creature and began pulling its skin down its body; it came away with a satisfying tear. It was a curse, he decided, his mind back on the car. *It's a dangerous thing to have a comfortable life founded on immediacy.* Everything and anything was available to him at the swoop of a drone. Maybe that was why his mother was always so patient; she'd never experienced that level of convenience; she only knew that things take time. His father, though, didn't share that quality naturally, though he seemed to calm down after Ajay, or rather *Karle*, left. *But being docile and patient is merely an excuse for procrastination. It's a smoother life to be efficient. Then again . . .* Ajay paused and looked up. *You can be efficient doing a job that needs to be done but it takes a long time. That's still productive.* He recalled how his frustration had got the better of him in the past. He swallowed and focused on skinning the cat; he picked up his wiper knife and cut into the cartilage between the meat and the skin.

Ajay berated himself out loud.

'What is it?' the Light asked, still sat by him, its device grooving into the sand.

'I should have wiped the blade.' Ajay, frustrated, rubbed the knife on his T-shirt, staring at the meat contaminated with sand and the cat's hair. He realised it was hardly the most sanitary of dining experiences, but he should try his best to avoid food poisoning or having to pick pieces of stray hair from his mouth.

'It's not like you're an expert at it.'

'And you are?'

'I did it now and again.'

Right, brilliant. He didn't want to ask for any more help. *I can figure this one out on my own.* He held the animal over his knee and with a final strong tug, its skin came off nicely.

'I'll clean it.' He stood.

'And discard its organs,' the Light added, hovering upwards with him.

'Right,' Ajay stuttered. *I should probably do that before cleaning it. Damn.* 'I'll get the fruit shards burning too.' He riffled through his sack to find the pile of dried fruit skin.

As night drew in, Ajay appreciated the heat of the burning fruit as he polished off the last of the meat, chucking the bone into the pile. So, another thing he'd discovered – silocat was delicious. Not quite as tasty or satisfying as the fruit, but it rivalled a camel burger. He almost couldn't believe how well it was going, this whole survival thing. He was smashing it – it would be about that time in the working day when he'd see his daily merit count hit its target. Something caught in his throat. He glanced at The Guiding Light. He didn't want to give it the glory, but it was the one who knew stuff; how to cook the silocat and the encouragement that he could catch it; it was the one who got the bolts off the car and kept him company while he fixed the wiring. It told him to burn the fruit in the first place, but it was him, Ajay, who knew to use the broken window shards to reflect the sun and start the fires. So he deserved some credit. It did know more than him, though. There was an unnerving feeling settling on him as he found it hard to admit his knowledge was inferior. He'd always been cleverer than the people around him. It was a belittling position not to be.

Ajay never would have trusted it with his life but over the last three days, he'd seen more of the Light's knowledge around, well, everything. The car, surviving, the best times of day to work. It was also refreshing to have someone to talk to who didn't have a vendetta against Command. It allowed a calmness to thrive, away from the chaos of the City and the scars people had from it. His conversations with the Light had centred around a few main topics: food, solar panels and batteries, Grandma and its life before – something Ajay was becoming deeply invested in. He straightened up, looking over the lilac sky, and spotted some clouds in the far distance. A storm? Hopefully travelling the other way. The air didn't feel humid enough; then again, the chill as night approached could be deceptive. The car would hopefully be enough shelter if it did arrive.

Warming his hands on the fire, he held the diary up to The Guiding Light.

'Shall we?'

'Now is as good a time as any,' it responded.

Ajay was beginning to like this girl. As she got older, she got sneakier. She'd planted a recording device in the living room of her house where her father held meetings with other resource workers. As a result, she retold the intricate details of how the Revolution was planned. It was historical gold. But it was unlikely people would care; tired, middle-aged, malnourished resource workers gathering in a small, dishevelled room wasn't anywhere near as glamorous as the rally cries, the valiant marches and the victory dances Command chose to focus on in their promo videos.

It seemed, though, that Osgar had hacked off the Revolution planners. Especially Hecter, whom Ajay pictured as a meaty man with muscles that made you step back.

'You're an absolute lunatic!'

Deva's attempt at a deep, masculine voice failed her as she described seeing Hecter, red-faced, marching towards Osgar and the crowd sitting on the sandy plain.

'You come here, from nowhere, and think you have the right to dictate what happens to our lives. These people need to fight.'

Osgar was calm. I remember because I expected him to maybe lash out or just ignore Hecter. But I clearly didn't know him as well as I thought I did. He just rested a hand on Hecter's shoulder gently and said: 'Violence won't lead to victory.'

Her voice went higher at that point – bouncier, light. Ajay concluded she'd got that imitation close, considering how The Guiding Light sounded through its device. *Then again, it's unlikely his voice back then vaguely resembled its current tone.* Yet another detail that kept bringing the question back; he couldn't even start to think how an actual consciousness could be coded into a device.

Ajay's attention turned back to Deva as her dictation dramatised:

Hecter let out a roar and went to punch Osgar's face, and no one stopped him, and me and the others in the crowd, we were on our feet, and not even my father tried to stop the first punch, though other resource workers did jump in to stop Hecter from going for Osgar again, who was now on the ground with blood around his nose – deep, dark blood – flowing and dripping around his face like a crazy big red splatter of paint.

'You didn't hit back.' Ajay hit pause as the night sky became littered with stars. 'Why not?'
'Violence or grumbling wouldn't have helped anyone.'
'You wouldn't have been helpless if you'd fought, though.'
'No, just angry and making someone else bleed instead.'

Ajay expressed how the guy would have deserved it. Hecter should have controlled himself, despite Osgar obviously causing havoc with their Revolution effort. It was a confusing feeling. The Revolution was a good cause, it led to a greater Tulo. Why wouldn't it want that? Ajay thought of the City, its wonders, not its faults. It was a glorious development from the world Deva lived in, so the violence in the Revolution must have been worth it. He stood, his knees clicking as he stretched his legs and lifted his eyes.

'A friend told me once . . .' Ajay paused, thinking of Haro in The Rogue with his dumpy stature and lazy eye, '. . . that sporadic violence creates chaos but strategic violence creates opportunity.' He appreciated the bright yellow of the moon as it crept into the darkening sky. 'Do you believe that?'

'Does a good person do bad things?'

'If it's to protect someone or themselves, then yes. That doesn't make them bad.' Ajay imagined what he would do if someone attacked Genni, or Grandma, or – his jaw jolted – Ace.

'There's more strength in taking the punches than throwing them. There are more graceful ways to show someone to change.'

Its words caused a wedge in Ajay's throat. All he could see were Ace's punches and the ones he threw back. He fixed on the moon, trying to let it captivate him so the image of Ace cradling his blood-spraying arm would leave. But it wouldn't; even the moon seemed to carry a red haze over it.

He was distant. Outcast. Lost. He breathed in the gathering night air, damper than usual. He looked back at the horizon to see the storm attacking the east of the desert where lightning forked down the canvas of the sky.

'Genni would love this,' he said unthinkingly at the storm, before sitting back by the charging car and glancing at some exposed wiring he'd fixed. 'She always said she'd like to come out here. To see more of it.'

'Why didn't she?' The Light glowed.

'No one ever did,' Ajay said curtly. 'Command advised against it. Dangerous.' He shrugged it off. 'There'd never be enough time, anyway.'

'People are always caught up.' The Light orientated itself towards the storm. 'But when you get out here, all of that melts away.'

'I dunno.' Ajay put his hands over his knees, his back firm against the car. 'Some things can't just disappear.'

'True,' the Light agreed. 'But the stillness, the rest – it helps.'

'Yeah, it helps,' Ajay choked. Before he could embrace any emotion, the ground started to rumble. *The storm. But it can't be – it's not close enough.* The shake vibrated through the car onto his back. It was only when he heard the patter of small feet and picking sounds that fear took hold.

Ajay flinched up at the car roof to see four eyes and a snout-like nose peering down at him. He scrambled away and the car was quickly engulfed by a colony of black, furry creatures with blue stripes glowing along their backs.

CHAPTER
EIGHTEEN

Ajay could feel it. A dead weight of dread dropping down the entire length of his body. Despite the innate fear as he scrambled from the car and watched the animals scurry quickly over the vehicle, all Ajay could focus on was the work he'd put in. The hours that could be wasted. The feeling intensified as he saw them chewing through the exposed wires on the roof that ran to the batteries; the wires he'd spent days reconnecting.

Hot expletives fired from his mouth and he grabbed The Guiding Light from the air, bounding forward and roaring at one that hung over the passenger seat window.

'Don't!'

The device's advice was muffled as the creature turned to Ajay, hissing through its keen teeth; its black fur stood on end and the blue lines across its back glowed with fierce warning.

He whacked it with the device, knocking it straight to the sand and the bang of its contact joined the coming thunder. It was no sooner that Ajay hit the creature again, killing it, that another launched itself off the car towards him. Quick enough to see it coming, Ajay turned and used the device as a shield. His body was forced to the ground and his biceps buckled under the weight as the creature tried to swipe and bite around the device, its eyes enraged.

'Let go,' The Guiding Light demanded. Ajay didn't listen as the first drops of rain splattered into the chaos. He held his neck back to avoid a claw in the face.

'Ajay, let go.'

He knew there was nothing else he could do. There was a moment of clarity as he looked at the hologram beneath the raving desert animal. *You can't help me. I don't know if you always can.* Ajay breathed out his doubt and relaxed his arms above his chest. His heart almost stopped as the device jolted towards him, along with the creature, before it took off skywards, throwing the beast across the sand. Ajay watched from the ground as The Guiding Light twisted itself back towards the car, still riddled with them, their blue stripes now luminescent through the increasing battering rain and stormy mist. But the glow of The Guiding Light was stronger. Just as thunder clapped above, a ripple appeared to shoot from the device accompanied by a sharp, high-pitched whistle; Ajay threw his hands to his ears and grimaced as he saw the creatures dart away, leaving only the mutilated vehicle behind.

When the noise stopped, Ajay jumped up and ran around the car, reeling at the damage to the wires. Several moments passed as he got drenched in the rain, staring coldly at it. Scraping a hand through his shoulder-length hair and over his shaggy, short beard, he resisted the urge to cry. *So much work.*

'Get in the car.' The device still held an unfamiliar, stern tone.

'Why?' Ajay leaned against the car, head in hands.

'Ajay, get in the car now.' It zoomed past him.

Ajay glared towards it, seeing another crowd of whatever they were, but their blue stripes were dull and only just distinguishable through the rain. They were barrelling towards them as lightning stabbed at the ground. Ajay didn't hesitate and threw himself into the car and cowered inside. For what felt like hours, he sheltered from the storm while yelling at the Guide when another group of creatures sprinted towards them. It would then let out its noise, scattering them back into the expanse of the desert. As he experienced the device fight them with ferocity and strength, all he could think about was something he'd never considered before. *Could this thing be a weapon?*

The next morning, Ajay felt safe to assess the damage as a post-storm chill blew in from the east. After the storm had passed, The Guiding Light had filled him in; the creatures were memepanyas, small nocturnal creatures who were attracted to electrical charges in plants, machinery or from lightning, so they were particularly active during a storm. They'd bled the car dry. Ajay smacked the bonnet. He breathed; eyes closed.

'Don't give up.' The device sat itself down. 'We can still do this.'

'I've got to start again.' Ajay stood, feeling the frustration twist and turn in his gut. *I'm sorry, Grandma. It's going to take me longer. Always letting people down. Ace. Genni. No. Stop.*

'Then let's start again,' it said. Its stern tone from the previous night had returned to being as soft as the sand.

Ajay's brain felt as frazzled as the frayed wires as he tried to process the setback, its trigger to his grief, and how the device's technology could still surprise, delight and scare him all at the same time.

'We may as well get going, while it's still cool.'

It made a good point, so Ajay shook it all off and got back to work.

He had grown to like it over the last three weeks. It was the only thing keeping him grounded from a darkness he wouldn't be able to control. A pit of anxiety over Grandma. A howl of grief over Ace. The frustrating mystery of the Guide. The car had been his saving grace.

So, what would happen if he fixed it? Would it all come back? The thought of having nothing to fix scared him. Maybe he wanted another storm so the memepanyas would come back. As he looked at the settled horizon, the moon starting to emerge in the night, Ajay knew he'd probably done it. Unlike the previous attempts, he had a genuine belief it would work. There'd been many false starts after he'd spent five days fixing the wires and got it charging again. They were all half-hearted chances based on a feeble hope that no other mechanism was degraded or frayed. As he pulled more insulation off a spare power cable he'd found in the glove box, he looked through the windscreen at the starter button inside. Its round silver trim was twinkling under the glow of The Guiding Light sitting on the bonnet. Ajay imagined the moment when he'd hit that button, and the car would shine into life like a fresh, colourful billboard flooding over a City street. It would be euphoric and disappointing, satisfying and devastating all at once.

Because after it was done, what would be left?

Only dark thoughts: Grandma or Ace haunting his existence like a repetitive song with a low promoter score.

He transferred the tube of insulation over the final tail of the exposed electric motor, taking longer than he needed to. Surely he'd be the first to fix a vehicle in the thick of the desert. *A record setter.* He grunted lethargically. *You've set records, mate. Bad ones.*

'What is it?' The Light's voice mirrored the smooth layers of the evening sky.

'Nothing.' Ajay squinted at the newly insulated motor. 'I think we might have done it this time.'

'What are you waiting for, then?'

'Also nothing.'

He hesitated, words on the end of his tongue. He couldn't express his gratitude. For all his vexation towards it, The Guiding Light had made some awful days bearable, and listening to more of Deva's diary had been a welcome distraction.

He jumped into the front seat.

'OK.' He reached forward and held his breath.

The click of the button was satisfying as it brought a moment of stillness. The desert breeze whistled through the windowless frames.

The car coughed and spluttered into life. The grunts of the engine eventually flowed into a beautiful mechanical purr falling over Ajay like the drop of a satisfying chorus. The dashboard lit up, all its dials and numbers luminescent as the car's fans lifted it off the ground and Ajay sat speechless.

'Go.' The Guiding Light erupted with excitement. 'Try the accelerator.'

Ajay fumbled and floored the pedal. The car jerked forward, lurching his body with it before it whizzed through the sand, grains blowing like a cape behind it.

Ajay felt joy take over his entire body as he beamed at The Guiding Light and embraced more of the hot breeze as they cut through the desert towards the mountains.

'I can't believe it.' He gripped onto the steering wheel. 'I can't believe it.'

'And now, onwards,' The Guiding Light declared childishly, its glowing arm pointing towards the horizon. Ajay let out a small laugh before it hit him.

Fixing the car isn't an end, it's a beginning.

I'm going to see the mountains.

CHAPTER
NINETEEN

The water was dark, foreboding and unknown.

Ajay didn't know what lay beneath, nor how far it went. As he sank deeper, staring into the chasm, he felt the weight of its frightening magnificence. But he wasn't scared. He would have expected to feel daunted by a dark, ominous abyss. What existed down there? If anything? What could come up and drag him down? Even with those questions in his mind, he was ecstatic to be in the water. As his oxygen wavered, he flipped his legs, flexing his body back and forth, higher and higher, relishing the touch of new, cool water on his arms. Cutting through the lake's shiny skin, the brightness of the sun warmed his face in the open air. Now on the surface, he floated serenely with his eyes closed. *This is bliss.*

Everything around him was taking him captive. He couldn't help but revel in it. The beauty of the mountains and the lake nestled between them like a glass cupped in a bigger power's hands. The freshness of the water, so unlike any chemical-infused pool in the City, or the rivers that were risky to swim in.

Everyone should enjoy this. Ace would have loved it.

An image came to life in his mind; he saw Ace swimming in the lake, whistling at Pearl as she makes her way in, giving him the finger jovially. Genni takes her time to get into the water, and Ajay chases after her, grabbing her by the waist, spinning her and hearing her squeal as he carries her into the water's grasp and they both splash forward together. Jaxson and Mila are bobbing close by, laughing at Blake who's trying to tread water while keeping his Tulo Ale can above the surface.

Ajay's eyes sprang open to reality, the sun and sadness hot on his chest. It wasn't until it moved behind a wisping cloud that he decided to swim back to the cobbled shore, where The Guiding Light sat by the resting car.

'Amazing, isn't it?' Its light grew taller.

'Yeah,' Ajay said quietly, sitting next to it, digging his feet into the stones by the vacant lake that was still, as if he'd never disturbed it.

'Are you OK?'

Ajay nodded. He couldn't explain the pain of their absence. It was always there, but there were moments when it stung so strongly it stole his breath.

Time passed as his skin dried and he dressed again, thinking of all the things he was missing, but then he considered what else he had discovered. The lake. Beyond the plain stretch of desert, up in the mountains, there was water and vegetation, including sweet plant leaves the Guide had encouraged him to try. There was more than anyone in the City ever spoke or cared about.

We should care. And then there's Grandma. Seeing the others so vividly in his imagination brought him back to her.

'Are you sure?' the Light asked again.

'I've been selfish.' Ajay tugged his T-shirt down. 'We fixed the car and I came here. I've just forgotten her.' He breathed back the urge to slam the open car door, perplexed that he prioritised his curiosity over Grandma.

Taking a moment to gaze at the high mountaintops, he thought about the journey he'd taken to get there; the heat, the noise, the jolting, the broken sleep. It wasn't the most comfortable way to travel, but it was amazing to see all that space. The wildlife seemed to be increasing, too; he'd seen wild lynxes, unidentified animals in the distance, more desert rodents and varying species of dry plants. What he hadn't seen, though, and he couldn't decide if it was unnerving or not, was any sign of Command. Not one resource plane. They might have figured out The Rogue's interceptions and the way they were smuggling people in, but they'd have to come out for resources sometime. Ajay had wondered where he would hide when they did, but he needn't worry about it, because despite his desire to see more, he couldn't stay.

'I've got to get back.' He forced himself into the car, visions of finding Grandma spinning around his mind.

The Light said nothing but floated in through the rear window.

'And I'll find her and bring her home.' Ajay hovered his thumb over the start button. 'I'll go to the Side and ask for information . . .' He pressed down hard and the car spluttered. 'Or maybe I should find that woman, but I don't even know her name.'

He thought of the woman with the birthmark as he peered into the rear-view mirror; the Guide was glowing but no noise came from it.

'Although there is Command. The drones will be everywhere and programmed to detect my face.' The steering wheel shook beneath his trembling fingers as the fans pulled the car up from the ground. 'I could wear my balaclava.' Ajay guarded his face as sand wisped up onto the seats. 'I don't know how to get into the City but we'll find a way.' He readied his foot over the accelerator. 'We'll find her and sort this out. You can help me.' He glared back through the rear-view mirror, a fire starting on his tongue. 'Would you answer me?'

'Ajay,' the Guide responded softly. 'I think you need to take a minute.'

He twisted his body round to the back seat abruptly.

'Why?'

'So you can come up with a better plan. Then, when the time is right, we go back together, even stronger than we are right now.'

Several, soft moments passed between them; Ajay hated that it had a point.

'I just need to make it up to her,' he said quietly.

'You will. In ways you can't even begin to imagine, but when you are ready.'

Ajay swallowed. He turned back and stroked the rattling steering wheel, battling to tame the beast in his thoughts. *You can't be selfish. But what if it's right? What if I'm not ready?*

Eventually he spoke back into the rear-view mirror. 'You promise we'll go back.'

'I promise.'

'And we'll find a way to save her?'

'Not just her.'

Ajay couldn't bring himself to even try to process what it was insinuating. *I'm no hero.*

'Let's go for a walk.' It lifted itself out through the window of the car and headed towards the lake, but not without calling back, 'Bring the diary.'

CHAPTER
TWENTY

As Ajay walked away and considered the cracks on the dry, rocky ground, he looked back at the car and wondered if it was the most rewarding work he'd ever done. It meant something to him and he couldn't figure out why. It was the best yet most meritless thing.

Leaving it behind, he marched on, pulling the fabric of the jacket he'd found over his shoulders. He followed the Light along a small creek where blooming plants started to creep along the ground; he watched toxlizards scuttle up the dry mountainside as more birds swooped above. As they emerged from a valley, the air tasted fresh as Ajay saw a memepanya scurry across the space in front of him. He paused, watching it run into the clasp of a large leaf which suddenly snapped over the creature's body.

'Did that just eat it?'

'No,' the Light seemed to laugh.

Ajay scowled.

'It's a mutualistic relationship. The Nadeo plant protects it from predators while it sleeps and the memepanya provides the plant with a small electrical charge, helping it grow faster.'

'So the memepanyas are only active in the evening or at night?'

'Mostly,' it confirmed, moving forward, 'or when there's a particularly strong storm coming.'

Ajay relaxed. *The car's safe, for now.* He couldn't bear the thought of them sucking it dry.

'You'll love this.' The Guiding Light streamed ahead of him. A raging rhythm of moving water invaded as they passed through another valley. Ajay was forced to a stop. Sharp fear stole his breath. He watched the Light move towards the large animal, big enough to ram him against the valley wall.

'It's only a helapin.' The Guiding Light moved towards it. 'Completely harmless.'

It was the size of a camel but with a purple tint to its skin. Collecting himself, Ajay stepped tentatively forward, and then he saw beyond the helapin. Fresh green plants hung down into a huge circular space, probably half the size of a City ring. Ajay stroked the tips of petals from blooming flowers as he listened to the sounds of creatures flying, skipping and calling above the roar of a sparkling waterfall.

Genni. Like the one in her painting.

Ajay slowly closed his mouth. He glanced back at The Guiding Light who was still by the helapin; he joined it. Ajay followed the gorgeously smooth arch of its lilac back and the small delicate tufts of hair along its neck. The eyes, too. There were six of them, not predatory but soft and gentle. Ajay lifted his free hand and stroked its back, its skin like velvet.

'I've never seen anything like this,' he said quietly, watching the Guide rest on the beast's back.

The Light then led Ajay towards the water. A bird flapped through his view. Ajay followed the creature, about the size of a Kakafruit, and found it resting on a branch, drilling its gold beak into the wood of the tree; moving so fast, it was hard to distinguish the yellow and purple spots throughout its mottled brown feathers. He heard the faint mumble of The Guiding Light's voice, not taking it in. As he moved forward, he spotted more of the life-giving fruit from the biggest tree, having fallen from similar trees around him.

'Has anyone been here before?' Ajay took his eyes up the waterfall that came down from the mountaintop into a glass pool.

'A few.'

'But surely Command explored the desert?' Ajay thought of the videos he'd seen on his father's Watch, and his own afterwards; the history after the Revolution, the building of a better Tulo.

'Yes, but other than the raw resources, it's not much use to them.'

'Progress is Strength,' he whispered; his mind turned back to the inevitable. Going back to the City. *How are we going to do this?* He sat cautiously by the pool and anxiously watched the felkar in the trees. It seemed to disappear, not fazed by his presence. Ajay fished the diary from his sack and instinctively wiped sand from its screen.

'Can't you just tell me what happened?' Ajay lightly flung the diary on the ground, its clatter disturbing the birds. 'We haven't got time for this. We should start our journey back.'

'I could.' The Light seemed to choke. 'But this next part is hard to talk about. So I'd prefer you to listen.'

He was waiting for it. The crux, the reason, the climax of the story.

It wasn't only the Revolution, but something else. Why else would she bury it? Assuming that's how it ended up where Ajay found it beneath the hugging tree. Ajay had plodded through Deva's in-depth account of the Revolution while he was fixing the car; the first night, how the rebels kidnapped the government's children to force a surrender; the resulting battle, the victory and the aftermath. Deva was a brave kid. She was celebrating in her last entry; they'd moved into the skyscrapers once occupied by the 'horrible enemy and their children', who were now 'safe and sound in the underground warehouse, until we decide what to do with them'. Ajay grimaced at the harrowing tone of her voice before curiosity held him.

'It's funny about Osgar, though, that man keeps disappearing,' she explained.

'Where did you go?' Ajay asked as the midday sun shone and he dangled his feet into the refreshing pool.

'Away.' The device shielded his head from the sun. 'When I came back to see people, it was brief.'

'How did you escape when they came for you?'

'My friends were loyal.' It flew down to sit by Ajay's hand, its glow mirroring the pool's shimmer. 'And clever.'

Ajay imagined a tribe of people working together to get him underground into someone's house or something.

'Each time it happens, I can't help but smile,' Deva said. *'But then it got hard . . .'*

'Sounds like she had a soft spot for you.' Ajay's smile was stolen by her next words.

They're planning to kill them all. Not only the old government and their families but Osgar's friends, too . . . I don't know if he and Father have ever spoken but Father and the others hate him beyond belief . . .

There was a pause.

Sorry, got to go, Mother's calling.

It went dead as the time stamp ticked down to zero on that entry.

'What . . .' Ajay fell silent and stared at The Guiding Light. He'd always known it, there was a reason a man's consciousness got stuck in that thing. *The answer is coming.*

He didn't hesitate, tapping on the penultimate entry and pressing play.

Listeners! So much has happened since I last spoke. It's been about six months. I'm now twelve and a half. I'm learning quicker than ever before. I have a teacher now, you see. Her name is Mrs Sully and we learn at an Education Centre. It's currently on the fifth floor of the third skyscraper but in the new city, it'll be an entire building. There'll be lots of them. In fact, I borrowed my father's camera the other day and sneaked into his new office and took a picture of the sketched plans for the City. I've given you a copy, have a look!

Ajay peered over the device, seeing a document appear, which he scrolled through; his intellect feasted as he recognised familiar places.

Don't you just love how the City will be laid out in one big circle? Oh, and with a sky train that spirals around it, dropping everyone off fast. And there'll be pipes deep underground, pulling water from the mountains. It's crazy but it's happening. I've been watching it all being built in the south from my window.

Ajay impatiently moved the player along, Deva's voice squeaking until he steadied it again.

As usual, he kept turning up every other day and then disappearing without a trace. But he hasn't been seen for a couple of weeks now. There's talk that he's not coming back and people are silly to be sad. I'm not sad and I know the truth.

The truth? His eyes locked on to The Guiding Light, which seemed to be vacant, its figure ebbing in a dim light.

It happened two weeks yesterday.

What did?

The Commanders had made up their minds. Tulo could not move forward while those of the old government survived: 'Their idleness will stifle our progress and that would make us weak.' That's what I heard one of them say through the recording after I sneakily retrieved my device from the meeting room. There were a few ideas thrown back and forth about how to do it; set fire to the warehouse, abandon them in the country; have an execution ceremony. And of course, those who followed Osgar were also part of it. If they followed his way of rest and laziness rather than technological and societal progress, Tulo would never reach its full potential. They too made us vulnerable.

As I listened to the recording of their latest meeting, I held Floppsy (remember my rabbit?) tightly for the first time in months and then I heard the soothing, calming voice of the man with no shoes.

'Please. Don't kill them.' I could sense a tremor in his voice; a sadness sitting uncomfortably in his throat. I heard the shuffles of chairs as the meeting's attendees processed his appearance. Until Brent burst out in rage.

Ajay felt his stomach drop as he listened to Deva's description of them beating him. The Guiding Light still didn't move, even when a small bird landed beside it, flapping its blue wings. Deva continued:

'Take me instead.' That's the words he said. I promise you, it's right here on the recording. He told them to take him instead, which I'm not stupid enough to realise was the best option for everyone.

Her voice turned to mumbles as Ajay stood and paced. He couldn't process it quick enough, an overwhelming

feeling locked itself across his chest. 'Why would you . . .'
He held his tongue when he heard a noise.

A sniffle. A grunt. A low, soft whimper.

He fixed on The Guiding Light.

It was weeping.

Ajay was caught helpless, feeling the weight of it. He
moved himself closer, letting its light mask over him.

'What happened to you?' he asked softly.

'Listen.'

Ajay picked up the diary with shaky fingers.

*It didn't take them long to arrange it. The plan, I mean.
It was the right decision, even though I still felt sad. If
they killed him in secret, his friends would believe he'd
abandoned them and come back to the City's plan.
Because what else would they do? After all, those
people still have the potential to contribute towards a
greater Tulo. It was even better than killing them all.*

Deva struggled.

*I can't tell you all the details, but I watched. I watched
as they took him to the forest. It was only an hour
later when I saw it burn.*

Ajay froze. *What burned?*

The largest tree.

The device quickly died with a lack of charge. They
both sat in solemn silence. Ajay tried to control his
wobbling lips. He sacrificed himself for his friends *and*

the monstrous government who, through their greed for water, had let men, women, children and *babies* die.

The feeling of his own inadequacy dropped on him harder than a lightning bolt. He had let so many people down. He was so Unworthy. He killed his best friend and yet the consciousness in that device had been sacrificial enough to die for people who didn't even know it. Ajay had always known he'd been selfish. But he'd ignored it. He'd buried his shame deep because he didn't know how to change.

'Ajay, it's OK.' The Guiding Light was weeping with him. 'It's OK.'

Ajay fell on his side, no noise coming out, his cries suddenly so deep and strong.

CHAPTER
TWENTY-ONE

Karle held his grandma's kind eyes as she stroked the side of his face. Her fingers were soft. Her voice calm. The storm outside rattled the windows. Her greying hair and ageing face glowed in the light of the device after it had finished its story. Karle breathed, his seven-year-old body shutting down into sleep.

'Goodnight, Karle.' She lifted herself from the wicker stool and kissed his head.

'Grandma . . .' He twisted in bed and stopped her at the door.

'Yes?' she smiled.

'Why don't we get as much merit?'

'That, my boy, is a bigger conversation for tomorrow.' She grabbed the door handle. 'But I will tell you this – there's one thing that's always better than merit.'

'What?'

'Each other,' she said simply before leaving him to a restful night's sleep.

'You OK?' The Guiding Light or Osgar asked after some time. Ajay was lying on his back, feet dipped in the pool; he was remembering, thinking, regretting. He didn't have the head space to respond, but turned his attention back to his uncertainty as he watched two birds dance together in the late afternoon light.

In one way, he'd convinced himself he'd got caught up in the device's emotion and everything he'd been bottling up for months had popped. *I might believe this. The evidence was there. Deva could have made it up. But I can't think why she'd have done that.* If it were true, Command were bigger crooks than he thought. Sure, the living Hevases and those at the top weren't around then, but they were celebrating a system that began with murder and the intention for more of it.

If it wasn't for Osgar, many generations of the City wouldn't even be alive.

'I need a drink.' Ajay sat up, holding his forehead.

'We should get back to the car anyway.' The device floated back towards the valley.

'Right.' Ajay remembered; the memepanyas would be out soon and he needed that car.

He splashed water over his face and caught his red eyes in the reflection. *It's time to change.* He puffed out air and gathered himself. Standing, he took a last glance at the green life around him, not able to process the overwhelming sense of peace he felt there. Closing his eyes, he listened; the sweet tweets of birds harmonised with the water pattering into the pool. It was, for the most part, the calmest place he'd ever been.

'Thank you,' he whispered to no one, before following Osgar out into the valley.

On their walk back, his mind a little clearer, Ajay realised he still didn't know something.

'How are you like this now?' Ajay watched his step over the running creek. 'You died? I doubt Deva knew you became what you are now, right?'

'No, she never knew,' it said as they turned the corner back towards the car. 'They came back for me.'

'Who did?'

'The organisation who sent me.'

Ajay paused.

'What do you mean?'

'I was sent here for a purpose, Ajay, by *them* to help people like you.'

'But how did they get you, a person, into a device like that?' he asked, his thirst for technological insight stronger than the other details.

'Something beyond what I can even understand.' It halted in the air as they grazed the lake. 'They programmed my consciousness into a device and replicated it – over and over.'

Ajay's brain suddenly went into overdrive, trying to decipher how that would even work. *How has someone been able to program an artificial intelligence that replicates a person? But the biggest question is: How do you do that so that every replicated device is essentially the same person? Because they'd have to sync with each other, where's the central base of information, how can they all react to their surroundings in the same way? I don't even know how it can do all that it does.*

'You said the diary would tell me how you work.'

'No, I told you it would tell you more about me. And it did.'

'But the things you're describing and the things you can do – they're beyond even X-Level Technology and

Command haven't even mastered that yet.' Ajay squatted by the lake, remembering what he'd read about X-Level; it still didn't make any sense. 'Don't you feel stuck?' he asked, eventually.

'Why would I feel stuck?' Osgar's tone lifted. 'They have allowed me to be with people, forever.'

Ajay considered how sobering that attitude was as he dipped his fingers into the still lake and smiled. 'So, it really was worth the walk.'

The Light laughed quietly. 'It was.'

Ajay let the fading sun mask his face and his mind turned back to the Side. They weren't perfect, but he realised he had been blinded by his selfish ambitions. They all worked solidly; they still had dreams, they still were driven, and sometimes they could be just as selfish, but there was something about the way they'd prioritise each other.

'Why did you say, in the stories, that the path of the City leads to destruction?'

'Striving for the wrong thing can kill you.' It settled beside him. 'Which is better, a life alone or one you share with others?'

'Just because you're gaining merit doesn't mean you're alone.'

'That's true.'

'Everyone wants to belong.'

'That's true, too. Being Glorified in and of itself isn't bad.'

Ajay wiped his nose, his head feeling scrambled.

'But we can't just work for other people,' Ajay sighed. He was tired.

'It isn't so much what you do, but *why* you do it.'

'That doesn't work.'

'Why not?'

'Because we are all fundamentally selfish. Even when we go to educate people, to *help them*, we're only doing it for the merit. So even if you think you have the right heart, it's still for you. There's no way out of that, it's who we are.'

'Do you really believe that?'

'I don't know what I believe.' Ajay sighed again, scratching at his long, wet hair. 'So the people who sent you . . . Where are they now? How far from here?'

'There's so much more I want to tell you,' Osgar insisted. 'But there are more pressing matters at hand.'

It hovered over the lake, skimming across it as if it were running on water. 'We must get you back. There are people waiting for you,' it echoed around the mountainside.

Grandma. Ajay sprang from his heels and jogged around the lake, meeting the device back at the car. He swung his body into the front seat and commanded the engine to start but he immediately cut it off again.

'What are you doing?' Osgar sat on the dashboard, shaking with the car's vibration as it powered down.

'I need a plan to get back in,' he almost whispered. He couldn't simply walk into the City.

'There's more than that to think about.'

'What do you mean?'

'You need to help Command.'

Ajay grunted, his hands tight on the steering wheel. 'Isn't Grandma our priority?'

'Not in the first instance.'

'What?' His jaw tightened.

'Ajay, for what's coming, Grandma won't be the one in the greatest danger.'

A nausea stirred up in Ajay's stomach. The Rogue. *Genni. His friends.*

'OK.' Ajay didn't let go of the wheel. 'What do we do?'

'We have time and we have a map.'

It took him a moment to remember; Deva's diary had a map of the City's designs. He threw the diary onto the dashboard, letting it charge in the setting sun's rays.

'A lot of things don't make sense right now.' Osgar's voice felt like gravity. 'You need to trust me, but Ajay . . .'

His brain was a shoal of hyperactive fish; so much movement but nothing distinctive coming out. *I can't trust him in everything, I don't really know him and I don't think I truly believe him. But, maybe, in time, I could. But what is he? Who is he? Where did he come from?*

'Ajay, you need to move. Now.' Osgar's urgency merged with the sudden shake of sound. Ajay flicked his head to the left; an army of memepanyas was avalanching down the mountainside. There was no hesitation. The car was gone before the creatures made it to the rippling lake.

CHAPTER
TWENTY-TWO

He'd trusted his gut and it may have delivered. *I never expected that.*

Callum hardly noticed the clunk of the plane landing and the grumpy whirr of its engines shutting down. His body lurched with the plane's impact on ground, his hand instinctively reaching for the strap above his head. He steadied himself on a box and thought deeply, reflecting on his trip to the City and what Fletch, the Watch engineer, had said.

Get to Ki and the others, fast. But the boxes. OK, sort them with the Distributors first. There are only two boxes.

Callum hadn't registered it fully; only two, medium-sized cardboard boxes of food and supplies had been snuck onto the plane. He scanned around the cargo, spotting a water barrel to the right of the industrial plane door. *Two boxes.* He rubbed the skin around his eyes, guessing only one person in the City was available to smuggle supplies. He knew there were fewer Rogue pilots too. Command had stepped up on their interrogation techniques, fewer people were getting through the reliability test and all the plane trips were limited.

Why weren't they passing anymore? Anxiety. A growing sense that The Rogue had no control, no plan, and they were never going to win. They're buckling under the pressure. The androids are probably picking up on it. Or they are being tortured.

Callum swallowed the thought.

We need more people. There are no people. But we've come a long way in the last ten weeks.

Callum stayed still, not ready to move, the sticky messiness of everything gluing him down.

But there's hope. A gut instinct has become something bigger.

'Oi, come on.' The plane door was hanging open, the settling engines blowing sand in as the pilot held Callum with pleading eyes. 'You want them to catch us?'

He didn't respond, but quickly stacked the two boxes and passed them to the pilot, whose name had disappeared from his mind.

Dismissively, he rolled the water barrel down the length of the plane and shortly followed it out into the orange expanse of desert. The pilot grunted with his labour, reaching inside the plane. He pulled out a battered, steel trolley and handed Callum an old Watch.

'Next Tuesday?' The pilot ran back to the cockpit. Callum had nodded in response before lifting the barrel and boxes onto the trolley, noting the degradation of its tyres. *Please don't get stuck.* He exhaled deeply, tapping on the Watch and ordering the trolley forward. Its wheels shot out sand as it bumbled over the plain towards the west side of the forest. Callum walked behind, thinking, wondering, calculating.

Could what Fletch said be possible?

'Is that all?' Poli said in disbelief an hour later when Callum arrived back at camp. He shrugged with conviction, understanding her frustration. She popped the top off one of the boxes and rummaged through the loaves of bread, tins and bunches of fruit.

'OK, it's not too bad. They've packed a lot in. We'll make do.' She sighed, retrieving a tatty piece of paper from her back pocket and writing the items down with a blunt pencil.

Callum didn't leave any time for pleasantries; no one did anymore. Their situation was hardening even the softest of them. He made his way through camp, striding between the families gathered around small fires, Fo Doktrin leaves boiling and children moaning with the green pulp around their lips. He arrived at his pit and slid his rucksack off, thinking more and more. *It could be possible.* He'd already used the radio function on the old Watch to communicate with Haro to call a committee meeting. *I hope they see it.* He didn't waste time, knowing they were probably waiting for him. He dropped his pit lid and trod over the foliage through another line of trees, the sun spotting through their heavy-leaved toppings. He wasn't wrong – the committee was waiting; Ki, Haro and Marta were standing in a small circle, the overgrown forest floor travelling up their legs. Callum always felt Maze's absence, the lack of his brusque presence reflecting how much they had lost.

As they turned towards him, Callum suddenly felt exposed and anxious. Vulnerable. Especially with the way Ki bent his eyebrows above his bloodshot, twitching eyes.

'Everything alright, Ki?' Callum asked as he reached them all; Haro and Marta exchanged an awkward glance.

'He thinks because *you* called a meeting you're going to suggest not killing Command again.' Haro crossed his muscly arms over his chest and eyed Ki with a condescending look.

'I am only aware of your true feelings,' Ki argued, considering Callum with questionable confidence.

'No, it's not that.' Callum wished it was, as he sat, feeling the heat of the ground seep through his trousers. 'We don't have time to argue over our differences. The people out there . . .' he pointed back through the trees, the others' eyes flicking in the same direction, '. . . deserve to know we're doing something more than increasing our food supplies.'

'Well, it's been better than nothing.' Marta grimaced and pulled her hair back.

'I know that.' Callum spoke sensitively. 'I wasn't taking anything away from what you've done.'

'Alright, so what's this about?' Marta joined him on the ground, more accommodating now he'd defended her months of effort to safely get more Climbers out into the forest.

'Why do I feel like you're about to change the plan?' Ki grew more exasperated, pressing his face into his hands. 'I don't think you appreciate how hard we've worked.'

'You're not the only one grafting.' Marta's face turned sour again.

'There's more to keeping this community alive than gadgets.' Haro sat ungracefully, almost stumbling over his own feet.

'Like dealing with all the shortages, and avoiding toxes every night.' Marta pulled at her hair again roughly. 'Who, by the way, are at it like wildfire.'

'They're . . . not gadgets!' Ki almost shrieked with frustration. 'They're what's going to save us.'

'Oh, grow up, Ki,' Marta laughed. 'You're acting like the plan is foolproof. It doesn't matter how many doors we blow up; we've still got to get into the City and have enough of us left to take control.'

'We know we're using the planes.' Ki held her eyes, the white sun dappling over his face. 'And we'll blow up more than doors.'

'We might not need to force an entry,' Callum cut in, one hand up. 'Please let me speak.'

Ki seemed to swallow something as he finally slithered down onto his knees and picked at his cracked fingers.

Callum closed his eyes briefly and saw the drones tasering him to the ground on the white, shiny floor of the shopping centre. Just a teenager, rejected and maimed because a system said he wasn't good enough.

We're all the same. The Side, the City and the Unworthies within it. We're all the same.

He enjoyed a deep inhale and saw the expectation around the circle. He began, not knowing where his words would fall.

'You know my intentions have always been to *show* the public that it's the system that needs to change.' Callum gulped. 'Well, I might have found a way.' Callum almost whispered, straight into Ki's broken eyes. 'A way we can take Command and each get what we want.'

After the three of them glanced at each other, Haro insisted he continue.

'Remember the Watch engineer I met months ago?' Callum started, scratching his forehead. 'Well, it turns out, I think he might help us.'

'You said that about Ajay,' Marta said bluntly.

'I know, but this is different. He doesn't know who I am.' Callum swallowed.

'So how could he help us?' Ki broke in.

'I'll explain, but I have to tell you that we need someone else's help first.'

'Who?' Marta asked.

'Lillie.'

'The drunk?' Haro grunted.

'Yeah, the drunk.'

Callum hadn't seen her in weeks, the alcoholic woman who had helped Ajay hack into the City before doing the same for The Rogue. Unfortunately, any mental stability she once had seemed to have disappeared with the lover she lost. The lover who reported her during a Command interrogation. Yet, for what Fletch had told Callum, and the consequences it could reap, he needed her knowledge. His head fogged over. *How did it come to this?* Their lives were in the hands of someone unreliable, but she was it.

She was their best bet, and probably, their final hope.

CHAPTER
TWENTY-THREE

They found her slumped against a tree, sitting in a puddle of her own vomit.

Having talked late into the evening, Callum splashed water over his heavy eyes. He and the others took tentative steps towards her as the twinkle of the wingsparks added some beauty to an otherwise tragic and disturbing scene. Under the glow of their old Watch lights, the four of them observed the empty ethanol bottles scattered around her like a growing mould. Stepping closer, Callum could hear the murmurs of her sleep. Intense cries. Whimpers. Different names escaped from her dry, ripped lips as her shoulders flinched under a long, tattered plait of hair.

'Are you sure about this, Cal?' Ki's words caught in his throat. 'Look at the state of her.'

Callum was unsure whether Ki's subsequent coughing fit was due to his own chronic *SkipSleep* withdrawal or the pungent smell which joined them as they encircled Lillie.

'She's the only one who will understand.' Callum glanced at Marta, her hesitant eyes full in the moonlight. 'Are you guys with me on this?' He moved his eyes from

Marta to Haro, whose crossed biceps bulged over the humid stick of his T-shirt.

'Yeah, we're with you, mate.' Haro unlocked his arms and rubbed his eyes. 'It sounds a better plan than what we've got.'

Callum nodded, thankful for the support they'd shown after he'd spent an hour explaining what Fletch, the man he'd befriended in the City, was doing and how it could help them. He knew he'd have to do it all over again with Lillie *if* she was even willing. Stroking a hand over the dead weight of his head, he realised he hadn't anticipated feeling such a deep wave of emotion on seeing her. The fatigue holding him wouldn't be helping, but the delicate sag of her malnourished limbs somehow made her look like a little girl, lost and broken. He decided not to ignore that sympathy, but to use it.

Maybe by helping us, she can find some sort of restoration. Some sort of release.

Wasting no more time, he approached her, breathing through his mouth.

'Lillie,' he whispered, shaking one of her bony shoulders. 'Lillie.'

Her scream, her jolting body and the clatter of a disturbed bottle took them all by surprise. Her bloodshot eyes bored into Callum, possessed with pain and wanting.

'What . . .' Her frown intensified with the bite of her voice. 'What do you want?'

'We need your help.' Callum squatted beside her.

Lillie's small head flicked to the others. She narrowed her eyes and pulled her clothes tighter around her frantically shaking body. Callum had assumed the bottles were emptied long ago; there'd been no ethanol supplies for days. Withdrawal also explained the vomit and her restless sleep. He wondered when she last ate.

'I am not . . .' Lillie turned her face away, eyes closing. 'There is no helping you.'

Callum looked to his support, all of them willing him to try again.

'We think we have a plan.' Callum swallowed. 'A strategic one – to take down Command.'

Lillie didn't reopen her eyes as she grinned, her voice rasping in the night air.

'Why you think I care about dat?'

'Because of everything they've done – and with what happened with . . .' Callum hesitated, knowing his next words would strike a nerve, 'with Martyn.'

He'd never met her supposed lover who had worked in Command and reported her during interrogations. Yet he knew enough to understand that it was his death that had sent Lillie to the bottle.

'Kid . . .' Lillie willed her eyes open and raised a shaky finger. 'Don't use him to use me.'

'We're not trying to use you.' Callum stood, looking down over her. 'You're one of us, aren't you?'

'I with no one.' She fumbled to stand.

'So, what are you going to do?' Haro cut in. 'Drink yourself silly until your body just stops?'

'That you, Haro?' Lillie squinted. 'Never seen you look so buzzed. You high?' A moment lingered before Lillie's gasp mingled with the patter of her steps. Charging towards Haro, her voice turned urgent. 'Where you get the stuff?'

'I'm not high.' He pushed her back. 'For Tulo's sake, Lillie, get a hold of yourself.'

Haro produced a pack of standard cigarettes from his back pocket, a tactic they'd all decided would calm Lillie down. She let out a strained giggle. Immediately, she snatched one from his offering hand and placed it between her wobbling lips. Waiting excitedly, her eyes flickered as Haro lit it up with a lighter and they all watched her breathe out her first relief of smoke.

'Where you been hiding these, eh, Haro?' She took another drag.

'Come on, this is serious.' Marta stepped forward. 'This isn't just about you.'

'I never seen you before, honey.' Lillie's feral eyes traced the length of Marta's toned body.

Marta's nostrils flared. 'Maybe that's because you've got your eyes closed half the time.'

'Ha! She's spritely, this one.' Lillie directed the laugh at Callum.

'This is completely pointless.' Marta spun on her feet, ruffling parched leaves beneath them.

'Alright, stop it. Marta, wait.' Callum exhaled deeply as Marta stopped, shrugging. 'Lillie, please, we're begging you. I need you. You're the only one with the experience we need.'

'Sorry, kid.' She blew smoke into his face. 'Even your sad scar won't change my mind.'

'Would some ethanol help?' Ki materialised a bottle from behind his back.

'Ki.' Callum bounded at him, blocking his view from Lillie's wide, thirsty eyes. 'We said that wasn't an option,' he grunted, displeased that Ki had been hoarding it for himself in the first place.

'I didn't agree to that.' Ki brushed past him, holding the bottle loosely. 'You help us and we'll get you all the drink you want.'

'That right, kid?' Lillie stubbed the cigarette out with her foot, eyes fixed on Callum.

'You don't need it. It won't make you better.' Callum spoke through his rising frustration with Ki.

'You don't get it.' Lillie shook her small head. 'I don't wanna get better.'

'But you can.' He stepped in closer. 'Look, after all this is over, we could have a Tulo you want to live in.' Callum felt the words burn his tongue; he didn't believe that, not if The Rogue tried to take control. They'd be clueless and would probably end up killing anyone in opposition to them merely to hold on to power, but he was hoping things would move in a way that meant something democratic would emerge. He hated how uncertain it was, but it was all he had.

'I like your hope, kid.' Lillie whispered so quietly he wasn't sure the others could even hear. 'But I'll take the drink.'

She didn't take her sad eyes off him as she prised the bottle from Ki's spindly hands.

'Fine.' Callum rubbed a hand over his increasingly tight forehead.

'Callum has met someone from Command.' Ki bounced on his feet. 'Someone who is going to hack into the new watches.'

'Impressive.' Lillie wandered back to the tree, popping the top off the bottle. 'How you recruit someone of such accolade?'

'I didn't recruit him,' Callum said.

353

'He befriended him.' Ki appeared frantic, the way he did when he was excited or scared. Callum struggled to tell the difference.

'Ki, would you just let Callum explain?' Marta held her fingers to her temples.

'Who is the new prodigy?' Lillie slipped down the tree trunk and took her first swig. Her gasps of enjoyment added a new toxicity to the air.

'His name's Fletch Aden,' Callum responded.

Lillie grunted into the bottle, almost choking on her next sip.

'You know him?'

She shook her head, wiping her lips. 'I didn't associate with squirms like him. I only remember him because his merit was the lowest on the staff board years back. He were a Command pet. What you done, kid? Drug him?'

'No.' Callum grimaced at her strong gulps. 'I took a shot in the dark.'

For the next twenty minutes, Callum told her everything Fletch was planning and how they'd take advantage. He almost didn't stop for breath as the night came to life. Insects scuttled around them and Lillie didn't move her misty eyes from him, her laughs and smiles becoming more conniving as the ethanol disappeared down her throat. All the while, Callum desperately hoped Ki wasn't going to give her any more. He needed her alert enough to hold a conversation. Eventually, he finished, and for a moment, they all felt the hot, sticky silence of the sleeping camp.

'I have to say,' Lillie slurred slightly, 'you're a manipulative sneak, kid. What you done to him and what you gonna do,' she belched, 'not pretty.'

'But will it work?' Marta demanded, her shoulders slouched.

'Technically speaking, as long as he has the right parameters in pace . . . place . . .' Lillie scratched at the flaky skin of her neck, '. . . and even doh he a squirm, he got the brains for that.' She darted her wild eyes between them before saying slowly, 'Yeah, it would work.'

A ripple of relief, excitement or fear spread between them. Callum found it hard to tell which, or whether it was a cocktail of all three.

'How long do you think it'll take him?' he asked.

'He tell you this yesterday? He said he'd done all the research?'

'Yeah.'

'A month or so.' She shrugged her petite frame and searched for the final drops in the bottle.

'Right,' Ki flung his hands together, 'so the next time Callum sees him, he'll get more information and you need to confirm or deny whether he's taking the right approach and explain anything we don't understand, OK? That will be the pivot on which our entire plan relies.'

'Oi!' She threw the bottle, pointing at him. 'Don't you take control. This is the kid's win. And when squirmy Fletchy finds out what he done to him,' her laugh turned Callum cold, 'poor worm gonna shrivel.'

'Come on, we have a lot to talk about.' Marta ushered them all away.

'Finally.' Ki almost skipped between the dark trees.

'Don't tell anyone about this yet, either. People will get excited too soon.' Haro lobbed another cigarette and the lighter at Lillie's feet, the way people threw old meat at a stray fox.

Callum wasn't sure he had the energy to talk about it all right now.

Which weapons will we need? How many? How do we get people into the City to be ready for when Fletch presses the button? Will he even do it? Can I even trust him? Can we trust Lillie to correctly confirm the information he gives me? Then there's the where, the how, the when, and how we'll communicate with each other once we're there.

Gathering himself, he started after the others, but not before having a final word with Lillie.

'You have to be at least a little sober when we talk.' He pointed fiercely at the scattered bottles. 'Otherwise there'll be no more. You got it?'

'It was nice work, kid.' She held the cigarette between her teeth, lit it and grinned. 'The dishonesty looks good on you.' He didn't look back as she cackled and sent more smoke flying towards the moon.

Six weeks later, Callum's hands shook on the gun across his chest. He scanned the final group now boarded on the plane, all of them anxious but ready. Everyone, except the children and guardians, were either on the plane or were waiting in apartments across the City.

He'd find out soon – could they force the change he wanted to see?

CHAPTER
TWENTY-FOUR

The plane roared across the sand, piercing its metal dominance into the delicacy of nature. Trees swayed backwards, refusing to bow down to its manmade oppression, and sand danced up to escape its heavy feet. As the great machine landed, Ajay watched from afar, all his nerves from the last few months mounting into an uncontrollable sweat. He could see small blocks of buildings in the far distance; the Side bubbled through a heatwave, reminding him of a simpler time.

'I don't think I can do this,' he stuttered, leaning against the car's bonnet, head in hands, his elbows shifting against The Guiding Light.

'We're going to take it slowly.' The device's metal warmed in an offer of comfort.

'That's sixteen in the last two weeks.' Ajay turned back to see the plane and a familiar sight; people as small as pinpoints disappearing into its back. It was only ever a few of The Rogue at a time, maybe four or five, creeping out from the forest at the last minute and sneaking aboard. The plane would then lift off smoothly and zip away, leaving only silence behind but surely taking trouble forward.

'That's got to be most of their strongest gone, don't you think?'

'Yes, I believe they're almost done.' Osgar floated away slightly before turning back to Ajay. 'It's time, Ajay. We need to do what we've planned.'

'I feel sick.' He closed his eyes, steadying himself against the car. 'You promise you're going to help me?'

'I'm right here.'

The words spoke into his heart, forcing a small smile over his ungroomed, shaggy face.

'OK.' He swallowed his fear and pulled up his long hair and tied it with a band. 'First step. Reha.'

The device moved back towards him and settled on the bonnet; Ajay took a moment to run through things. It had come too quickly; it only felt like yesterday when he was listening to Deva's diary, hearing about all the turmoil and unknown events of the past, her and Osgar's story softening the hardest parts of his heart. And yet more than two months of planning had flown by, despite his efforts to slow down time. Ten weeks of questioning if it was the right thing to do. Endless days of guilt for not going straight back for Grandma, despite knowing he wasn't yet able to help her. Not without a feasible and well-thought-out route to get home.

But in all the obstacles and challenges along the way, one thing had always been clear. Reha was his way in. Reha – Osgar had told him her name – that friend of his parents with the large birthmark, who had always kept one eye on him. And even on Genni, whom he loved. He'd almost forgotten it was Reha who dropped Genni on his doorstep the night of her *SkipSleep* overdose. That driven, strange lady with the dirty home and Glorified teaching gig was in some ways his only hope. Ajay knew, without any evidence other than his gut feeling, that she would help him despite everything he'd done.

'So, how does this work?' Ajay moved his hands over the device's number pad, usually used to select a story reference. 'Am I meant to type in a number or just say "ring Reha"?'

'I've heard you.'

Immediately Osgar's holographic figure morphed into a green beating mesh of lights accompanied by a mellow ringing tone.

'Will she be able to see me?' Ajay fumbled, wiping down his hole-ridden, overworn T-shirt as if it mattered.

'Not if you don't want her to.'

'OK. Fine.' Ajay's mouth felt dry as the reality of speaking to someone who was not an unexplainable form of artificial intelligence fell on him heavily. Especially Reha, who he hadn't treated too kindly the last time they'd met. She was only trying to get him out of the City, away from the possibility of being arrested for hacking into his Watch. If only he'd listened, then he wouldn't have run home and found Ace and . . . *I can't think about him right now. Just focus. But I doubt I can even begin to—*

'Hello.'

Reha's deep voice injected into the desert.

'Hi . . .' He fumbled. 'It's, erm, it's . . .'

There was a pause on the other end.

'Ajay . . .' She sounded uncharacteristically cautious with her words. 'Is that you?'

'Yes, I need your help.'

'I gathered that. How did you find a device? Are you in the City?'

'It kind of found me.' He stroked his arms to battle his internal chill. 'And no, but I need to get in. I'm a few miles out from the east forest.'

'You been with *them*?'

'I was in their camp, but I was never *with* them.'

'I thought as much.'

'Then why did you ask?'

'To check, I guess. Though I . . .' She paused then sighed. 'Never mind. You do realise you're dead if Command catches you?'

'Yes, I'm aware.' Ajay started to relax. 'It doesn't make me feel so great.'

'No, I don't imagine it does.' Reha let out a small laugh before a sincerity returned to her voice. 'You've caused a lot of pain, boy.'

Ajay fought against the ache in his chest, knowing that any thought of Ace was only going to cloud his focus – and focus was something he desperately needed, for what he was about to do. They'd been over it several times the last month when he'd questioned his sanity or even his ability to pull it off, but as The Guiding Light and his own logic had reminded him, there was no other way.

'I know,' he eventually said. 'But I want to try to prevent any more.'

'What do you mean?'

'The Rogue is coming back.'

Ajay expected her sharp intake of breath.

'When?'

'I don't know exactly, but with their movements, I'd guess very soon.'

'Are they using the planes?'

'Yeah.' Ajay narrowed his eyes towards the still throbbing green light. 'How did you know that?'

'They've been cutting the resource plane routes for weeks; it wasn't hard to figure out.'

'They publicised that?'

'Oh no, but I bother to dig deeper into what's going on.'

'You'd think they'd stop them altogether.'

'And stop collecting the materials for the extension projects?'

'I guess not. Progress is Strength, right?'

'Only when greed isn't in the picture.'

Ajay left the profound statement, or lesson, or whatever it was to the side. He had to stay on track.

'I've been reading that Command's interrogations are intensifying,' Reha continued and Ajay could imagine her strong, petite frame hovering over her device, arms grasping the side of a desk. 'Which is why they're moving; they're running out of time to have any edge.'

'Right,' Ajay agreed, having already wondered how long it would be until they caught the pilots on the inside. 'So, I have this plan. One I've been working on for months.'

'With his help?'

'Yeah, with his help.' Ajay smirked at the device. *This woman really does know everything.*

'OK, Alpha and I are all ears.'

Ajay heard a patting through the device and assumed that she was comforting her fox.

'I'm coming back because I believe I can help with whatever type of attack is coming. It wouldn't surprise me if it was technical, rather than outright violent.'

'What makes you say that?'

'They wanted me to hack into the new model when I was there,' Ajay admitted, pulling his balaclava over his face to shield it from the beating sun. 'I was their plan A. They must have found a plan B.'

Reha breathed deeply. 'You think they're in the Watches again?'

'Somehow.' Ajay nodded. 'But I don't think they'll be stupid enough to do the same thing. When I left them, I made it clear that wouldn't work.'

'How do you know they listened to you?'

'I don't.'

'OK,' Reha grunted.

'So,' Ajay ignored the slight sarcasm, 'my plan rests on a few details I need from you.'

'Sure. Go ahead.'

'Do you still meet with your friends in the River House?'

'Yes.'

'And it has an emergency escape door?' Ajay visualised it the same way he had for the last few weeks. A rusted door with a round, manual handle that would open out into a depressurised chamber with another door leading to the river. He only knew they existed due to his limited knowledge of the Underwater Bar Disasters, being sure he'd read something about staff failing to operate the doors quickly enough to get anyone out.

'Of course,' Reha confirmed.

'Does it open?'

'I don't know. I've never tried. It's old but I don't suppose it's not functional. Why?'

'I'm coming into the City through the water pipes.'

Reha let out a low, deep murmur. 'You'll die.'

'There's no other way.'

'Can't you sneak onto the planes with The Rogue?'

'There's no way. And anyway, then what would I do? I can't walk the streets like they can, no one knows their faces like they know mine.' Ajay stroked his long beard, knowing drones were advanced enough to see past it. 'I need to get in completely undetected and the pipe system is the oldest and probably the least monitored route in.'

'You don't know that for sure. You can't go in there on a hunch.'

Ajay lifted the device from the bonnet, giving himself some thinking time and a chance to move his numbing legs. Walking away from the car, he stared into the device, trying to communicate his desperation to Reha that this plan was the only one that would work, and that without her, it was nothing.

'OK, sure.' He spoke patiently. 'There are a lot of unknowns with this. But there are also a lot of things I've thought through. Just give me a chance to explain it.'

'OK, boy.' Reha breathed heavily, adding weight to the moment. 'I can do that.'

CHAPTER
TWENTY-FIVE

'You must be terrified.'

Reha whispering those words kept replaying in his mind. They made Ajay want to cry, or heave, or run. His insides were screaming with fear, but he couldn't give the fear a voice because if he did, he'd never do it. Bracing himself, he knew he couldn't turn back and be a coward and besides, he wasn't alone.

Staring over the browned circular hatch nestled beneath the desert sand, Ajay had one eye back on his car a few metres away, knowing that this time, he wasn't coming back for it. How easy it would be for him to drive away. How straightforward to set off across the sand, and let Command and The Rogue tear the City apart, and he would stay ignorant of how it all unfolded. For every sense of how easy that would be came a reminder of how to live selflessly. *I can't abandon them. I owe Grandma. I owe Genni. I owe Ace.*

'OK.' He knelt by the hatch, Osgar floating beside him. 'At least we've got here again.'

'So far so good,' Osgar said, as Ajay closed the map from Deva's diary they'd used to find the access hatch to the water pipe, as they had done a few weeks before.

Ajay scanned the sand, imagining the 4 metre-wide pipe beneath him, strong water rushing through its veins, pumping life into the City around two miles away.

'It's depressing that this was the easiest part.'

Ajay didn't hide his discouragement as he fiddled with the tight cuffs of his climbing suit. He'd forgotten how tight it was. Quite naturally, he couldn't help the doubt from creeping in. There was every possibility he was about to die. That fact was real to him from the moment they started talking about accessing the City through the water mains. The more he thought about it, the more he became aware of the anxiety that was binding him. Everything scared him and the conversation with Reha had only fuelled his concerns further.

He didn't know if he was going to have enough air for the few hours it would take him to crawl over the maintenance ladder along the top of the pipe. He didn't know if he would be able to breathe long enough underwater, just as he didn't know his plan if he even made it there, as he wasn't sure of The Rogue's strategy or timings. He didn't even know how Grandma was, despite Reha trying to encourage him that 'she was safe enough' when he'd asked. *If she's in custody, they can't be treating her well.* He also wasn't enthralled with the idea that Reha needed someone else involved in the plan at this point.

'So, you think the door would open?' Ajay had asked about the emergency escape door in the River House.

'I guess so.'

'Do you think you could test it in the next hour or so?'

'Yeah, I could send someone down there. Let me make a call.'

'No.' Ajay stopped in his pacing over the sand. 'Don't involve anyone else. Not yet. I can't compromise anyone any earlier than I need to.'

'Well, you need to.'

'Why?'

'Because I can't swim, boy. And I'd be of little use to you if I tested the contraption and drowned as a result.'

Thinking about it again, Ajay was flummoxed that Reha was the type of person not to excel at everything, especially something as fundamental as swimming, probably the most merit-worthy sport. Despite his annoyance, Ajay had accepted there was little option. *If I even get there.*

'Boy, you're going to die.' Reha's words in his head. Over and over.

'Ajay,' Osgar's voice snatched him from his thoughts. 'It's time to go.'

'I don't think I can do this.' Ajay tried to steady the wobble of his bottom lip as he lifted the plastic cover to the numbered keypad sitting in the middle of the circular hatch.

'We'll take things step by step together,' Osgar comforted. 'Just like everything else we've done.'

As he stared at it through fearful tears, he saw it all – what happened with Ace, being trapped in The Rogue; the storm and his escape; finding The Guiding Light before truly discovering it; Deva's diary, the rhythms of the waterfall, the gazzen and the stars. Then came all his planning. The maps, the strategy, the risky way he attained the hatch's access code, and then finally speaking to Reha; all of it danced together in the glow of its light, like a moving film, and Ajay didn't know the ending. He breathed, deciding to use the adrenaline to his advantage and not waste any more time.

'Right, step by step,' he whispered. Without hesitation, he keyed in the four numbers he'd known for two weeks, betting that Command wouldn't have changed them in their neglect of updating their oldest system. As the light above the numbers turned green, he took one last shaky breath and spoke a word of good luck to himself. It was nothing too profound, just something Ace would have said: 'Go smash it, lover boy.'

He aggressively pulled down his balaclava and jumped beneath the sand, taking the moment with grace because he knew full well – it could be the last time he ever saw the sun.

Ajay forgot to breathe in the shock of the darkness.

He'd never been in a space so void of light. The only reference he had was the hot ladder steps beneath him, wetting his hands as he crouched and held on. He could feel the erratic tremors of his heart; he could taste the old sweat on his balaclava as his quick breathing sucked its dirty fabric in and out of his mouth. He closed his eyes to steady himself, but the roar from the gallons of rushing water in the pipe under him sent him off-balance.

'Where ... are ...' Ajay fumbled, '... you? I can't see.'

'I'm here.' Osgar's voice bounced off the concrete ceiling above him. The device finally floated around Ajay, its light giving him at least a little relief.

'I didn't expect it to be this dark,' Ajay panted, now able to see the shake of his hands.

'You closed the hatch quickly.' The Guiding Light swirled. 'Give yourself a second to adjust.'

'I know, I just wanted it closed, as we discussed.' Ajay wiped his sweaty upper lip, the humidity working hard on his hydration.

'Let's get moving, then.' It turned. 'I'll go before you.'

Saying nothing, Ajay felt the warmth of that assurance, and as it increased the power of its light, he was pleased to see more of the path ahead. The ladder stretched out like a train track into the dark distance. Beads of condensation sat on the pipe's surprisingly non-mouldy surface, and dozens of desert critters cowered from the light, scuttling down to the lower parts of the pipe.

'Urgh,' he grimaced as he embraced more of the slimy, hot touch of the ladder between his fingers. He looked back at the hatch. *It's closed. The drones can't get in if it's closed. If they even send drones. They'll send someone or something out here. They sent that guy out when we disturbed the sensors the other week before we got the access code. So, they'll know someone is down here. They're coming for me. No, it's OK. You always knew this, Ajay. You've got your suit on, its technology was good enough for The Rogue, it's good enough for you now. Just rest on that assumption – another assumption, yes, but it's all you've got. Maybe they'll have drones waiting for me there. Reha is right.*

'Boy, you're going to die.'

He tentatively crawled forward. The device lit up the way before him and all he could do was trust that he'd make it out the other end.

'Can we stop? My legs are shot.'

This must be the worst experience of my life. Get me out.

'Two minutes.' Osgar turned back, shining into his eyes and lighting up the ladder under him as the pipes started to slope down even deeper. They'd made it beneath the Outer-Ring rivers, meaning only one more to go before the Inner-Ring.

Two minutes. That's all I've got.

Ace.

What I did to Ace was the worst experience of my life. How could I ever compare this? It's hard and gruelling and at this moment, I don't think my calves will ever recover, but I can't ever go through anything as painful as ... what ...

Ajay flinched as he saw it nestled under his legs.

'What is that?' he whispered calmly, staring down at the blue, red and black snake coiled up like the Command symbol. He didn't move, despite the intense cramping in his calves after crawling for a few hours.

'Beautiful, isn't she?' Osgar took his light closer.

'Don't.' Ajay pushed the device away. 'You'll alarm it.'

'Her.'

Ajay panted quietly, anxiety and humidity teaming up to make him sweat. 'Will she kill me?'

'No, Ajay.' Osgar floated in again and the snake lifted its head smoothly, causing Ajay to shuffle backwards into the dark he'd come from. He watched as the snake stroked itself across the circumference of the device, almost to find comfort or friendship. It was only for a moment, before it seemed to settle soundly back to sleep.

'Come, we're almost there.' Osgar turned slowly.

Ajay scuttled himself over it, ignoring his fear. Several more minutes passed and thinking about everything he'd seen in the desert, both the dangerous and ethereal, seemed to help the time go more quickly. Because the next time he looked up, Osgar had stopped, his glow showing Ajay a problem.

'Ah, no.' Ajay felt his heart drop to his aching legs.

He blinked at the way the pipe dived down and split into five, like a serpent with multiple heads. He'd never believed the map would be up-to-date but he'd hoped. With how many sparkles of water had reflected up off chambers, he guessed they were now at the Inner-Outer-Ring. It would make sense for there to be new pipes, it being the area of the City with the most growth.

'OK.' Ajay yanked his balaclava off in a futile attempt for some air. 'I just need to . . . breathe.' He let out every emotion in his escaping breath while staring at the five different routes. 'Are we going with what we talked about?'

'Yes, straight ahead is the best bet.'

'The best bet? We can't get this wrong.'

'I know.'

Ajay stared at the ceiling, his nerves fraying at the thought of drones above him, scanning the streets and failing to see the heat of his moving body, if the suit was working.

'It's the most logical approach. It would make sense.' He pulled his balaclava back on, justifying their decision. *New pipes would be added to the side of the original as the City grew. The map I had was the original so it would make sense for the access to the Inner-Ring to be this way.* He cursed incessantly as they continued.

After another half an hour, he looked up and blew a sigh of relief at a blue shimmer in the inky abyss. He stared down through a glass hatch to see an empty chamber beneath him. Two doors with windows sat on either side of the tight depressurised room, working to hold back the aggression of water, its presence reflecting through the glass. He glanced behind him as the ladders continued straight ahead and then jutted off to the left and right. With his memory of the map, the chamber below was the correct access point to the river.

'Shall I ring Reha?' The device sat on the hatch, blocking the chamber from Ajay's view.

'Yes.' Ajay swallowed some vomit.

The figure dissolved again into the green throbbing light and Ajay could feel every beat of its ringing. The clear tone of Reha's voice ripped through the tunnel.

'Boy?' Reha sounded urgent. 'You there?'

'Yes, yes.' Ajay opened his eyes, having squeezed them shut. 'I'm here. I'm ready. I'm at the riverside hatch.'

'You're inside?'

'No, just above.'

'Can you go in while we're connected? I want to make sure there's the manual switch before I get Lorcan ready again.'

'OK.' Ajay fought through his guilt of pulling this Lorcan into danger, even if he had tested the River House door. He didn't deserve the consequences of conspiring with an outlawed criminal if the plan went south. Yet if Ajay had learned anything over the past few months, it was that he couldn't act alone because others had strengths he didn't. Like Reha's knowledge of Command, or Lorcan's ability to swim, or Osgar's awareness of the desert.

He pulled open the glass hatch and jumped down into the chamber, scraping his left arm against the wall. It was tight but tall enough for him to stand. He examined the door which led to the river and stared through the small window on its top; he saw only clear water. Scanning down the door, it was all as he expected; a large wheel handle and at the bottom, a smaller door to fill the chamber safely.

'Yes, it's here.' Ajay spoke up towards the device floating above his head. 'And there's the handle to open it.' He rested a shaking hand on the mini rusted hand wheel before standing and feeling along the rim of the larger door to find the automatic door release module. Memories flooded through him; many nights under the stars discussing the need for Command to refill the rivers after periods of dry weather to always keep the City aesthetically pleasing. Not that any of Command's vain initiatives mattered to him now. *This is it.*

'What's the number on the door?' Reha said.

'G260,' Ajay said, squinting at the fading speckled digits.

'Not G261?'

'No, G260.' Ajay clutched at the neck of his suit. A shuffling came down the line as Reha failed to respond, drawing Ajay's stomach into itself.

'Reha?' he said, grinding his teeth.

'You're in the wrong chamber,' Reha said, sharp as a blade.

'No, that's impossible. I used a map. The River House is by the Ttex building, which makes it closest to the chamber on the west side.'

'That company moved years ago. How old is your map?'

Ajay didn't know how much Reha knew about Osgar's background. Did she know about the diary? He doubted it. Regardless, that information was immaterial for his current situation.

'What do I do?'

'Climb along to the next tunnel, to the right. It won't be far.'

'Are you sure it's right?' Ajay's jaw was tight, staring into the glow of The Guiding Light.

'Yes.'

'Your map is the latest?'

'It's thereabouts.'

'Thereabouts? The longer I'm down here, the more likely they'll get to me, if they're looking.'

'I get it, boy, but I'm pretty sure. You'll just have to trust me.'

Ajay felt the rattle of his brain, trying to remember the positioning of the chambers on the map. He placed a hand over the bulk of the diary, sat in his trouser pocket beneath his suit. Tempted to retrieve it and sit to figure out whether Reha was correct, he knew he didn't have the time, nor did he believe it was the right thing to do. He didn't always have to figure things out alone. Other people were as good an asset as any device or algorithm. But that didn't stop the hollow feeling in his chest.

'OK,' Ajay said finally, swallowing his unease. 'What do I do?'

'It's only the next chamber along, but to the *right*,' Reha said as static fizzed through the light of the device. 'Ring back when you're there. I'll sort Lorcan.'

Reha was cut from the call. Ajay didn't hesitate. Without a word to Osgar, whose glowing figure lit his way, he pulled himself through the hatch above and out into the tunnels. Something within him knew he needed to move quickly, a sort of gut instinct or hunch that someone was watching him. He gripped the ladders tightly as he flew down the right tunnel shaft and onto a new curve of pipes. Following it along, he darted his eyes over the ventilation systems, down the grimy walls and up over the dripping ceilings above. In his speed, he wondered if he'd seen the eye of a small camera, but he didn't stop to check. Clenching his jaw, he ignored his shallow breathing, involuntary moans of panic and the cramp of his legs as he could see the new blue reflection on the pipes up above. Somehow the sight of his goal sharpened his focus and he could feel his heartbeat slowing down. He dropped into the chamber, almost identical to the one before, except for the number on the door.

G261 shone clearly under the glow of Osgar's light as he floated by the steel frame and flicked his figure back to a green ringing throb.

The conversation with Reha was quick and practical; her guy was ready; the door was correct and there was no time like the present. So, after Ajay took a huge calming breath, he crouched down and shifted the hand wheel on the lower hatch – once, twice, three times until the lock clicked. Pushing, he heaved his weight into it, pressing against the force of the water behind. The water trickled in before the door flew open and Ajay stumbled against the back wall, his breath taken as pain ricocheted like bullets down his back.

Water spilled fiercely at his feet.

His breathing quickened.

The blue water rose with the desire of a predator.

Up his body, towards his face.

Ajay turned his neck upwards and circled his lips to gasp his last few breaths. He was under the water's power. He hoped it would show him mercy.

Under the surface, bubbles popped from his mouth but Osgar's light filled his eyes, its waterproofed frame self-suspended next to him. Thrusting forward, he grabbed the larger door's handle and turned it, already feeling the lack of oxygen.

'Keep calm.' Osgar's voice rumbled through his drowned-out ears.

Ajay settled his panic and the handle clicked. Pushing the door forward, he was met with a wide-open space of water, knowing he only had about a minute of breathing time left. *I can't go up for air. They could be waiting.*

As his body floated into the river's grasp, he felt the jolt of its current. He was forced to grasp the door's handle to stop losing control. He then remembered what they'd discussed, just as Osgar voiced his thoughts.

'Hold onto me.'

Ajay tumbled through the water and crushed both hands either side of the device. They lunged into the river with the power of a speedboat motor. It forced them down against the river's manmade movement and as the way cleared, Ajay could see the foggy shimmer of the skyscraper apartments above the surface and the moss-covered walls beneath it, and there in the distance was a dark rock that soon became a building, and as they surged forward, the speed drying out his skin, the building presented a door, and the door was open, and there was a man, a man with a tank on his back, but then the man was gone, and Ajay felt a darkness close in on him, like he was being shut inside a black box, and when they reached the man, and something was put over his mouth, and he was pulled through the door, he willed himself to hold on as his eyes shut.

CHAPTER
TWENTY-SIX

The light was all he could see. His eyes were wide, bloodshot, wired, focused on it; his body was suspended in water, a strong arm sat tight around his waist, but the light was still all he could see. He could sense the air moving from the mask around his mouth into his throat and into the great expanse of his lungs. Still, the light was all he could see and it became all he could hear.

'It's OK, Ajay. Breathe.' The light throbbed as the blue water waltzed with the white of its sparkle.

Ajay obeyed, inhaling deep through the mask he was holding. The door to the river had already been closed and as he lifted his head, he watched the water level above creep towards him. He looked to the man. Lorcan. Dark-haired with a full face, he was holding his breath, staring at Ajay with a solemn look in his eye, before giving him a questioning thumbs-up. Ajay mirrored the gesture and the two of them bobbed there for what felt like minutes but could only have been seconds.

When the water level in the chamber was low enough, Lorcan swam up with the weight of the oxygen tank on his broad back, his head disappearing above the surface. Ditching the mask, Ajay followed. As he emerged, a gigantic gasp escaped and it was as if he was breathing a whole new type of air.

The noise of their simultaneous pants echoed around the chamber, both treading water silently until the water drained completely. Lorcan didn't hesitate in his movements. Ajay noticed he was quite well-built as he briskly opened the opposite door. Pulling it open, the man bounded into a barely lit room; shelves lined the walls, full of oxygen tanks and lifejackets, and a large safety notice was taped to the back of another steel door. Lorcan threw the black, chipped tank off his back and lobbed Ajay a red towel that had previously been folded on the floor.

Ajay watched him rub his own towel over a large mole on his neck, and deliberated on how to thank him. Though the disgruntled body language and the audacious looks weren't hard to decipher. *This guy doesn't want to talk to me.* Ajay questioned why that surprised him; he was hardly popular, but somehow the sour energy felt personal. *Does he know my parents? I bet he knows my parents.*

Lorcan moved quickly, forcing open a final door and drowning the room in blue light, revealing the large space of the River House behind.

'Hey, thank you ...' Ajay shouted after him instinctively, throwing his towel over his shoulders, having dried his beard.

'Yeah.'

Ajay stepped into the River House and watched him walk towards the bar at the other end. As he did so, he nodded at a group of people taking up the sofas and armchairs. Every set of eyes was on Ajay, who looked down at Osgar, floating at his waist. Boldly, they went together towards the group, and Ajay spotted details that surprised him about the building last time. The photos on the wall, the shelves of Guiding Light devices at the back, the comfort and the water rushing above their heads. It wasn't until he readjusted to his surroundings that worry caught him. *Why are all these people here? There are at least ten of them. Where's Reha?*

As soon as he thought of the question, he saw her by the bar with Lorcan. He didn't hesitate to rush over, dismissing any polite instinct to let them finish their conversation.

'But she needs to know,' Ajay caught Lorcan saying, frustration riding through his thick brows. *Who needs to know, what? About me?* Ajay didn't have time to focus on the peripheral details of the situation so he shook them away.

Reha put a firm hand on Lorcan's chest, her ageing eyes flicking onto Ajay.

'It's OK. We'll deal with it in a minute,' she said to Lorcan quickly before pulling her long, tattered hair over one shoulder and turning to Ajay. He took her in; the wrinkles around her strong brown eyes and the bobble of her skin over the birthmark that ran down her cheek.

She didn't greet him with a smile or a handshake. Instead, she merely raised her eyebrows and sighed.

'Didn't think you'd be making friends, did you?' She nodded subtly in Lorcan's direction; he was now perching on the end of an armchair, joining all the others in watching them.

'I didn't try to,' Ajay answered honestly.

'Probably wise.' Reha let the moment sit before asking: 'You OK?'

'Yeah, I'm fine. Reha, what—'

'So, it wasn't today,' she interrupted, smiling slightly. 'Your day to die.'

'What are all these people doing here?' He ignored any small talk and stepped in closer, his tone tight.

Reha appeared surprised but not unnerved. 'You really thought we could keep people safe by ourselves?'

'Well, no. But I don't know how long it will be until The Rogue does something.' He kept his voice low. 'Everyone in this room is now in danger for conspiring with me.'

Reha didn't flinch but casually leaned on the bar. 'Boy, we've been living outside of the law for years.' She snorted. 'What makes you think they'll come down here now?'

'Probably because they already know I'm here. My break-in won't have gone unnoticed.'

'Well, we'll just have to hope that they've lost you, won't we?' Reha said it so simply, as if that was the obvious way to look at the situation. Without producing words he didn't mean, Ajay breathed and looked down at the quiet device beside him. *Remember why you're here.*

'OK. Fine. What now, then?'

'Tell them what you told me.' Reha handed him a hot cup of coffee and gestured to the sofas. The two of them walked towards the group of strangers, Ajay feeling sheepishly disillusioned by their presence. Lorcan was still looking at him with a defensive eye, there was a tall, skinny guy whose stature reminded him of Ki from The Rogue; a petite woman with square glasses and a cute bob haircut, and about eight others who he didn't look at long enough for him to make any distinction between them. In that moment it was hard to take each person in isolation because they all stared at him the same way; was it judgement or intrigue? Fear? He hadn't missed the feeling of not knowing what other people were thinking and that anxiety, he knew, had the power to control him. But he wouldn't let it. Not now.

'OK, Ajay. Tell them why you're here.' Reha sat next to the woman in glasses and pointed to the armchair on the far side.

Ajay sat, despite the discomfort of his sodden clothes. He tentatively placed his mug on the central coffee table. Coughing to clear his throat, he took the opportunity to steady his mind, and choose his words carefully, so he could be as clear as possible.

'I've been watching The Rogue's movements.' Ajay swallowed, darting his eyes beyond people to the walls around them. 'Many of them are already in the City. They're planning something.' He let a silence settle as people moved uncomfortably and exchanged nervous looks. 'I believe they've done something to the Watches again. What, exactly, I'm not sure, but I've come back to try to stop them from making things worse than they already are, and I felt that Reha could help me do that.' He glanced at her focused eyes. 'So, I contacted her and here I am.'

'Do you think it's to do with the pictures?' The woman with glasses sat forward, cradling a cup of coffee. 'People's ID photos have been playing up.'

'That's a glitch, Trixy,' Lorcan huffed before snapping at Ajay, 'how do you know all this?'

'Lorcan...' Reha appeared startled, as if the aggression was out of character.

'What?' Lorcan crossed his arms over his wide chest. 'I want to know why he thinks we should trust him.'

'That's a good point,' the skinny guy broke in from another seat.

'I was with The Rogue.' Ajay tried to reassure them even though their reaction was, he appreciated, completely natural. 'I've seen their anger and their hurt and their determination—'

'You were with them?' a larger woman remarked, and Ajay felt offended by her fearful eyes. *Please don't fear me.* A heat of pain crawled across his chest. *Of course she's scared of me. I'm not the man you think I am.*

'Why were you there?' Lorcan moved around the sofas and Ajay thought he saw his fists clench.

'They . . .' Ajay paused, realising his failure to lay out any context. 'They kidnapped me.'

'Right . . .' Lorcan scoffed, his brown eyes drilling into Ajay's. 'And why would they do that?'

'Because they needed my intelligence.'

'Your intelligence?' The skinny guy raised one of his long, thin eyebrows.

'Yes.' Ajay clasped his clammy hands together. 'To get into the Watches . . . I don't think they—'

'And how did you get out?' The skinny guy cut across him.

'I got lost during a storm, but I can explain exactly what happened, I just don't have—'

'And how did you get into the water pipes?' Lorcan continued.

'Lorcan, how is that relevant?' Trixy placed her mug on the coffee table.

'Seems suspicious to me – how could he do that alone?'

'That is again a long and complicated story, I doubt I have time to explain it all now.'

'Well, that's convenient.' The skinny guy let out a sarcastic snort.

'Would you two stop that?' Trixy scowled. 'You really think this guy would bother coming back if there wasn't something going on?' She pointed at Ajay with a strong finger. 'He's literally outlawed. He's basically dead just by being here. I know this is hard, especially for you, Lorcan.'

Ajay darted a look of confusion at Reha that went unnoticed. *Why especially for him? What did I do to this guy?*

'But give him a chance,' she finished before turning in urgency to Ajay. 'What's your plan? Do you know what they're going to do, if and when they get here?'

Ajay opened his mouth to speak but was startled by a sudden rush of noise. Running footsteps flew down to the entrance with an open eagerness. The rhythm of their hurry echoed his uneasy heart. *Command? They've found me.*

'Have you seen ... the news?'

Her familiar, wheezing voice ricocheted through the room.

Ajay went cold.

Everyone turned to see her excited smile dissipate into something between shock and fury. *She's here.* Reha's eyes darted around uneasily. *Why is she here?* People shuffled on the sofas or drank from empty cups. *How is she here?* Despite the moment choking him, every cell in his body communicated its innate hunger to escape, so Ajay stood. And then he froze.

'You're here.' Genni held his gaze as he processed the unsurprising anger in her tone.

He was suddenly thirsty; he could feel the sweat building under his arms and between the webs of his fingers; his legs were heavy, like all his weight was being driven down into his soggy boots.

She's here.

He didn't know what to say, feel, think or do. For a split second, as he took in her gentle features, it didn't feel real. He was never intending to find her; he never wanted her to see him again. He didn't want to pull back all the hurt, shame and heartbreak he knew he'd probably caused her. And yet there she was, standing right in front of him with a mist in her beautiful eyes and Reha by her side.

'Ajay has come back to tell us about The Rogue. They're planning something.'

He had never heard Reha speak with such sensitivity. He said nothing, but lowered himself slowly back to sitting. *Why is she here? How do they know each other? Am I sure this isn't a dream?*

'OK,' Trixy stood, her back to him. 'We should all talk. Over there.' She walked quickly to the other side of the room.

Ajay addressed only the palms of his dry, ripped hands as the space grew colder with the group leaving him alone.

'What do I do?' Ajay moaned at Osgar floating beside him. 'How is she here?'

'Just stay put.'

Ajay's heart wobbled as he looked up again. 'She's leaving . . .' He watched her escape from the group, striding fiercely through the exit. 'I should go . . .' Ajay hesitated and corrected himself. *Not your place, mate.*

Not moving, he instead observed a heated exchange between Reha and Lorcan before he followed Genni up the steps to the riverside.

Are they together? The question hit Ajay full in the chest; jealousy and shame stole his focus. *Is that why that girl said my presence was hard 'especially' for Lorcan? Are they together?*

Sighing, Ajay pulled his head to his knees, his hands gripping his matted, drying hair. *Focus. The Rogue. But – are they together?*

'Just give me a moment with him,' he heard Reha order the others, all of whom quickly moved to the old bar.

Ajay squeezed back the tears as Reha's presence settled into the next seat. He didn't look up.

'How do you know her?' he sniffed.

'A lot has happened since you've been gone, boy. It's a long story.'

'Did you try to help her? Told her that you saved her life?' Ajay didn't move but remembered Reha watched over Genni by dropping her on his doorstep when she overdosed on electrified *SkipSleep*.

'No, she has no idea about that.' Reha curled a soft hand around Ajay's wrists and pulled his hands from his head. 'Ajay, she found me. She went to the Side to meet your parents.'

'She did what?' Ajay straightened, shock stealing any further movement.

'Last summer.' Reha nodded and smiled. 'She's grown desperately fond of them. So much so she might have just saved their lives.'

'Saved their...' Ajay fumbled, an urgency for information so strong his words scrambled. 'What?'

Reha's mouth opened but her voice was beaten by the ping of her Watch, followed by hurried gasps and alarmed murmurs from the group behind them. Their immediate uneasiness was also written on Reha's face as she swiped at her wrist repeatedly. She frantically flicked up screens and patted them down again.

'What...' she breathed in disbelief.

'Reha, is it yours too?' The skinny guy ran over on his long legs, fear cascading through his eyes.

'Yes,' Reha stood quickly. 'I'll do a restart.'

'I've tried that. It's not changing.' Trixy followed from the other side of the room, pushing her glasses up her nose. 'Do you think it's another sort of glitch?'

'I have no idea,' Reha mumbled, swiping at her Watch, a sad realisation emerging in her thinking eyes.

'What is it?' Ajay stood to join them, his lack of a Watch bothering him for the first time in months. 'What's happened?'

'Here, look.' Reha came closer, flicking her head between him and the others. She thrust her wrist towards him, placing her Watch under his nose and whispering, 'Do you think this could be them?'

At first, the information on the screen blurred with its impossibility.

But it only took him a moment to steady his thoughts and swallow back his fear, for he knew it had begun.

CHAPTER
TWENTY-SEVEN

Their mumbles of anxiety and looks of distrust danced with the twist in his stomach. Callum steadied himself against the dust-laden window ledge, being careful not to shift the closed curtain of the dark, tenth-floor Outer-Ring apartment. Vacant for so long, but currently aswarm with twelve others like him – members of The Rogue preparing to attack. Except it was all taking too long. Callum breathed, counting back from ten.

'Cal.'

Seven, six, five.

'Callum.'

Ki's wail forced open Callum's eyes and strengthened his knuckled grip on the windowsill. Callum took in Ki's grievous voice, straining through the Watch on Callum's wrist.

'What's going on? We need to go. When is Fletch doing it?'

Callum had learned to swallow Ki's erratic, anxious episodes. They were probably a result of the years of dodgy *SkipSleep* withdrawal, or his personality, or his unknown obsession with killing the Hevases. Callum didn't know, but this time, it felt contagious. He could feel the nervous energy tingling up his legs and strengthening across the shortness of his breath. Still looking down at his borrowed Watch, he saw the score of an older Rogue colleague static on its screen. The one he saw every time he came into the City with the Watch on his wrist. M-139. Callum had never had a score, no initiation, no meaning, no worth in *their* eyes. He was waiting to show them all how it felt and how things should be different, but doubt opened within him like the pages of an old, paper book.

I've put my trust in a man I don't even know. I've put all these people's lives in his hands, in the faith that he would do what he said he would do.

'Callum?' Ki's urgency through his Watch, speaking from another apartment across the City, fell over him vacantly. 'Is it happening? The longer we stay here, the less likely this will work. Callum.' Ki's voice muffled as a fog descended over him, cutting out his senses.

What have I done? What have I done?

'Hey, stop that.' Charlene's voice resounded through the Watches. Callum felt her presence behind him. 'He's here with us, calm down.'

'Why isn't he responding?' Ki floundered. 'Oh my . . . we're going to die . . .' he gasped, unnerving people in Callum's room, their concerns popping over them like the crackles of a fire. Callum turned to face Charlene's suspicious eyes.

'OK, Ki.' Charlene lifted her wrist to her mouth. 'Just take a moment.' She pursed her lips. 'Breathe. Give me a minute while I ask Callum what's going on, OK? You flipping out over the line isn't going to help anything.' She pulled one side of her long, greying hair behind her ear, glancing back at Callum, who started to feel more connected as her blue eyes caught his own.

Ki obeyed, the communications going silent. Charlene sighed, hands on her hips.

'What's going on? You're not talking to us.' Charlene glanced at the others, who listened attentively despite her attempt to keep her voice low. 'It's freaking people out. It's freaking me out.'

Callum nodded, understanding, but he couldn't find words. *What if he's not going to do it?*

'So?' Charlene insisted. 'What time did your friend say he'd flick the switch?'

'He's not my friend,' Callum managed, parting his lips like they were stuck together. 'And he's late.'

'How late?' Charlene whispered and readjusted her laser gun, pulling her slim frame into an unnatural posture. He stayed quiet.

'Cal, how late?' She gritted her yellowed teeth.

'An hour.' Callum breathed, still holding on to the windowsill as if letting go would mean he'd fall.

'An hour?' A woman jumped up from a tattered desk chair, which spun on her exit. 'He's an hour late.' She paused, yielding her own weapon. 'This was a mistake, all of it. How do we know this isn't a trap? That this fella hasn't sold us out to Command?'

'It's not a trap.' Callum shook his head. 'There's no way he's in it for Command. He might have just got nervous, or something has taken longer than he expected, and anyway, he said around 3 o'clock. Not dot on.' He hadn't looked at anyone as he spoke, only at his legs, encased in his combat trousers. 'Once it happens and Command react, we'll walk right in. All of us.'

'Not all of us,' a man on a stool grunted, chewing his tongue. 'Only the ones that are left.' He raised his voice and pointed beyond the stained apartment door. 'How do we know they're not looking for us, right now?'

'Alright, alright. This isn't helping anything.' Charlene held her hand up to the man and turned back to Callum. 'You're leading this, Cal. If you say we wait, we wait. But we better tell Haro and the other groups so no one does anything stupid.'

Charlene's wide eyes communicated one thing: so *Ki* doesn't do anything stupid.

'Yeah, OK, we better send someone to them.' Callum choked at the weight of everything. 'That's what we said. It's too dangerous to use the Watch comms here.'

Another thing Ki hadn't listened to.

'I'll go.' Charlene pulled her hair back, breathing in the clammy air, before setting down her gun and throwing a casual shirt over her vest.

Callum thanked her as he pulled off his headband and twisted it between his fingers, commanding his nervous tears back. *I felt so sure that he would do it. He still could.* Callum remembered the first time he met Fletch. He could almost feel the fire in his eyes, burning with resentment and malice, and then flaming even hotter with the passion of his plan. One he thought he came up with himself, but really, Callum had always been planting seeds. He had never wanted to deceive anyone, but it was necessary and times were desperate. But maybe he wasn't as convincing as he thought, and Fletch had figured him out, and now he'd left *him* in the lurch along with all the others. *I could contact him. No. That would be too suspicious, I don't want to put him off.*

Every breath was a struggle as he watched the abysmal scene of people losing hope. He finally let go of the windowsill, his legs feeling unsteady beneath him, and twitched the thin curtain open slightly, staring down over the City, seeing the billboards compete with the brightness of the sun.

He scanned along the tops of the buildings, squares of glass and concrete and plants merging down towards the glistening of the river. His eyes took him along its concrete bank, in and out of the sea of people, as if he were down there with them. *If this happens, it's happening to them. All of them, destroyed, everything taken, because of me. No.*

Because of them.

We're only showing them who they are.

His wrist vibrated. Then a stark, sharp cheer in the room.

He didn't hesitate to lift his wrist and when he saw it, he let a blow of relief escape through his dry, cracked lips. He instinctively glanced back at the City from behind the dust-covered curtains to see people jerking to abrupt stops like products on a jammed conveyor belt; tattered shopping bags dropped to the ground, hands were raised to mouths, and people urgently ran to one another, all cowering over their wrists.

Callum stared back down at his borrowed Watch to see the score now mirrored on every Watch in the City.

A score of M-0.

END OF BOOK THREE

393

AUTHOR'S NOTE

Working as a young person in this modern, busy age isn't easy. Through school and education, we are encouraged to believe that achievements, grades and accolades determine our worth. A lie only supported through comparison culture on social media, where we're given a controlled and edited version of other people. Crazy expectations and unrealistic ambitions can then leave us feeling discontented, discouraged and uninformed about the value of our work.

Don't misunderstand me. I'm not saying don't dream. These books are me, a writer bordering on thirty, pursuing a dream that her books might mean something to people. But when our dreams are motivated by our own success rather than a powerful *why* which empowers others, things start to get icky. If we strive our entire lives to be 'it', to make constant 'impact', and always overachieve merely for short-term validation from a world that overall, let's face it, doesn't care about us, we are missing out.

This past year has been the toughest of my life. You may have noticed the first part of this book's dedication was to my mum. In July 2023, my mum was admitted to hospital after presenting signs of dizziness and confusion. A week later, she was on a ventilator. For four months, Mum was in a heavy coma induced by a rare autoimmune disease attacking her brain. Then in November 2023, Mum passed away and, as a person of faith, I believe went home to a God who loves her more than anyone here ever could. I'm not highlighting this story for sympathy or to pack an emotional punch, but to invite you into my learning that 1) our past can empower us and 2), everyone is valuable. While working hard and striving for excellence aren't bad things – in fact, they are *good* things – they become insignificant in the light of pursuing and loving each other. I was so thankful for the relationship I had with my mum, but it came through intentionally connecting, intentionally investing, and intentionally forgiving.

Knowing her was worth more than any job, award or bragging right.

As hard as it is some days, I'm choosing not to be chained down by the disappointment of her loss, but to be empowered by the honour it was, and still is, to be her daughter. And whether someone is a shopkeeper, a lawyer, a plumber, a doctor or unemployed, they are all worth more than their titles or bank balance. While we can't have close, meaningful relationships with everyone we meet, we can give them our respect and our love, even if it ends up costing us something. Thank you for giving my writing a chance and I hope, in some way, that I have communicated my heart while keeping you gripped to a cracking story.

But just you wait, book four, the final one in this series, is a corker.

ACKNOWLEDGEMENTS

It's funny when writing a series and you come to this time again. As always, I want to thank my husband, Stephen, for always believing. Big thanks to Malcolm Down, Sarah Grace, Sheila Jacobs, Liz Carter and my sister-in-law, Sarah Jenkins, for assisting me in publishing, editing, designing and providing maps to bring Tulo alive once again. Thank you to my entire family (on both sides) for being a rock as we all battled through a hard year together, but a special shout-out to the ones making babies (you know who you are) – being an auntie is honestly the biggest joy. To all the friends who have prayed and supported me, thank you, thank you, thank you! To Dad, for more than this book, I want to say thank you. Despite what you've been through, you have never failed to show up. I can safely say that your strength and encouragement has enabled me to persevere and 'not be chained down by the past, but empowered by it'.

Finally, to Jesus Christ, who has changed me in so many ways, but his life and love prove that even the smallest can be Worthy. Thank you.

Whoever can be trusted with very little
can also be trusted with much . . .
(Luke 16:10, NIV)

GET READY FOR THE FINAL INSTALMENT

Be 'in the know' for book four

Join my mailing list for all writing updates including the title and cover reveals for the big finale!

In addition, you'll get access to my newsletter – 'The Dystopian Digest' – to enjoy dystopian book recommendations, giveaways, exclusive author interviews and more. If you love dystopian worlds and stories, it's not to be missed.

Join by visiting lgjenkins.com or scan the code.

**Find me on TikTok and Instagram too –
@lgjenkinsauthor**

And remember, have a happy merit-making day!

ABOUT THE AUTHOR

Lydia Jenkins is an author, booklover and coffee drinker. When she isn't immersed in writing dystopian worlds, you'll either find her reading in a coffee shop, playing netball or spending time with friends in 'sunny' England.

Sun of Endless Days was her debut novel and she hopes to encourage others in their purpose, worth and faith through writing for years to come. Follow Lydia on Instagram and TikTok to keep up with all her antics – @lgjenkinsauthor

REVIEW THE
MERIT-HUNTERS SERIES

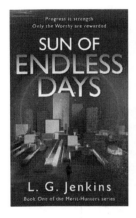

on Amazon, Goodreads
and everywhere else online

READ THE SPIN-OFF NOVELLA,
SET IN THE CITY OF TULO . . .

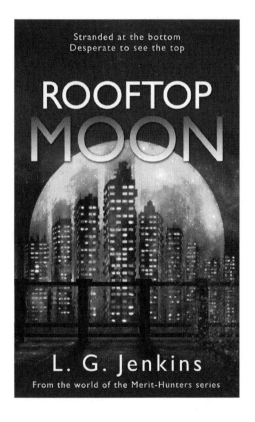

Visit **lgjenkins.com** to
download Kole's story for free